Replay

The Playbook Series
Book One

L.A. SHAW

Replay - The Playbook Series Book One

Editor: Mackenzie at Nice Girl Naughty Edits

Cover Design: Concepts by Canea

Formatting: L.A. Shaw - Vellum

To all the dreams we never thought were possible...

Author's Note

Please <u>Scan</u> or <u>Click</u> the image below for content warnings

Playlist

Music plays an important role in our writing process…
So, please enjoy our <u>Replay</u> playlist.

PROLOGUE

Berkley

E ven though the sun is disappearing past the horizon, the pool party surrounding me is still in full force. It's summer in Nori Beach, which means if we aren't taking the boat out to one of the islands, we're sipping by the pool.

But today feels different; I can't shake the impending doom.

I place my beer on the small table beside my pool lounger and close my eyes, trying to drown out the noise. I thought alcohol was supposed to numb your emotions, but all it's doing is stirring up my fears and anxieties about Nate leaving for Texas.

Needing the reminder he's still here, I open my eyes to find him.

There he is… We still have time.

Nate glances over his shoulder from where he stands a few yards from me with some teammates, giving me a wink like he has any time he's far from me today. Most days this summer, we've tried to stay away from the crowd to soak up our time together. Being that he's leaving for college sooner than most of us for football workouts, I pushed the selfish part of me aside and planned one last hurrah at my condo's pool. Especially since everyone wants to say their goodbyes to him…

The superstar.

The future QB for Texas Tech.

The boy I'm trying desperately to hang on to.

Something is off, though, and it's worsening my anxious thoughts.

Chasity, my keep-at-an-arm's-length friend, sits on the lounger beside me, along with Graves, who has his arm slung over her shoulder.

"Want to play flip cup with us?" Chasity asks with the typical mischievous look she has spread across her face.

"Maybe later." I shrug.

"What's wrong?" she pries, but she isn't the type of friend I tell those things to.

God, I wish my mom was here. I know she'd reassure me that everything's going to be okay.

"Yo, Nate!" I hear one of his teammates call out, causing my eyes to find him again.

"This is Nikki." He points to one of the girls walking up with him, a gorgeous brunette. "She's here on a family vacation, but she's going to be a freshman at Texas Tech this year, too."

His eyes find mine, likely knowing my insecurities are raging about all the girls who'll no doubt flock to him in Texas, but I give him my best smile. A reassurance that I don't feel one bit.

"You know good and well, that bitch only came because she heard he was going to be here." Chasity sneers, and I wish she was sincere in looking out for me, but there's no doubt, if given the chance, she would hop on the Nate train too.

The girl's eyes light up when she sees Nate standing there in all his tanned, muscular glory, and my stomach sours.

Fuck this. Maybe I just need more alcohol to forget everything.

"Y'all still down for flip cup?" I rush out, trying to focus on anything else.

I see Graves's eyes light up. "Yep." Standing, he gives me his hand to take as he helps me up from my seat.

I don't look over at Nate, not wanting to see him being polite to this girl who wants my man. In the next few days, when I stay here in North Carolina, and he moves to Texas, she will have much easier access to him. And if it isn't her, there will be so many others falling at his feet.

Nate has never given me a reason to feel insecure, but I can't shake my growing unease.

Whispered words skate across my neck. "You are too gorgeous to question your relationship. And you know it will be like that every night for him in Texas."

I know Graves's words are true, but Nate loves me. I try to remind myself again that he's never given me a reason to question that.

A few minutes into our game, I feel Nate behind me. His eyes burn a hole in my bikini-clad body from where he stands with Graham Leblanc, one of our best friends who graduated last year.

I'm being toxic as fuck right now by feeding into the attention of the one person Nate doesn't get along with, but for some reason, I can't stop myself.

Two rounds later, I'm several more drinks in. I sneak a peek over my shoulder to where a pissed-off Nathan stands, clenching his fists. I bite my lip, liking that he's just as jealous over me as I am over him.

Graves leans closer and rests his hand on my hip. "You suck at this game."

I tilt my head back, laughing, because he's right.

The next thing I know, Graves is being pushed to the ground, and I'm being pulled from the table. "Sorry to break up your little bonding session, but I've had enough of his fucking hands on you."

Everyone's attention zeroes in on us, likely whispering about how uncharacteristic this is for the happy couple we are, but the alcohol buzzing through my system has me not caring in the slightest. I let Nate's firm grip on my hand guide me into the back door of mine and my dad's condo. Neither of us says a word as he drags me down the hall to my bedroom.

As soon as he shuts my door, I'm in his face. "What the fuck, Nate?"

"What the fuck is right, Berkley. You know how bad he wants you. I was trying to let you have your fun, but fuck... I want to go out there and break his fucking face in." He takes a breath, running his hands through the longer strands on top of his head. Strands I love to twirl with my fingers. Strands that make me want to vomit just thinking about someone else lying beside him, running *their* fingers through his hair instead.

His hazel eyes penetrate me when I don't respond. "I stood there for thirty minutes picturing you and him doing this every weekend at Mountain Ridge, until one weekend, you let him fuck you."

I rear back like I've been slapped. I don't want Graves, not in the slightest. I want Nate and only Nate, but I don't say that. I'm too pissed he could ever think such a thing about me. "Like you are one to talk. I saw you with your newest friend, so I chose to drink and forget this fucked-up situation."

"You have no idea how fucked up this situation actually is," he grinds out, and the anguished turmoil that was on his face earlier today is back in place. "And for your information, I shook her hand and politely excused myself to find you."

"I just..." The alcohol hits me suddenly, and I lie on my bed, the long day of sun and booze taking over my body. "I feel like I'm drowning in my insecurities right now, and I fucking hate it," I whisper.

Moving closer, he releases a heavy breath and pushes the hair from my face, his tone softening. "There is nothing to be insecure about. No one will ever be you. I wish..." His hesitation has me opening my eyes, finding his pained ones. "I wish you would've just let me have Coach get you a spot with me in Texas."

I shake my head, because I fear that may be the biggest mistake of my life. "I just can't leave him," I mutter, eyes burning with emotion as I turn onto my side, wanting sleep to overtake me. I want to wake up tomorrow and pretend this never happened.

The bed dips beside me, and Nate wraps me in his arms. He kisses away the tears that trail down my cheek as he reassures me. "I'll never love anyone more than I love you, BB."

My doubts melt away in his embrace and, finally relaxed, I drift off to sleep. But I swear I hear him whisper, "He ruins everything," before I pass out.

The sun creeping into my room the next morning stirs me awake. I try to fight it, but the queasiness in my stomach won't let me. Bits and pieces from the end of the night flood back into my mind.

Nate isn't touching me, but I feel him beside me in the bed. I want to roll over, wrap my arms around him, and tell him I'm sorry for last night and that everything will be okay, but when I notice him lying there awake, staring at the ceiling, dread like I've only felt one other time in my life consumes me.

Getting out of bed before I lose my shit, I make my way to the shower, pretending I don't notice he's awake. The water cascades over my sun-kissed skin, and I try desperately to convince myself that I'm thinking too much into this, and that everything is fine. He's probably just nervous about leaving and likely upset with me for ruining one of our last nights together, instead of just coming to him and talking about how I was feeling. We've always had a mature relationship in that regard, but last night, we were the furthest thing from mature.

I remind myself of how perfect things have been the last two years since I moved back to Nori Beach. From the very first day my eyes trailed up that tan, muscular body that I later learned purposefully overthrew the football on the beach, just to have a reason to run over and talk to me. He was unlike anyone I had ever seen, with his dreamy hazel eyes and his captivating smile. I think I fell instantly. Every day since then, he has fiercely adored me and brought so much happiness back into my life. Which is why the thought of losing him floods my mind with an onslaught of crippling fear.

My nerves skyrocket again when I leave my ensuite bathroom and find Nate sitting on the edge of my bed.

His eyes meet mine, and I swear he looks like he's been crying. My heart plummets, and that sickening feeling hits me again. All the positive thoughts from the shower are churning into negative ones as my gut sours.

No... no... no. We have a plan. Don't do this, baby.

Please.

He gives me a weak smile. I swallow roughly and walk beside him to where my clothes lay on the bed.

Nate picks up my simple blue panties and, without a word, he bends for me to step into them. My towel falls to the ground, and he slides them up my legs. He gently kisses my stomach, not sexually like he normally would, but somehow even more intimately. Almost like it's the last time he knows he will have me like this. My stomach lurches beneath his lips at the thought.

"Blue..." he whispers, gently touching my panty line. Tilting his head up to mine, he continues, "Blue was the color of the bathing suit you had on the first day I saw you on that beach. I couldn't take my eyes off you. And then you spoke to me... I've been so fucking gone for you since that exact moment."

My heart flips at his admission, but my brain tells me not to let my guard down.

He presses his eyes together before grabbing my shirt and slipping it over my head. That's when I notice a tear escape the corner of his eye, and I feel like my throat is constricting. I want to say so much, but no words come out.

As his eyes meet mine, he reaches for my hand. "Lay with me, BB."

The sound of the nickname he gave me steals the air from my lungs, and I suck in a breath before lying beside him.

"Nate," I whisper, hopelessness seeping into my tone.

"Just let me hold you," he says as he buries his nose in my hair. I feel his body trembling as he holds me, mine doing the same, and I can't take it anymore. With my heart beating out of my chest, I push out of his grasp and stand up on shaky legs.

When my eyes land on his broken-hearted ones, I lose it. "Don't do this, Nate... Look at us!" I yell, but it's tired and raspy, filled with emotion as I point from my tear-stained face to his. "Why would you do this to us?"

Desperation etches his features as he jumps off my bed and tries to pull me back toward him. "BB, just let me explain."

Head shaking, I shove him back. "Don't call me that when you are about to shatter my heart and soul all over this room."

He closes his eyes again, and when he opens them, he tries composing his emotions before speaking. "Berkley, deep down, you know this is for the best."

"No, Nate! No, I don't. Don't fucking tell me what I know!" I shout, not caring who hears. Tears stream freely down my face and cheeks now, the image of him blurring before me as I choke back a sob.

He pulls on his hair, turmoil coiling up his entire body, and with how upset he is, I don't get this at all. Why is he doing this, when it's so clear he doesn't want to?

"What happened to us giving long-distance a shot? What happened to us being able to make it through anything?" My voice grows louder with each question, pleading for him to make sense of this.

"I just don't know if I can handle it," he whispers, looking down at the floor before back up at me. "What we have is too perfect to ruin it with the shit we did last night, and I think that was just a glimpse into what our future holds. Maybe you think you are, but I'm not mentally strong enough for long-distance."

I ignore the pang in my chest at the truth in his words, the truth I've been pushing out of my thoughts for a while now. "I thought we were supposed to give it a try..." I trail off, sounding as unsure as I feel.

"Then what? End up hating each other because last night is on repeat every week?"

In this moment, I know I love him too much to not replace that with hate. "If you do this, I'm going to hate you either way."

"One day, you'll understand why I had to do this."

I huff a breath, numbness taking over. "Whatever, Nate. Just get out of here with that cryptic bullshit." It's silent for the longest minute as I try and fail to process what's happening. It feels like a nightmare. Leaning back on my desk to hold myself up, I tell him, "You are ruining us before we even had the chance to try."

He reaches for me again, and I feel like my heart is physically being torn apart in an irreparable way. If he touches me again, how does he expect me to let him go?

When his fingers brush my cheek to cup my face, I recoil. I can't do this.

"BB, please," he mutters as I push away from him. "I don't want to end things like this. Please, don't make me—"

"Leave!!" I scream to cut him off, my voice breaking through more tears. Biting my tongue, I refuse to beg him to stay. It's no use. His mind is clearly made up.

He stares at me for a few seconds, and just when I'm about to yell at him again, unable to take another second of the pained way he's looking at me, he walks out of my life for good.

I just wish he would have given me back my heart when he did.

My mom once told me being in love could be the best feeling in the world, but love could also damage you in a way nothing else ever could. I was a stupid, stupid girl who didn't listen to her mother, and now I get to learn the hard way exactly what she meant.

THE HOWLER

Mountain Ridge University

| Volume 20-02 | August Update |

SUMMER UPDATE: NEW QB TO GRACE THE MOUNTAIN RIDGE FOOTBALL FIELD

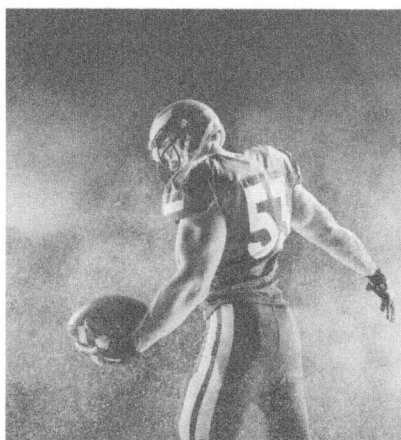

Following MRU's surprising defeat last year, the team has recruited Nathan Outlaw, a new QB from Texas Tech, to guide the MRU Wolves this season. With his remarkable performance with the Texas Tech Red Raiders, fans are hopeful he will bring success to his new team and lead the Wolves to this year's National Championship game.

ONE

Berkley

No matter how many times I reread the headline, the outcome remains the same. Nate is in Mountain Ridge. Here, at my college... What a welcome-back gift to receive after being away for the summer. Just when I start to feel more like myself than I have in two years, this Howler Report gets thrown in my face.

My feet continue to run along the trail, almost in sync with the pounding in my chest as my mind races.

I've done everything in my power to keep all things *Nate* securely locked away in Nori Beach. Never to be seen or discussed again. There are many reasons why I haven't returned to my hometown, and Nate is one of them. How dare he transfer here, after what he did to me...to us. He can't possibly think this is a good idea.

Nope, stop that right there. That's where you are wrong, B. He doesn't think of anyone but himself. That's for damn sure.

I pick up my pace, officially lapping several older speed walkers decked out in matching tracksuits. I wonder if the people I'm passing can feel the swirling emotions radiating from me. I'm trying my best to keep it together and convince myself it will all be okay. But the fact that I've completed my tenth lap around the trail proves otherwise.

I've never been much of a runner, but over the past two years, it's become a sort of therapy for me. It helps me clear my mind and keeps me level-headed. Running in nature certainly trumps running on a treadmill, and Ridgeway Park has some of the most gorgeous views I've ever seen. Not only does it have a running trail surrounding a large pond, but it also has hiking trails, mountain views, and sports courts.

There's a bit of a breeze today, but the August sun is still hot on my back. Stopping to catch my breath, I wipe the sweat from my forehead and seek out the closest bench to stretch out before heading home.

Ridgeway Park is pretty busy for this time of year. The town is usually quiet during the summer. Yes, families live here year-round, but the university students take over when in session. And considering school doesn't start for another two weeks, the only students in town should be those who never go home and the fall sports teams. Meaning, Nate is already here. I thank my lucky stars I haven't crossed paths with him yet, even though I've only been back for less than twenty-four hours. But I know it's inevitable. I'm just glad I now have time to prepare.

"Hey, beautiful." A voice sounds from beside me catches my attention. My gaze flits in his direction, finding Carter walking my way. His brown eyes trail from my eyes, down my body, lingering on my sweaty chest. Taking in his handsome face, I smile.

"Carter, what are you doing here?" I ask, surprised to see him. Our plan was for him to come by my apartment after my shift at The Wolfpack. I lean into his embrace, loving the familiar scent of his cologne.

"I had to get out of my house. The new roommate I was telling you about has a superstition about cleaning his socks. Fucker smells so bad. So, I figured I'd come to the park, assuming you'd be here."

Chuckling, I grab my water, taking a large gulp. "Yeah, I don't think I could survive that."

"I missed you," he says, touching my hip. "Two months is a long time. How was Spain?"

"I missed you too… It was amazing. Sooo gorgeous. Still can't get over how old everything was."

"Well, I'm glad you're back."

"Thanks, I'm glad to be back too." I smile at him, trying to mask my thoughts of Nate. Did Carter know all summer that Nate was joining his team? From what I've read, the transfer portal closes in April… So, he must have known. *Is that why he was pushing to be exclusive?*

I've known Carter Graves for quite some time, since we both graduated from Nori Beach High School. When we first started hanging out, it was just as friends, but eventually, we evolved. At the end of last semester, I felt like maybe I could feel more for him, but instead, I ran away to Spain. So, although he desperately wants to be, Carter is not my boyfriend. I've sworn off those. Just the thought of putting myself in a situation to get hurt again scares the hell out of me.

"How's practice been?" I question, wondering if he'll mention the team's new quarterback?

He hesitates for a moment before answering. "Coach has been running us like crazy this week. I'm so fucking sore and so damn hungry."

"You're always hungry," I quip as I gather up my things. Is he just waiting for the right time to break the news to me?

Carter laughs and pulls me into him. His tall frame towers over my 5'2" self. I look up at him, admiring his big brown eyes and tanned skin. He licks his full lips before he leans down for a kiss. Hands roaming over my hips, he cups my ass before he pulls away.

"Hungry for you," he whispers, and I playfully swat him away. My body responds to his touch, but my brain is too fucked up to want what's clearly on his mind.

"I'm serious. Two months is a long time, Berk. I'm a desperate man."

Rolling my eyes, I grab his hand. "Come on, let's go back to my apartment. I need to shower. We can eat and catch up, then I can get ready for work."

The walk to my place is less than five minutes from the park. It's located in downtown Mountain Ridge, where most of the off-campus housing is. There's my apartment complex, several sorority and fraternity homes, and then there are the sports houses, which are basically fraternity homes in a sense with just a little more of a sweat smell to them. At the center of the sports housing is The Wolves Den. The elite players live there, including Graham, a friend of mine and Carter's from Nori Beach. As of last semester, there were only football and hockey players living there, but that changes every year.

Walking into my apartment, I'm welcomed by silence. Bellamy and Darby aren't back yet. I, however, live in Mountain Ridge year-round. Nori Beach is no longer a place I wish to visit, so I've made Mountain Ridge my home. Although it may be lonely at times, I'd rather be here than face the life I left behind.

Carter walks right to my kitchen and opens my fridge to inspect its contents. "How about sandwiches?" he asks, pulling the essentials out.

"Sounds great. You're lucky I went food shopping this morning," I tease as he opens a bag of chips to snack on while he makes us lunch.

"I'm going to shower. Be out in a minute," I say as I head down the hallway to my bathroom before he has time to ask to join in. I should be jumping his bones after two months and, normally, I would be, but I can't seem to get a certain someone out of my head.

While I wait for the water to heat up, I text my girls.

ROOMIES💋

ME

Miss you people... come back to meeee.

DARBY

Ahhh! Miss your face.

BELL

Welcome back to this side of the pond.

ME

For real. When are you guys coming back?

BELL

Possibly sooner than I thought. I don't know how much more family bonding time I can take.

DARBY

Woof... sounds like torture.

ME

Yeah, sounds like you should come back tomorrow. You literally live like thirty minutes away... Okay, thanks 😌.

DARBY

Jackie and I are going away this weekend before she goes back to school. So, I'll probably head there on Monday after she leaves.

BELL

Aww, that's so sweet. Hope you enjoy it!

ME

Aw okay! Well, enjoy your lovas weekend. And I'll see you both soon. Bell, let me know when you're coming.

BELL

Sounds like a plan.

I step out of the bathroom in my robe, with my hair wrapped in a towel. Carter takes one look at me and laughs. "I don't think I'll ever get used to you looking like that."

Rolling my eyes playfully, I sit next to him. "It's granny-chic."

"You keep telling yourself that."

"Listen, you can't judge until you've experienced the robe life. Until then, zip it."

"Okay, granny, eat your sandwich before I do," he teases before taking the final bite of his own.

Carter, refusing to go back to his smelly house, walked me into town for my waitressing shift, then headed over to a friend's house to play Call of Duty. It's a Monday, so I'm not expecting to make a lot of tips, but anything will help. Especially after the way I ate and drank my way through Barcelona and Madrid, I'm broke as a joke. Usually, Mondays during football season are a gold mine shift, but it's still a bit too early for that. At least there's baseball…and thankfully, the Carolina Bulls have a game tonight.

Strapping on my apron, I begin my prep work, checking the utensil rolls, ketchup, and salt and pepper shakers. I jot down today's specials, then head to the bar, where my manager Phil Oakley is wiping down the bottles.

"Hey, kid! How was your trip?" he asks with a genuine smile across his face.

"It was life-changing, but I'm glad to be back."

"Oh, I bet you are. We missed you. Well, I think Tiffany did the most." He laughs, and I join him.

I help Tiffany and Phil by watching their crazy clan of four kids whenever they need me. It's great money, and their kids are hysterical. I swear their youngest, Gwen, will be a stand-up comedian or an actress one day.

"Well, I'm back and don't have classes for another week and a half…"

Phil's eyebrow quirks. "Oh, she knows you're back, probably giving you at least forty-eight hours to adjust before she unleashes the beasts."

I notice a table has been seated in my section, so I wave off Phil and walk over to greet my first guests of the night.

Several hours later, my friend Graham strides through the doors, followed by a herd of hulking forms. My stomach sinks immediately... If Graham is here, does that mean Nate is with him too?

I make my way over to greet him, and he wraps me up in a big hug. "Hey, B, is there room for us in your section? There are..." He pauses to count how many of them are huddled in the entryway. "Seven of us."

Taking a deep breath, I nod, then gather a bunch of menus and have them follow me to a table. Nervously placing the menus, I step back and eye the guys Graham has with him. When I realize Nate isn't here, I can't tell if I'm relieved or disappointed.

Frickin' fool.

They're quick to order their wings and burgers, and I gather up the menus after delivering their drinks.

"Oh, we might have a straggler or two. Would you mind leaving a menu?" Graham asks, right as I'm about to walk away.

"Yeah...uh, sure. Here ya go." I smile and walk away, but my knees shake with every step. Nerves ripple through me. What if the straggler is you know who?

I need to get my shit together. Regardless of if I see him tonight, tomorrow, or a week from now...it doesn't change the fact that Nathan Outlaw will be attending my school and be the center of everyone's attention. So, I'm going to have to get used to the fact.

Can't fucking wait.

Taking a deep breath, I start loading up my tray for their table's second round of drinks when I hear a throat clear behind me. My eyes go wide, and my heart skips a beat before I turn around. But to my surprise, it's Graham.

"What's up? Did you need something?" I ask, but the look on his face tells me otherwise.

He gives me a half-hearted smile and nods for me to step off to the side with him. "You were supposed to text me when you got back... I wanted to talk— Shit, B, I know you've probably heard..." Trying to gather his words, he hesitates. His hand sweeps through his sandy blonde hair as he looks at the floor and then back at me. "Nate is here in Mountain Ridge."

I take a steadying breath before responding. "Yeah, I read about it this morning. Great welcome-back surprise for me," I say, sarcasm dripping from every word.

"I'm sorry I didn't tell you sooner. I found out right before you left to study abroad, and I wanted you to enjoy your trip. I know you purposefully don't follow his sports updates, so I was hoping I could tell you when you got back so you weren't stressed about it during your time away."

"Thank you, I appreciate that. But I'm okay." I stand on my tiptoes and wrap my arms around his six-five frame. Graham's probably the biggest softy I've ever met, and I'm so glad to call him a friend. He's basically like an older brother to me at this point, and seeing how he cares just proves that further.

He raises his eyebrow, and I laugh. "No, for real, I am. I have a lot going for me, and I have Carter too. I'm good. Don't worry about me."

Maybe the more times I say it, I'll eventually convince myself.

"One last thing..." Graham starts. "He's moved into The Wolves Den."

Of course, he has...

"We knew that empty room wasn't going to last long," I tease and finish loading up my tray. Carter wanted that room, and even though Graham and Carter are friends and know each other from back home, Bellamy's stepbrothers, who just so happen to be Graham's cousins, hate Carter, so they didn't vote him in.

As I follow him back to the table with a tray in hand, I try my best to come to terms with my new reality. Long gone is my safe haven; Nate has now infiltrated yet another place where I felt at home.

I've spent the last two years ignoring my past... Now, I have no other choice but to deal with all six foot two of it.

TWO

Nate

"You're looking strong out there, Outlaw. Dare I say, even stronger than you did before your injury," Coach Price says from behind his desk. Pushing the images from my mind that Graves has on repeat after his taunts during practice, I embrace the coach's words.

"Thanks, Coach, I'm happy to be here and excited to see where this season takes us," I answer honestly. Getting injured in the last game of a record-breaking season is a tough pill to swallow and not one I took easily. Especially after feeling like I had already lost my world when I went to Texas.

"We're happy to have you, bud." He beams. His tough exterior from practice just a few minutes ago is nowhere in sight. I try to hold back my smile, but damn, it feels good to hear that. To go from a coach who so easily replaced me to one who took a huge chance on me makes me extremely proud to deliver.

Thankfully, for my former team, our second-string quarterback was able to take us to the championships. I hate to say, as excited as I was that day, jealousy I wasn't used to feeling when it comes to anything other than a certain blonde crept deep into my bones, planting seeds of my likely unfortunate future at Texas Tech. And just as I and many others suspected, my former coach told me I would take the position of QB2 for my junior season. To say I was pissed is an understatement, but you know what they say… When one door closes, another door opens, and by the end of my spring semester, I already had several new offers. Mountain Ridge and two other Division 1 schools were the top three I narrowed it down to, and I would be lying if I said the thought of being at the same school as Berkley again didn't make that decision for me.

He taps his pen on his playbook. "The shotgun offense seems to be working really well. You and Wynn are in a great groove, and I think for the game next week, it's the way to go."

I nod. "I agree. Tennessee's man-to-man defense won't be able to keep up with Wynn."

Coach leans back, pushing his chair away from the table. "Hell, our best defensive backs can't keep up with him. As long as he stays healthy, Wynn has a big future." Standing, he walks around to me and pats my good shoulder. "As do you, Nate. I know it's been a rough year, but I'm serious. I see a different fire in your eyes."

I try to focus on his compliment as I say my goodbyes, but the mention of our DBs takes me back to one in particular. The one who has avoided me like the plague since my arrival, even though I've known him since I was twelve years old. The same one I've seen post pictures with Berkley more and more over the past two years, but mainly with others in them and never with a label. I've suspected and stayed up late at night, spinning stories in my head about if they're dating, but he chose today to break the silence, and it took everything in me not to break my fist across his face.

She's mine now… Stay away from her, Outlaw. She's in my bed every night, saying my name. And she'll be in the stands wearing my number next Saturday.

When I let the anger settle and allowed his words to play on repeat, I was somewhere between crying and puking. It's my own fucking fault…. Or maybe it's *their* fucking fault, but either way, I chose to walk away.

The locker room is mostly cleared out when I finish up with Coach, but I notice Graham, my best friend and one of the top tight ends in college football, sitting on the bench near my locker.

I nod at him, urging myself to let the animosity go before I speak. "You didn't have to wait on me. I'm going in with the trainers to ice my shoulder anyway."

He stands up and slings his bag onto his shoulder as I'm opening my locker. "I just wanted to check on you. You seemed off at the end of practice."

I wait for a moment to answer. I know it's not Graham's fault, but I feel unreasonably pissed at him. My emotions get the best of me as I slam my locker shut and meet his gaze. "Is she with him?"

"Wha… Where did that come from?"

"Just fucking tell me… Is she with Graves?" I force out the last part, not even wanting to speak it into existence.

"Look, Nate…"

"No, don't sugarcoat it. Tell me." I level him with a demanding look I've never given him before.

He holds up his hands, shaking his head. "Whoa, whoa, boss…don't come at me like that. You are the one who broke up with her, remember?"

I fucking knew it. The side of my fist hits the cold metal of the locker, and my head falls against it with a shaky huff.

"Fuck, man," Graham hisses out. "I'm sorry, Nate, but she's my friend too and, honestly, I didn't know if you'd care."

The tiredness of practice and the anguish I feel over being so close but so far from her finally take over my body. I sit down on the bench, eventually lifting my head to see how concerned he is. "Of course, I still care. Why do you think I always ask you about her? No matter how hard I've tried to move on…I still care. I always will."

At that, his concern seems to melt away, and he shakes his head in frustration. "I just don't get this shit, dude. If you are still so fucked up over her, why did you end it? Especially how you did."

I pull the strands of my sweaty hair, whispering, "You don't get it. It's not that simple."

The door to the locker room opens and our roommate, Nola's, eyebrows pinch together as he takes in our tense body language. "Y'all good?"

"Yeah," I say as I pick up my stuff.

"The trainers were looking for you, so I told them I'd come find you before they wrap me up." He pauses for a beat and smirks. "But I got dibs on blondie's table."

I roll my eyes at him and chuckle, not wanting my other teammates to know the shit going on in my head. "I'm coming."

"I'll see you both back at the house. I think the twins got back while we were at practice," Graham says, but grabs my arm before I walk away. "We good?"

"Yeah, it's not your fault. See you at the house." I lift my fist, and he taps it with his, watching me suspiciously as we both head our separate ways out of the locker room.

Graham Leblanc has been my friend since I made the varsity football team in the seventh grade. He was captain of the middle school team that year and took me under his wing. That bond grew when I joined him in high school two years later, and again, he immediately pulled me into his fold. That's Graham; if you are his people, he always looks out for you. Which is why I was thankful Berkley had him here at Mountain Ridge these past two years.

I follow behind Nola into the trainer room. "How's your ankle feeling?" I ask him.

He smiles, nodding. "Solid. Like those passes you keep throwing me."

I smirk. "I was just talking to Coach about how well that's working." Nola and I have only been practicing together for a couple months, but our chemistry on the field is unreal.

"Ice that shoulder up so we can get home. I'm cooking breakfast for dinner tonight," he says as he winks at the athletic trainer and hops onto her table.

Brody Wynn, otherwise known as Nola, was born and raised in New Orleans and is the epitome of "rizz" in the urban dictionary. Even as a sophomore, he has already made a name with the ladies on campus. He's also the best wide receiver I've ever played with, and he's a hell of a cook in the kitchen.

After a long shower, during which I contemplated all my life choices on repeat, I decide to torture myself further by opening my closet door to stare at the picture collage on the back of it.

I trace my finger over her pouty lips and clear blue eyes. She's heart-breakingly beautiful.

The week before everything changed, Berkley had surprised me with a picture collage for my room in Texas. She even included a few with us and my younger sister, Willow. The same sister who wouldn't speak to me for two months after she found out I broke up with Berkley. She was only fifteen at the time and, unfortunately, I think myself, along with our parents, ruined her idea of true love all within one short year.

"Yo, dinner's ready. If you want any, you better come on..." Graham's voice trails away as I hear his feet pounding down the steps.

"There's the superstar," Maverick teases from across the table, where he sits beside his brother, Cash.

I raise my hands, smirking at them. "In the flesh."

"Sit your asses down and bow your heads," Mav demands, and after having a few "family meals," during their visits this summer, I already know what he's about to say.

"Dear Lord, bless this food, bless the hockey puck, and the gridiron. And bless Nola's parents for teaching him how to cook." He even tops it off with one sharp clap, like we're finishing a team huddle.

I chuckle. It's the same prayer every time. According to Mav, his gigi made him promise to bless his dinner every night. She knew Cash and Graham wouldn't do it, so he took the responsibility like he always does for his twin and cousin. However, somehow, I feel like he's the least responsible of the three.

"This looks like a five-star brunch," I say, taking a bite of the eggs Benedict. I swear, even the presentation looks like something from a fancy restaurant. From what Nola has shared with me, his parents own a restaurant in New Orleans that was like his family's second home growing up.

"Fuuuck. This slaps, Brody," Graham moans, still chewing his food.

Nola chuckles. "Damn, it must be good if you are using my first name. I don't think you've called me that since the first day of training camp last year."

"He's right, though," Cash says as he shovels food into his mouth. Both he and Maverick are huge guys who likely have to eat a ton of calories to bulk up during the off-season of hockey.

"Thank you." Nola nods proudly.

"Bellamy's coming back tomorrow. She was asking if we're going to do our before-school get-together here like we did last year?" Maverick asks, and my heart flutters at the mention of Bellamy, who I learned over the summer is not only the twins' stepsister, but also Berkley's best friend.

Will Berkley come too?

I've stopped myself so many times from seeking her out since I heard she was back from studying abroad, but I don't want to bombard her after everything I put her through.

When I realized she blocked me after our breakup, I started writing down thoughts and conversations to her. I know it sounds pathetic, but it was the only way I found to cope with it and still be able to focus on football.

I've been contemplating writing something to deliver to her. Something to break the ice about me being here, and hopefully a way to get her to talk to me.

Graham's answer pulls me from my thoughts. "I say we do it Sunday night, since it'll be our last light day before school starts back up, but keep it just football and hockey. Invite only."

"Bet," Mav says. "But then after y'all whoop that Tennessee ass next Saturday, we're throwing a big one here that night."

"I like the sound of that." Nola whistles.

Cash turns his attention to me between bites. "How's Mountain Ridge treating you so far, Nate?"

I think about it briefly before answering honestly. "I like it. It feels more like home."

"I bet it's nice being within driving distance of your family." Nola's expression is one I haven't seen him wear before.

"Yeah, my dad and sister will be able to come to more games, so that's nice."

"Sister, you say?" Maverick asks, raising his eyebrows.

"Like fuck..." I level him with a stare.

He just chuckles, raising his tattooed arms in surrender. "Okay, okay."

"QB, what's up with you and Carter Graves? I know y'all grew up with him," Nola asks as he looks between Graham and I. "But I haven't seen you interact with him really at all." He must have missed the little stare-down we exchanged at the end of practice, or maybe he didn't and that's why he's asking.

"That pussy bitch," Maverick growls.

"What?" I ask, remembering Graham telling me they didn't vote Graves into the house, mainly because of the twins.

"He tried to fuck Cash's girlfriend, Tori, freshman year. He knew exactly who she was too. No one disrespects my brother like that. I'll never trust the punk." He shakes his head. "I don't know what the fuck *she* sees in him."

His words have heat crawling all over my skin. I fucking hate they know her as being his.

"Yeah, he's always been like that," I bite out and turn to Nola. "I don't have shit to say to him, so nah, you won't see us interacting, unless it's with my fist in his face."

"I knew I liked you." Maverick chuckles. "So do you know Berkley too? I can't imagine anyone from her hometown not knowing that girl... The first time I saw her, I thought I had died and gone to heaven. But Graham threatened our lives if we even tried anything with her."

I smirk, giving Graham a look of appreciation. "Good." Surprisingly, I don't feel jealousy at hearing this; I just hope she knows how beautiful she is. Berkley has always been one of those girls who's gorgeous beyond words and her own comprehension. No matter how many times I told her. My heart literally aches thinking about the way it feels to have her smile in my direction. I consider how much I should tell them, and I surprise myself again by deciding to open up.

"Yeah, I know Berkley..."

I close my eyes, trying to articulate the overwhelming emotion I feel thinking back to that day and all the months after. "I'm the one who broke her heart...and ripped mine out in the process. So as hard as it is knowing she's with Graves, if that's what she really wants, I deserve to sit here and watch. Doesn't mean I have to fucking like it or make it easy on him, though."

They all sit there in silence for a few seconds before Cash asks, "Did you break up with her because of the long-distance relationship?"

Again, I answer truthfully. "That's what she thinks."

THREE

Berkley

If I hear the name Nathan Outlaw one more time, I'm going to lose my fucking mind. It's bad enough I'm currently avoiding all my favorite places in Mountain Ridge to ensure I don't have any accidental run-ins with him, but listening to basically every guy and girl in town talk about him is driving me mental.

I wish I could rewind the clock eight months and prevent the stupid injury that ultimately caused him to leave Texas Tech. Yes, I knew about his injury when it happened. Even though I blocked his number and his socials, it's all Graham and the twins would talk about. But never in a million years did I think it would lead to him transferring here, of all places.

Bellamy joins me while I sip my smoothie in the quad before we head into the campus bookstore. She came home yesterday after only four full days of me begging her. Darby is still away on her "lovas" weekend, but she'll be back by tomorrow night. I need them both here. I crave to feel some sense of normalcy again.

"Are you aware that you're literally scowling at the world right now." She takes my cup and steals a taste, her green eyes shining back at me with mischief.

"Am not," I retort.

"Are too. I swear if we weren't synced up, I'd say you were getting your period," she quips.

I take my smoothie back from her and gulp it down. Attempting to fix my face, I smile at her.

"I was deep in thought… That's my thinking face."

"Thinking of he who shall not be named?" she asks, flipping her long red hair over her shoulder.

"Shut up!" I swat at her arm playfully. She's well aware of my history with Nate and his now sudden presence at MRU, since that was part of my case I pled to get her back to me. She, Darby, and my friend Lottie were my guiding lights during my freshmen year. My beacons leading me out of the depression hole I dug myself after he left me.

She chuckles in return. "Well, if it's not him, then it's certainly enough to have you all kinds of wound tight. Are you backed up or something?"

I stifle the laugh threatening to spray my strawberry-peach smoothie out my nose. "Backed up?"

"Yeah! I know two months is a long time not to get laid, but I'm sure you and Carter are making up for lost time, no?"

I roll my eyes to hide the truth. One would think we would be banging like rabbits after a summer apart, but that's not the case. We've had sex once, maybe two times since I've been back. I find myself making up every excuse to avoid being intimate with him. My brain is not in it…at all, and I refuse to admit where it's traveling off to.

Remaining silent, I continue to sip my smoothie while Bellamy switches topics and starts talking about how gorgeous some of the new hockey players are. I listen contently as she gives me a rundown of every player, their positions, and whether they're single, as well as what parties will be coming up this week. I've been friends with Bellamy for over two years, and well aware of how she hides her inner turmoil with boy talk, partying, and jokes. She's the epitome of a girl who never takes life too seriously. A great person to have around, but I just hope one day she's brave enough to face the demons she tries so hard to hide.

Regardless of who she is swooning over, Bellamy is definitely a stan for hockey, whereas I prefer football. She also always has the inside scoop because her two stepbrothers, Maverick and Cash, play on the MRU team. They also happen to live in The Wolves Den, along with Graham, Nola, and now Nate.

This is what I mean when I say his presence is everywhere. I can't even enjoy going to The Wolves Den, which used to be our favorite hangout spot. We even host Sunday dinner there since their place is huge and so much nicer than our condo. UGH! Why does he have to ruin everything?

"Come on, grump, we need to get moving," Bellamy says before taking my smoothie one last time and slurping it.

"Fiiine," I protest as I stand with a groan. "Let's get this over with so we can go float in the pool."

"Oh, you're not working later?" she asks as we walk side by side to the bookstore.

"No. I don't usually work Sundays. Why?"

"I figured you were, and that's why we're on campus at the ass crack of the day to buy our school shit."

"Oh, stop being dramatic… It's not that early."

"Is it lunchtime?" she questions.

"No."

"Then it's too early!" she whines, and I shake my head at my night owl bestie.

We remain silent for a few moments while she checks the messages on her phone and then glances in my direction. "What's that look for?" I ask, noticing the nervous gaze she gives me. Like she wants to tell me something but isn't sure how to.

Thinking about her words, she bites her lip. "So, I told Cash and Mav I would hang at The Wolves Den tonight. This was before I knew Nate was their new roommate. They're having a little party before classes start this week. I can totally cancel, or…you could come?"

"No, it's fine. Go and have fun. Carter had mentioned going to the party the other day, but I think we decided to just stay in and chill."

"Are you sure? I would much rather hang with you and not watch a bunch of girls hang all over those boys." She slings her arm around my shoulders.

Yeah, that's what I'm trying to avoid as well.

"If I change my mind, I'll totally let you know," I say, just as we enter through the store doors. "Come on, let's make this quick; the pool and some sort of fruity drink are calling my name," I add, trying to raise the mood.

Even though I really don't want to be around Nate, or the girls who will be throwing themselves at him, I can't help but wonder what his reaction would be to seeing me for the first time.

After a fantastic afternoon floating around, drinking, and soaking in the last licks of the summer, Bell and I retreat to our apartment. She's busy getting ready for the party, and I'm mentally planning what Netflix movie I want to watch as I wait for Carter to come over with our pizza.

Speaking of which... I walk to the front door to double-check that it's unlocked. Opening it up to check the handle, I see an orange bag lying on our welcome mat. I pick it up, leave the door slightly ajar, and head into the kitchen. The orange bag turns out to be UTZ Honey Barbecue chips with an envelope taped to it, my name scribbled across the front.

I'd know this chicken scratch anywhere.

My heart nearly stops as I take a seat and rip open the envelope.

Hey BB,

It's me... Nate. Probably the last person you want to hear from, but here I am.

Literally.

I'm sure by now you've heard I trans-ferred to MRU.... I also know you likely don't give a shit, but I do. And I wanted to be the one to tell you I'm here, but I also didn't want to bombard you.

I'm not here to ruin anything for you. I'm sure this will go unanswered, but I've wanted to ask you these questions so many times, so I figured I'd write them instead.

How do you like Mountain Ridge?

Did you decide for sure on teaching, or did you change it up?

Oh, and I hope this is still your favorite flavor of chips.

I miss the taste of honey barbecue. And I never take a sip of Diet Coke without thinking of you.

I heard you work at The Wolfpack... What should I try from there? Do they have good wings?

This last one I know I shouldn't ask, but... Graves? Really, B?

Does he remind you of home? Does he make you think about me? Is that why?

Honestly, I feel fucking crazy writing this, but you blocked me, and I have no idea how else to talk to you at this point without showing up at your job or stalking your building.

I don't expect you to be my pen pal, but could I see you? Maybe we can talk so things aren't so awkward when we're all together.

-Nate

In a state of shock, I place the letter on the table before picking it up and reading it over for a second time. Letting out a long sigh when I finish, I put my face in my hands, digesting whatever the heck that was I just read.

I don't know how to feel. It's been two years since I last heard from him. An unwanted flutter takes flight in my belly, a sensation I've shut down for too long.

It's like he couldn't think straight while writing. His thoughts were all over the place. Almost as if contacting me made *him* uncomfortable. I picture his tall, hulking form anxiously writing this letter, not knowing how I'd react. The nerves he must have felt when he dropped it at my front door, along with my favorite snack. It almost makes me feel bad for him...

Shut down that fucking thought right there!

I hope he's as uncomfortable as he sounds.

I audibly scoff again as that flutter dissolves and morphs into tension... *Doesn't want things to be awkward when we're around each other. I'm not the one to blame for our situation.* Maybe he should have thought of that before transferring to MY school. Who does he think he's, asking if my being with Graves has anything to do with him, or home, for that matter? Like he has any right to ask.

And just like that... I've changed my mind about the party tonight. I'm going to show my face, and I'll be on Carter's arm as I do.

Bellamy waltzes into the kitchen, just as I'm about to stash the letter away before Carter arrives. Even though Nate remains a topic we tiptoe around, I don't want him to see his note.

She steps closer, eyeing me suspiciously. "What's that?"

"The reason I'm going to that party tonight." I hand the letter to her and wait with my hands on my hips for her to finish.

"What the fuck, B? After all this time...*this*." She shakes the paper for emphasis, her face pinched. "This is how he contacts you."

I'm already nodding, eyebrows raised as much as my hackles. "I know, right! But Carter's going to be here any minute, and I really don't want him to see this."

"Okay, okay, we're going to need to unpack this with Darby when she gets back. How dare he." And this is why she is my best friend. Literally taking the thoughts from my head.

We'll unload all of this during one of our many weekly roomie hangouts. I need to wrap my head around it fully beforehand. I've been trying my best to keep it all together and not lose my shit over a stupid boy who broke my heart. Besides, I'm over it and him...right?

"And B..." she says with a mischievous grin on her beautiful face.

"Yeah?"

"Ignore his ass tonight. You're going to make him regret every second of every day he lives starting tonight. And then this week, I'm taking you shopping for the sexiest, tiniest bikini that ever was because we're throwing a pool party next Sunday, and I'm going to make sure he's there."

I can't help it, I smile. The thought of a jealous, regretful Nate excites me much more than it should.

Seconds later, Carter comes through our front door, freshly showered and sporting a handsome grin, holding a delicious-smelling pizza. Ugh, why can't I just fall head over heels for this one... The one who actually wants me?

Bellamy takes the letter and walks down the hallway with it, leaving me with an *I got you* wink.

"Hey, beautiful," he says, giving me a quick kiss, and then dropping the pizza onto the counter. "Did you pick out a movie for us?"

"I did, but I was thinking… If you want to go to the guy's party tonight, I'll go with you."

"You guys should definitely come. It'll be so much fun!" Bell squeals as she reenters the kitchen. "And we have pizza! This night just got so much better."

I laugh as she prances around the kitchen, eating a slice. I appreciate her superb acting abilities.

"Oh…uh, yeah, sure. I think it'll be fun. And if for any reason you want to leave, we can go," Carter says, loading his plate up.

He seems a bit unsure, and I don't know if it's because he doesn't want to go, or because he knows Nate's going to be there. Regardless, I can't let his presence hold me back anymore. What we had is in the past, and it's time we act like adults and move on, and if that means going about my normal life, even though he'll be there every step of the way, then so be it.

But moving on doesn't mean I won't enjoy making him regret breaking my heart.

Because I have moved on…haven't I?

I can do this… I can do this. I chant on repeat, hoping my heart will adopt the same mindset as we walk up the driveway.

As we pass a familiar blacked-out pickup truck, my heart begins to race faster.

We can hear the low bass of whatever Graham's newest obsessive song is playing from outside the house. The steady beat does nothing to calm my nerves.

Carter lightly squeezes my hand, drawing my attention to him as we approach the stairs. My stomach churns with every step.

"You look gorgeous tonight, B," he says with a soft smile.

"Thank you," I reply sheepishly. I look down, assessing my outfit choice for what feels like the tenth time. After ripping through my closet and Bellamy's, we landed on a pair of cut-offs, a tube top, and a pair of Bell's cowboy boots, with my hair styled in loose waves. I feel good, confident even…especially with the tan I'm sporting.

We step through the front door, and I am immediately surprised by the size of the crowd. Leaning over to Bell, I whisper-shout, "I thought this was supposed to be a small thing."

"Shit, I thought so too!" she laughs back, then grabs my hand. "Come on, I see Mav over by the kitchen."

I mouth to Carter, *follow me* as Bellamy grabs my hand and leads us through the crowd. But as we step into the kitchen, I feel as if the wind has been knocked out of me.

Well, here goes nothing.

FOUR

Nate

I should be downstairs partying, but instead, I'm trying to get my shit together after dropping that note off at Berkley's. I eye the playbook on my nightstand, wanting to torture myself further, but I leave it where it sits.

Fuck, I have to reel in it before our first game next weekend.

*But she was right there…*just a few feet away. A door was the only thing keeping me from seeing her. And now I have this unsettling need to lay my eyes on her. After Maverick told me earlier that Bellamy said she was coming solo, I'm even more upset I didn't get to see her there.

I pull on a fresh pair of joggers, not feeling like getting dressed up tonight. When I pick up my phone, I notice a notification. My buddy, Greyson, who I used to work summers with in Nori Beach, texted me.

GREYSON

I'll be the one in the stands on Saturday, internally cheering for you.

I smile for what feels like the first time today at the image of my broody friend in the stands on Saturday. No doubt his girl will be there, too. They live about thirty minutes away on the outskirts of Richmond Hills.

ME

Glad to know I'll have at least one fangirl in the crowd.

ME

BUT seriously, I'm happy you'll be there. If we win, y'all should come over to The Wolves Den for the after party.

GREYSON

Sounds lit. I'll talk to Lottie.

GREYSON

I know you are busy, but if you ever want a break from college life, you're welcome out at the house anytime.

He's reading between the lines. We haven't talked much during my time in Texas, but his girl and Berkley have remained good friends, per Lottie's Instagram. And besides Graham and my dad, he was the only other person who called me out, knowing there was more to me breaking up with Berkley than I had led on.

ME

Thanks brother. I might take you up on that sooner rather than later.

I tuck my phone in my pocket and head downstairs. I can feel the vibration from the bass of the hip-hop song playing in the living room under my grip on the staircase banister. Taking a steadying breath, I try to let go of my bad mood and be the easygoing QB my team needs me to be. I spot two of my roommates in the kitchen and head their way. This party isn't the small get-together they described it as, but I kind of figured it would end up being that way. My dad has always reminded me not to let fame and glory get to my head, but I'd be lying if I said I didn't enjoy my teammate's praises as I greet a few of the guys from our offensive line on my way to the kitchen.

"Superstar, what you drinking?" Maverick asks, opening the fridge like he's Vanna White showing me my prize.

Graham reaches in before I can answer, grabbing me a Blue Moon that I'm sure he bought with me in mind. It was always our beer of choice in high school. I don't drink much during the season, but tonight, I could use the taste of nostalgia.

"Thanks." I nod at Graham, taking the bottle from him.

"Sorry, we don't have orange slices, your highness," Maverick taunts.

Laughing, I flip him my middle finger. "Fuck off."

His attention goes over my shoulder, and a big smile takes over… "Amy!" he shouts and starts in that direction.

"Oh my god… Rick, don't fucking call me that." I hear a sultry southern voice reprimand, and I turn around to see a gorgeous redhead being swept up in Maverick's arms.

"I feel like it's been forever, Sis." Okay, so Amy must be short for Bellamy.

"Don't call me that either." She playfully swats him. "And I just saw you, like, a week ago."

I don't hear what's said back because Bellamy didn't come alone.

There she is. The piece of my heart that lives outside of my body.

My pulse quickens, and my toes tingle to move toward her. Beautiful long blonde hair, maybe even a little longer than the last time I saw a picture of her. Pouty lips covered in gloss, making me bite my own lip at the memories that flood in. My body aches for her to turn that beautiful face in my direction like she would have two years ago, seeking me out and then gracing me with her perfect smile. "She has a smile that can light up a room" was never a phrase I understood until the day I saw Berkley.

Her eyes finally land on me, but it feels nothing like how I remember. I think the biggest lineman in the league could hit me, and it would hurt less. No reaction, no emotion. Nada. Zilch. The only thing I get is her holding my gaze for a few beats longer than a glance before she turns her attention behind her. *To him.*

I take two steps toward them, but Graham grabs my arm. "You need to think before you do something stupid and push her even further away," he whispers, and I stare at them, considering his words.

My attention moves from them to where Graham's hand is wrapped around my arm, then to his face, and he continues, "Come on, let's go out back for a few. Get yourself together, and if she wants to talk to you, she will later."

I look back, and the sight of Carter Graves's arm slung over her makes me feel murderous, especially when he whispers something in her ear, and she smiles. The only thing that has me following Graham is that smile on her face. It's nothing compared to the smiles she used to give me. In this moment, I don't care how fucked up that is.

As we walk out back, I think my heart may beat right out of my chest. I try box breathing, but I'm having a hard time catching my breath. Dropping my beer, I bend over with my hands on my knees, feeling like I just had the air knocked out of me.

Nothing could have prepared me to see her in person, even more so on his arm, and with absolutely no regard for me. I don't know what's worse.

My anger turns inward...and the others who affected the choices I made back then. I've questioned myself every day since I made that life-altering decision, but today, I'm not just lying in the bed I've made; I'm suffocating in it.

I pick the beer up and chug what doesn't spill out.

"Slow down," Graham mutters from beside me.

"Put yourself in my shoes and tell me how you'd feel," I growl.

"Yeah, well, you made your bed, Nate." Get out of my fucking head, Graham.

"You think I don't fucking know that."

"I think you have to face it now, being here, seeing her. If you won't tell me why you did it, maybe you should tell her the truth. She deserves that, and maybe it would make this shit less awkward."

"It's not that easy." Even though Graham's always suspected there was more to the story, I haven't shared the truth with anyone but my dad. It felt wrong to talk to people about it when Berkley didn't even know.

"Just think on it. Whether you can ever get past it all and be together or not, she deserves to know the real reason you broke up with her. She hasn't been the same, Nate... I think she's settling with Carter."

My eyes narrow on him. "Of fucking course, she is."

"Just chill. Your team is all here and riding the high from how well practice went this week. Don't ruin that."

Exhaling heavily, I nod, and Cash walks up just in time for me to smooth out my pissed-off expression.

"Y'all good?"

"Yeah, as good as I'm going to be."

"What happ—" His attention is drawn to the door that opens to our patio area, where his stepsister, Berkley, and Carter walk out to the backyard, joining the majority of the partygoers. "Shit, never mind. I will gladly tell Carter to kick fucking rocks if you want me to."

"Nah, he would get too much satisfaction out of that. Dude has been trying to get under my skin since we hit puberty, and he finally found a way."

My center walks up to me, right as I finish my sentence. "Hey, QB...my girl's best friend was asking if you're single."

I chance one more glance toward Berkley... *Come on, BB, look at me. Give me something.*

"Yeah, I'm single, but unavailable. Thanks for looking out, Big John."

If she doesn't have blonde hair, blue eyes, glossy lips, and the initials 'BB,' I don't want her.

"Probably for the best. She's a bit of a clinger."

We all chuckle at that.

When he walks away, Cash's tone is low as he says, "Yeah, if you got it that bad, fucking another girl, no matter how many times, isn't going to make you see anyone else but her." I don't miss the way Cash watches his stepsister when he says it and not his girlfriend standing just a few feet away.

"Yeah, I tried that and quickly learned that void could never be filled."

Nothing would change my reality. Nothing would turn their brown hair blonde or their green eyes blue. No one's smile would light me up with one glance. *Nothing would make them her.*

She walks back into the house as Carter talks to some of our teammates. Staring him down, I follow her inside. I know it won't take him long to notice we're both gone, but I don't give a fuck.

"Can I grab a beer for Carter from the fridge?" she calls out to Graham, who's talking to a girl I don't recognize.

"Help yourself, B," he says over his shoulder.

Standing back, I watch her open the fridge, trying not to stare at her cute bubble butt and failing miserably. I notice her pink painted nails reach for the Blue Moon. *That's right, baby...think of me.*

With her lip between her teeth, she stares at it for a few seconds before putting it back and grabbing a Michelob Ultra instead.

I'm speaking before I can stop myself. "What? You don't want to taste me on his lips?"

She jumps, turning to face me, but recovers quickly with a sneer. "That would mean I'd remember what you taste like... Sorry to disappoint."

Her words break through me like hundreds of tiny shards, but deep down, I know she's lying, what we had is unforgettable.

"So we're going to play it like this, huh? Just going to walk in here and act like you don't even know me. Like there aren't a thousand memories between us."

"Yep. Left those in Nori beach the day you walked out on me." She tries stepping around me, but I move, blocking her into the kitchen. Berkley puffs up her chest and raises her eyebrow, letting me know she isn't the least bit intimidated by me.

I want to reach out and touch her, but I remind myself I gave up that right two years ago, so instead, I ask what I've been thinking about all evening. "What about my note? Did you even read it?"

Still standing her ground, her clear blue eyes feel like they dig into me. "Yes, and fuck you and your questions. You being here is like a slap to the fucking face, Nate."

It's like a smack to the face to me too, BB. I wish she understood, but how could she? She has no clue.

"I know none of it makes sense, but that's why I want to talk. I want to explain."

Do I? Am I willing to tell her the truth? Fuck, it feels like it was all for nothing.

"Berk, you okay?" I hear Graves ask from right behind me, and I've had enough of him this week.

Turning around, I shove my hand into his chest. "She's a big girl. Back the fuck up. We're talking."

"Fuck you, Nate. She's my girlfriend," he growls, pushing my hand away.

His words sear through me, and I grab him by the shirt. "You got exactly what you always wanted, didn't you?"

He tries removing my grip, but it's no use. "This isn't Nori Beach. You don't run shit here."

Huffing a laugh lacking humor, I raise my eyebrow at him. "That's what you think."

Suddenly, Graham is beside me. "Nate, let him go; you're drawing attention."

Carter puts a fake smile in place. "Yeah, QB, we wouldn't want people to see your true colors."

"You are one to fucking talk," I say, shoving him hard as I let him go.

"The girls can stay, but you need to go, Graves." Cash's voice joins this shitshow.

When I face Berkley again, Bellamy's by her side, scowling in my direction. "Actually, we were all leaving." She turns her attention to Cash. "Your little girlfriend is looking for you out back."

Ignoring whatever that's about, I keep my eyes on Berkley, whose face is full of rage that's pointed in my direction. But I'll take anger over indifference from her any day. Wanting to spur her on more, I reach into the fridge as the three of them start for the door.

Calling out with the Blue Moon in my hand, I taunt, "BB, you want a beer for the road…or maybe Graves does?"

"Don't call me that…" she hisses.

She looks around at a few of my teammates, who are now watching the drama unfold. An unhinged smirk takes over her face, and I brace for impact. "As far as the beer goes…if my memory serves me correctly, you like things up your ass. So that's exactly where you can shove that." She nods to the bottle.

Berkley thinks she embarrassed me, but I don't give a fuck; it just adds fuel to my fire.

I tilt my head, matching her smirk. "But BB, I thought you said you didn't remember anything."

She flips me off over her shoulder, taking Carter's hand in the other. I squeeze my fist, imagining I'm breaking his wrist, but instead, I do something else I know will piss him off.

"PS: I only like *you* touching my ass."

By the way Carter slams the front door, my jab landed as intended.

I may have gotten the last word, but right now, as I watch her leave through the window, it does fucking nothing for me. My chin falls to my chest. *Fuck.* I didn't intend to fight with her, especially the first time we came face to face again. But what the hell else did I expect?

I fucked up, and this is my price to pay.

THE HOWLER

Mountain Ridge University

Volume 20-08

SURVIVING OR THRIVING?

Hope everyone has had a good first week back in action. Who else is excited for the first home game of the season?

Tomorrow at 3pm the Wolves take on The Tennessee Vols! We expect the student section to show out for this one. Word is our new QB is taking us all the way this season so don't miss out.

FIVE

Nate

"Hey, ol' buddy," my dad greets me, closing his laptop as I walk up to his table at The Wolfpack. I can't help but search the staff members' faces, even though I already know the answer. *She isn't here.* Because when my dad suggested meeting here for a quick lunch, I pathetically asked Graham, who confirmed that Berkley didn't work on Fridays. No matter how badly I want to see her again, I don't want to put her in an awkward situation because she and my dad were always tight when we were together.

And after I caught a glimpse of her across campus on Wednesday, and she immediately turned and went in the opposite direction, I know for a fact she doesn't want me to just show up while she's on the clock.

My dad stands up, wrapping me up in a hug.

"Glad you're here," I say, loving the familiarity of his embrace.

"I wouldn't miss your first big game." He nods toward the chicken breast and salad he ordered for me since I don't have a lot of time between class and reviewing game film before practice. "Now eat up. You don't have much time."

"I'm sure she texted you, but your sister was so torn about not coming. She'll come to the next game with me, for sure."

"Good. I'm glad she listened for once." I take a bite of my salad, chewing before I continue, "I remember how fun the weekend before senior year was in Nori Beach, the last taste of freedom before the end of summer."

My dad chuckles, closing his eyes briefly. "Don't remind me. I try my best to be fair and give her the same freedoms you had, but I worry about her ten times more than I did you." He shakes his head. "Sorry, bud."

"Well, you knew I had Berkley keeping me straight." The words are out of my mouth before I even think to tamp them down.

A sad look takes over my dad's face. "Have you seen her yet?"

I swallow thickly at the memory of last Sunday and nod.

"Not so good?" he asks, probably from the solemn look on my face.

"Yeah, it didn't go quite as planned. She's umm..." It kills me to say it. "She's dating Carter Graves now."

"Well, shit..." My dad huffs in surprise. "I didn't see that coming. She's so far out of that dude's league, it isn't even funny."

Couldn't agree more with you, Pops.

The waitress walks up to check on us and refill our waters. "Hey, you're our new quarterback, aren't you?"

I smile up at her. "Guilty."

"Well, you know if y'all win tomorrow, you'll have to come eat this every Friday before a home game." It's her attempt at flirting, but the only thing I can think about is whether she knows Berkley or not.

I chuckle in good fun. "For sure. Couldn't do it without this chicken and lettuce."

She smiles. "Let me know if you need anything else, QB1."

My dad and I both thank her, and he jumps right back into our discussion about Berkley.

"Have you thought any more about being honest with her?"

I push the salad around my plate with my fork. "Yeah, a lot, actually, but then it feels selfish of me to do it now, like it was all for nothing, and then it might end in the same result for her...or maybe it won't. Maybe now that it's all said and done, it wouldn't change much. I don't know. It's never not on my mind, but I'm not sure what to do."

He sets down his burger and puts on his serious face. "I've always been team you-being-honest-with-her, but after a conversation I had with your mom the other day, I *definitely* think you should be."

I drop my fork at the mention of my mother. "You talked to her?"

He looks at me incredulously. "We have two children together, one who lives with me full time. Of course, I talk to her."

Shaking my head, I roll my eyes. "Yeah, okay, well...what did she say that made you feel the need to bring her up?"

"For one, she wants to come to a game, but I told her that was a discussion she should have with you, not me."

I don't respond to that because, honestly, my mom is a sore subject, and I don't have the energy to worry about seeing her right now.

"But she also told me something I found interesting. She said that Berkley never goes home to Nori Beach. She hasn't been back in over a year."

My eyebrows pinch together. "That doesn't make sense. Why wouldn't she go there? Unless her dad comes here often."

I make a mental note to ask Graham if he's seen Mr. Black.

"I don't know, Nathan, but I think it adds to the fact that you and her need to have a real conversation. Put your pride about Graves aside and talk to her. I want to see my son happy again, even when he's not on the football field."

I consider his statement, swallowing roughly I reply, "Okay, Dad...subject change."

He takes a sip of his water. "Okay, okay. How you feelin' about tomorrow?"

I smile at that thought. "I'm excited. We have a good thing going. I love being back with Graham. And my other room-mate, Nola, is untouchable; we have real chemistry on the field. He's going to make me look good."

"I figured you and Graham would fall back into it. Even in high school, you guys had the Mahomes-Kelce thing going on. I'm excited to see this other kid play. How about your defense?"

Offense scores points, defense wins ball games. I remember him saying this to me since I was in little league.

"They're giving me a run for my money in practice, so that's a good sign. They do have a hard time keeping up with Nola, but I'm telling you, he's just one of those players. He'll no doubt be a first-round draft pick in a few years if he stays healthy."

My dad and I continue eating our meals as he fills me in on life back in Nori and my free-spirited sister's latest antics.

As soon as we finish eating, I notice a man out of the corner of my eye approaching our table. We both look toward him.

"Hey there, gentlemen. I'm Phil, the owner of The Wolfpack." He reaches out, shaking my dad's hand first, then mine. "Outlaw, glad to have you here."

The Howler report plastered me in my practice jersey across the front of their release today, so I guess I'm easy to spot.

"Thank you. The food and service have been great. Just meeting my dad for a bite before film."

"Well, I just wanted to say hello and ask a favor of you." He looks bashful with the last part of the statement.

"Sure, what's up?"

That's when I notice the jersey he has slung over his shoulder. "I have your jersey and was hoping you'd sign it so we can put it on the wall with the other legends," he says, pointing to the wall behind where we sit.

"Of course, I'd be honored." My first thought is that Berkley will see it every shift. Now I just need to work on her not admiring it with disdain.

He passes me a Sharpie, and I sign my name and the number two on the back of the jersey. "All set."

"My son's going to go crazy for this. He's been a fan since we watched you at Texas Tech," he says, holding up the jersey.

I smile at that; I remember being a young fan idolizing my football heroes. "What size is he?"

His mouth drops open before saying, "Seriously?"

I laugh, smiling. "Absolutely. I probably won't have time this weekend, but maybe I can swing it by on Monday."

"Anytime. And he's a youth medium or maybe even a youth large, so he can wear it longer. You have no idea how excited he's going to be."

"Happy to do it."

He pats me on the shoulder and shakes my dad's hand again. "Hope to see you both in here again soon. Your meal is on the house."

We both tell him he doesn't need to do that, but he waves us off and heads toward the back.

"Nice guy. I should try to get his kid tickets too," I say, and my dad just smiles at me.

"I don't tell you enough how proud I am of you." He glances at his watch. "I don't want you to be late. You better get out of here. I'm going to stay and work on my laptop a little longer."

"Okay, I'll see you after the game tomorrow, right?" I confirm with him as I stand.

"Of course, ol' buddy." He hugs me and kisses the top of the head. "I love you."

"I love you too, Dad." Through everything, my dad has been my constant, and I want him to have his own happiness, not just living for me and Willow.

I take a few steps away from him and turn back. "Let me hear them."

He smiles, knowing exactly what I want.

Positive manifestations for tomorrow.

"Four touchdowns." Holding up four fingers, he then points one at me. "One of which you run into the end zone yourself. And a big win over Tennessee."

"I like the sound of those."

I'll be writing them in my playbook tonight and adding one of my own.

Berkley in the stands, wearing anything but Graves's jersey.

BERKLEY

"If I don't eat something pronto, I think I might die," Darby groans, linking her arm with mine as we walk through campus. The attempt is quite comical with our height difference.

"Hey to you too," I chuckle.

"First week of classes always kicks my ass. I need a pick-me-up if I'm going to make it out tonight."

"Ahh, yes, the Kappa Sigma party. How could I forget," I tease.

"Oh, stop, you know damn well if you weren't babysitting, you'd be there, right alongside me and Bell."

"Yes, their parties are wild... Just don't forget Bell is super-human and doesn't get hungover, and Cash and Mav will be dragging us to that field first thing in the morning. So don't try keeping up with her."

"Yeah, yeah. I know my limits." She waves me off as we enter the café.

By the time we sit down with our order, Bellamy joins us at our booth with her signature iced coffee in hand. Looking pissed as hell, I might add.

"You're never going to believe this. Remember, I was all excited about the new psych professor this semester? Well, there were some schedule changes, and now I have Professor Douglas. Ugh, shoot me now."

"Professor Douglas, the major creep? Like, don't sit in the front row with a skirt on, Professor Douglas?" Darby confirms as she throws her brunette hair into a high ponytail.

"Yup, that one!" Bellamy says, groaning as she steals a piece of fruit from my bowl.

"I'm sorry, Bell. Is there any way to drop it?"

"I wish, but because I was late to declare my major, I'm behind on my prerequisites. So no, I need this class this semester in order to stay on track to graduate."

"Ugh, I hate that for you; that creep shouldn't even have a job. Guess it's sweatpants and hoodies for you this semester." Darby tries to lighten the mood.

"Yes, and sit wayyy in the back," I add.

My phone vibrates with a notification, and flipping it over, I see a message from my friend, Lottie.

> LOTTIE
>
> Greyson and I will be at the game tomorrow…
> Where are you guys pre-gaming?

"Lottie is going to the game tomorrow and wants to know tail-gating details. Where are we meeting?"

"Aww, yay! I miss her. Let me confirm with Mav. He

mentioned something, but I totally spaced. Tell her I'll text her later and let her know," Bellamy says.

ME

Bell said she'll talk to the guys and let you know. Can't wait to see you and catch up!

I haven't seen Lottie since the beginning of the summer, so we definitely have a lot to catch up on. Now that she's declared her major, she's been on the western campus, so I won't get to see her as often in the quad and between classes as we used to.

LOTTIE

Okay, babes, I'll see you tomorrow! Xoxo

Looking at the time on my phone, I realize I need to head to The Wolfpack to meet Tiffany and grab the kids.

"I have to go soon. Picking up the rat pack at three," I announce, and start cleaning up my tray.

"Alright, I have basketball workouts in a bit so I'm going to chill… I love playing but damn am I going to miss happy hour Fridays. Darby says with such a dramatic flair, I can't help but laugh.

"Okay, Drama, you'll survive sans happy hour. Just think by the spring you'll be back at it and you won't have to use a fake id anymore."

I leave the two of them to debate the significance of getting to happy hour on time and head across campus toward The Wolfpack.

I've tried my best these last few days to take the long way through campus, so I don't have an accidental run-in with you know who. But today I have to hope for the best since I'm already running behind to pick up the kids, and the quickest way to town is straight through the quad. I'm looking forward to seeing those munchkins tonight. A summer away is a long time, and I've missed them like crazy. I've been watching them since my second semester freshmen year when I got a job at The Wolfpack.

Shit, shit, shit.

Fuck my luck because, of course, dead straight in my path are Nathan Outlaw and Nola, swarmed by their adoring fans. Ugh, it makes me want to puke. Keeping my head down, I trudge onward, right past the groupies and the two men who seem to be eating that shit up. I chance a glance in their direction and can't help but notice the superstar smiles they're both sporting as they chat with the gorgeous girls pawing at them.

The two of them together are a dream. Nola has always been big with the ladies with his caramel brown skin, green eyes, and endless charm. Making him a well-sought-after member of the MRU football team. He's handsome as hell, but in my eyes he doesn't hold a candle to the guy who stole my heart years ago, Nathan Outlaw. He's so damn good looking, it hurts. His brown hair is perfectly tousled, curling ever-so-slightly at its ends. The hazel of his eyes shines brightly, and I'm sure every girl's heart stops dead in its tracks when his attention is focused on them. And don't even get me started on the new sleeve of tattoos he's sporting. Ugh. I haven't given myself permission to ogle the new addition openly, but it's massive and extremely detailed. Everything about him is fucking perfect, and it drives me insane.

Slews of comments and curses come to my mind, but I bite my tongue and pass without a word. *Good job, B,* I internally praise, patting myself on the back. I can't let the sight of him dampen my mood because, let's be real, I'm going to be seeing a lot of him.

But I don't think I'll ever get used to seeing the swarms of girls, and that's why I blocked him on all my social media. I didn't want the constant reminder of something that was no longer mine. That he was now free to be touched by anyone other than me. And walking past what I just saw stirs up a fuck-ton of those old emotions. Jealousy rearing its ugly green head yet again.

I stew for the entire walk to town. Replaying the dumb smile that he gave to every one of those cleat chasers. I arrive at The Wolfpack with a few minutes to spare and make my way inside to wait for Tiffany, releasing a breath that I'm now in the clear.

I'm waiting by the bar, sipping on a Diet Coke, when I hear my name being called.

Wait, that voice sounds familiar. Whipping my head around, I find Mr. Outlaw walking in my direction.

"I thought that was you," he says with a genuine smile. The sight of him thaws my heart from the frost that has slowly crept in over the last few days.

Snapping out of my shock, I give him a genuine smile right back. "Brian." I lean up to hug him.

"It's been too long. How's school going? Still doing education?" he asks. He's always been such a wonderful man. Fully invested in his kids' lives, their happiness, and their successes. Which means, while I was with Nate, he was invested in me, too. My chest twinges at that thought.

"I love it here, and yes, early childhood education," I beam proudly.

"Always thought you would make a wonderful teacher. So much patience and compassion. You're going to do great." His hand squeezes my shoulder lightly.

"Here for the big game?" I ask, knowing he's one of those parents who's at every practice, every tournament, and every home game if possible.

"Wouldn't miss it for the world. He scared the crap out of us last year when he got injured, but I'm glad MRU had the wherewithal to approach my boy."

"He'll do great, I'm sure," I say, trying to tiptoe around the topic.

"Listen, I know it's not my place or any of my business...but I'm going to say it anyway. I think you two should talk. Clear the air, maybe start the school year off on a better foot. It's been two years of radio silence, so I'm sure you both have a lot to say. I told Nate the same thing today. He has some things he needs to get off his chest."

My stomach sinks at that. What else could he need to tell me? Taking me back to that last night we spent together in Nori Beach, my mind spins with scenarios. "Yeah, you're probably right," I say with a sad smile. I mean, he's not wrong. It would make life easier if we were to talk...but am I ready to hear what he has to say is the real question?

Mr. Outlaw takes a look at his watch. "Well, I gotta go. I'll see you in the stands tomorrow," he says, rather than asks.

"Go, MRU," I cheer, and he hugs me goodbye with a chuckle before walking out the doors.

I close my eyes and regain my composure, just as tiny squeals fill the air.

With my arms splayed wide open, I spin toward the stampede of kids heading in my direction.

"You're back!" the oldest, Josie, says as she dives in for a hug.

"I missed you guys so much," I say while rustling PJ's hair, who decided to latch onto my leg.

Jack stands a foot away, looking at his feet sheepishly.

"What are you, too cool to give me a hug?" I ask him, reaching out to pull him closer. He smiles and wraps his arm around my middle.

Tiffany comes through the doors, holding on to Gwen, looking like she just stepped out of a windstorm.

"Oh, thank heavens you're back. We've missed you so much!" Tiffany exclaims as she leans in to give me a hug.

When she puts Gwen down, I'm expecting the littlest to dive at me, but instead she eyes me cautiously, and I squat down to be at eye level.

She juts her chin out at me. "You're back," she says, all nonchalant.

I stifle a laugh. "Yes, I'm back."

"Was it worth it? The trip and all?" PJ asks from where he's still clutching onto me.

This time it's Tiffany who's holding in her laugh. "I did have a great time, if that's what you mean."

"Well, I guess I'm happy you had a good time. But was it worth leaving me?" PJ asks, his big doe eyes doing their job to guilt me.

"Aw, I missed you all terribly."

Gwen hesitates for a beat longer, then comes crashing into my arms, and I hold her close. She pulls back slightly. "You missed me most."

"Is that so?"

"Mmmhmm, but shhh." She grins, then wraps her arms around me again.

With all their love surrounding me, I feel my body decompress from the stress of the last two weeks. Being with them brings me back that sense of normalcy I've been craving, and I can't wait to spend the rest of my night catching up with my favorite kids. This is exactly what I need, and I know they'll keep me busy enough that I won't dwell on tomorrow.

Just as I grab the to-go food from the counter, I hear Phil calling out Jack's name. We turn to face him as he walks out of his office, a maroon shirt in his hands.

"Jack, I thought you might want to help me hang up the newest addition to the jersey wall."

He beams at his dad, more than happy to help him.

"I was waiting for you to do it… Look, buddy. I got Nathan Outlaw's new jersey. He signed it, too!" Phil beams as he holds out the jersey for his son to see.

And just like that, another piece of my life has been infiltrated.

Seems like I'm destined to forever see reminders of him through my shattered rose-colored glasses.

Six

Berkley

While sipping my morning coffee, I stare at the envelope sitting on the table. *Another letter.* After running into Mr. Outlaw yesterday, and his remark about me and Nate needing to talk, I'm not sure if I want to read what's scribbled inside. Because I know deep down, my guard is starting to slip. It was easy to stay angry and hurt when I cut off contact, but seeing him and being around him is another story. *Especially with the way he looks at me…like I'm still his.*

I stumbled across it this morning when I got back from my early morning run. I almost choked when I saw the familiar handwriting again. Both Bellamy and Darby are still sleeping off last night's party, so it's just me, my coffee, and the fucking letter.

Releasing a sigh, I relent and open the seal.

> I know we got off on the completely wrong foot, but somehow, knowing there's a chance you'll be in the stands today comforts and excites me in a way I haven't felt in a long

time. Please don't throw this away... This is
something I wrote as a way to work through
my feelings of my first home game in Texas...
- Nate

There's another sheet of paper tucked under the first, so I
carefully unfold it and read on.

Freshmen Year- Sept 1st

Tomorrow's our first home game of the
season, and the number one thought on my mind
isn't about the plays that we'll be running or
the routes that I need to be looking for on
each possession. It's not even on winning the
game itself. My mind can't stop spiraling at
the thought of you not being there. You won't be
there, you won't call or text, you probably won't
watch it at all. I can't blame you. I did this.
I ruined us.

My heart constricts at the agony in his words. Confusion
floods my brain as I read both papers for the second time.
Flipping each sheet over to see if there is more…desperately
seeking more.

And there, on the flip side of the first note in small letters, is
one last request from him.

Please don't wear his jersey today.

God knows how long I sit staring into space as I try to piece back together my thoughts and emotions running rampant. It's not until I hear the slight dragging of the kitchen chair next to me that I come to with a jolt.

"You okay over here?" Bell asks.

I stare at her blankly, handing her the papers. Gnawing at my lip as she reads them.

"Damn," is all the response I get as her gaze locks on me to gauge my reaction.

"Shit, B. I don't know what to say…"

"Yeah, you're telling me," I scoff.

"The only thing is…for someone who broke up with you, he seems awfully torn up about his decision."

"What decision?" Darby asks, wiping the remnants of sleep from her eyes as she enters the kitchen.

"The note writer struck again," Bellamy answers, then hands the letters over for her to inspect.

I remain silent as she reads them, waiting for her take on what we just read.

"Have you two talked yet?" Darby asks.

"No, and I ran into his dad last night, and he was being all cryptic and shit. Alluding to the fact that Nate had some things he needed to get off his chest."

"Listen, I was all for Team Hate Nate, but I think you guys should talk. There seems to be more to the story," Bellamy says as she takes a sip of her tea.

"Fuck, guys, it was so easy to keep the memory of him locked away, never to be thought of again. But now…now, I don't know how to feel. And I hate it," I admit. These letters are strong reminders of the reasons I fell in love with him years ago.

Darby comes behind my chair and wraps her arms around me. "I know this can't be easy for you. But at the end of the day, we're Team Berk, so you tell us how you want to proceed."

"I just want to get through today and, hopefully, by tomorrow, I'll have my thoughts together enough to have a real conversation with him." Even if seeing him in his jersey will likely be the worst kind of torture.

"That sounds like a great fucking plan! Also, not to add fuel to the fire, but…" She does quotations with her fingers. "Don't wear Graves's jersey… Does he not know you at all?" Bellamy laughs out.

Once upon a time, I wore an Outlaw jersey every chance I had. It's one of the things I could never part with.

I cringe, knowing I've led Nate to believe there's more between Carter and I. Especially after he dropped that girl-friend line at the party last weekend. Even though I enjoyed the way Nate's fury blazed at his words, I didn't appreciate Carter making such false claims.

"Sounds like we need to start drinking asap," Bell says and heads into the kitchen. "What will our tailgating poison be today, ladies?" she asks as she scours our liquor supply.

"Whatever it is, make it strong," I tell her with a sigh, folding up the notes and carefully placing it back in the envelope. "I'm going to need it."

Why do the bathrooms need to be so far away from where we parked? Is my main thought as I weave my way through the cars, trying to find our tailgating party. I swear we weren't this far.

Shit, am I lost? I chuckle to myself.

We pre-gamed at our apartment, which probably wasn't the best idea, but I can't hide the fact that I'm having a great time. Lottie and Greyson are here, and I love having her around. We got really close her first year dating Greyson while in Nori Beach. Then we both enrolled in Mountain Ridge and were able to remain friends, regardless of Greyson's lasting friendship with Nate.

I find Maverick's Tahoe clearly differentiated by its bright blue color and its 'CRSHBROS' license plate. The nickname Cash and him have earned on the ice. As I walk around the side, I pause at Lottie's words.

"Yeah, I couldn't believe it either. They were so in love. Like the couple G and I looked up to," she says, then adds, "Although he never admitted anything, Greyson swears there's more to it. There had to be. According to him, Nate was so torn up by the breakup, you would've thought she was the one who broke it off."

Emotion clogs my throat, breath catching at her words. We were the best; we were endgame. Until something happened, and lately, everyone seems to be confirming my recent suspicions that there's more to the story than Nate led on.

"That's the vibe I'm getting as well," Bellamy replies.

"I just want Berk to be happy. So whatever that takes, I'm all for it," Lottie says.

"Well, I think our girl is super confused. It takes time to digest it all. But I know she'll get to the bottom of it," Darby adds, and I smile. Even though I stumbled upon a conversation I probably shouldn't have, I know they're all just looking out for me.

"Why you being a creep over here?" I jump at the sound of Maverick's voice behind me.

"Shit, you scared the crap out of me." I grab my chest to dull the pounding, unsure if my heart is racing from being caught off guard, or the thought of what my conversation with Nate might reveal.

He slings his arm over my shoulder. "Come on, B, we still have another hour before we head in."

"I need another drink. *Or ten*," I proclaim, muttering the last part to myself.

"We can fix that. I need a partner for beer pong. You in?" Maverick gives me a wink.

As our team lines up on the fifteen-yard line, the crowd roars to life. The sound of howling wolves fills the air. With less than a minute on the clock till halftime, and the end zone within reach, another touchdown and extra point would put us at a 14 to 7 lead.

I swear I'm going to have a bloody lip with how badly I'm chewing on it. It's almost like time slows once the ball is snapped into Nate's waiting hands. He looks to the left, but Nola is surrounded. Then he looks to his right, where Graham can't shake Tennessee off his tail. Tennessee's defensive end is closing in on him, so he makes a dash for it.

Nate charges up the left side of the field, zig-zagging his way past Tennessee.

"Holy shit, he's running it in!" Cash yells as we all cheer.

A brick house of a linebacker lines up to take out Nate, and we all let out an audible gasp as Nate dives over the pile of players and lands in the end zone.

The fans go wild. Howling and cheers are all we can hear as maroon puffs of smoke signal MRU's touchdown. Nate points to the section of the crowd where his dad is sitting several rows over and closer to the field. My heart squeezes at how it used to be me he'd point to, then he'd lift his hand up in a half-heart for me to complete from my place in the stands. I quickly shake off those memories as the team kicker, Pike, lines himself up and easily gets MRU the extra point.

There's a small celebratory gathering of the team before they head off the field. The cameras zoom in to catch the team's high, and I can't stop myself from staring at the jumbotron as it focuses on Nate. The close-up reveals the underwater scene expertly tattooed on his throwing arm. And not just any scene, an octopus.

"Did you hear me?" Bellamy yells over the noise, smacking my arm for my attention.

"Sorry, no. What did you say?"

"I said, I hope they keep this up. The party will be even better with a win under their belt!"

"Yeah...uh, sounds great," I mutter, half listening and half staring at the jumbo screen.

"Whatever, you're not even paying attention," she teases, then turns to the rest of our group and howls along with them.

She's not wrong. I'm not paying her any mind, too busy staring at the tentacles wrapping around his bicep and forearm. *An octopus... What are the chances?*

· · ·

"Says here they can change their color and shape to match undersea objects." I read aloud from the display next to the octopus's tank.

"Did you know they collect treasure too?" Nate whispers in my ear.

"Really? What kind?"

"Usually rocks or shells, but sometimes they collect shiny objects too."

"They're so fascinating," I say, pushing my face up even closer to the tank to see if there are any others hiding.

Out of nowhere, a suction-like sound erupts behind me, and I jump. I find Nate close behind me, acting all innocent.

"What the hell was that?" I ask, swatting at him.

"What was what?" With a grin, he places his hands on my hips and pulls me flush against him.

"That noise… Did you make it?"

"Not sure what you're talking about. I'm just educating you on octopus behavior," he teases, sucking on my neck.

Pushing him away, I scold him with my eyes. "We're on a field trip…at an aquarium. You can't get me all hot and bothered."

"No one's around… Besides, it'd be hot to hook up in the predator cave, no?" The smooth timber of his voice has goosebumps spreading over my skin as he presses his growing erection against me.

"I'm here to learn. So, if you could be so kind as to remove your growing extremities from my vicinity," I tease, then turn back to the tank to try to cool off and not take him up on his offer.

"You'd be my treasure," Nate says as he wraps his arms around me. Butterflies swirl in my belly as I look at him over my shoulder.

"It's true. You're the thing I treasure most in this world." He kisses my cheek softly, and I feel my knees buckle.

This guy means the world to me, and I to him. Nothing will ever tear us apart... Nothing.

"He's looking at you again." Bellamy's voice pulls me from my memory.

I turn my attention from the jumbotron to the sideline, and one thought stirs on repeat as I stare back.

Why did you give up on something you treasured, Nathan Outlaw?

NATE

"All I Do Is Win" by DJ Khaled blares through the stadium, and the crowd goes crazy when the jumbotron zones in on my team heading back onto the field as the halftime clock dwindles. The adrenaline rushes back through me with every step. We had one hell of a first half, and after our locker room pep talk from Coach Price, we're ready to finish strong.

I find my dad in the stands as I jog past, and he lifts two fingers. His reminder to me that I have two more touchdowns to go. Feeling more confident than ever that I'll carry out his manifestations, I salute him. He's always believed in me, but after my injury and being replaced so easily, my ego was taken down a few notches.

I keep walking, and like so many other times today, my eyes flit past my dad to where Berkley stands with her roommates and the twins. Her blonde hair in two braids is almost long enough to touch her exposed back. The tan skin right above her ass in those tiny jean shorts makes my dick twitch inside my jock cup. She's such a fucking stunner.

Deep down, I know she didn't do it for me, but I can't say that when I saw her right before the first snap of the game, that I didn't feel pure relief. No Graves jersey in sight, just her tight, tanned stomach on display with a wolf stretched across her maroon crop top.

She has her back to me, talking to Bellamy, and I allow my gaze to trail down her toned legs. Even though I can't tell from here, I can almost guarantee she has on a pair of Air Forces.

"Wipe that drool off your mouth and let's go get 'em." Graham nudges me, putting on his helmet.

I steal one more glance, and this time, she turns in my direction. I expect the smile to drop from her face when our eyes meet, but it doesn't. She holds my gaze for a few beats, and I squeeze my hand at my side, so I don't lift it up and give her the symbol I used to at every game in high school.

"Seriously, Nate, come on. We got work to do."

He's worried my head isn't in it, but he has no idea how much just one simple look from her drives me to do my best. Hell, just her being here lights a fire under me.

Yes, she's on my mind, like always, and especially after my dad's admission about her not going home to Nori beach. I plan to go out there and win this game first, and then at some point this weekend, I'm going to find out what that's all about, one way or another.

"I'm coming."

He smacks my ass, and then a shit-eating grin takes over. "Sorry, I forgot ass play is your thing."

Because he and my other roommates are as mature as thirteen-year-old boys, they haven't let Berkley's comment go.

"How about you stay away from my ass, and I'll get you a touchdown this half."

He winks. "Bet."

I head through the back entrance, out to where our family and friends are waiting. I'm smiling from ear to ear. It feels good to still hear the buzz of the fans when leaving the stadium, happy with our win today over Tennessee.

As I look for my dad, I'm met by the most beautiful girl in the world instead. Standing in between my roommates and hers, I'd give anything in this moment to walk up to her, pull her into my arms, and kiss her silly. But I have no right to do that anymore. I can't rewind the clock and change other people's actions, nor can I change my own.

There's the superstar!" Maverick cheers. I finally peel my eyes away from Berkley as I make my way closer to the group, giving the twins a bro hug.

The win feels good. Four touchdowns, one that I ran into the end zone, just like my dad predicted, and a pick six from a crazy interception by our rookie linebacker. On top of that, Nola and Graham scored too. It was an epic first game and there's only one thing that would make it better.

And all five foot two of her standing in front of me.

"Hey, ladies, did y'all have fun?" I greet Berkley and her friends.

"I personally love hockey more, but there were a lot of good views out there today, so I ain't mad about it," Bellamy says, raising her eyebrows, and Cash's flaring nostrils have me chuckling.

"I'm just here for the secret sauce," the brunette beside them chimes in and takes a sip from her cup. I recognize her as Darby, who Graham pointed out on campus earlier in the week. She's on the women's basketball team, and not nearly as prickly to me as Bellamy is.

"You and half of the student body." I laugh because it's the first game of the season, which means, the majority of the campus is drunk right now.

Allowing my attention to wander where it really wants to be, I look right at Berkley. "How about you, BB?"

"Could have been better..." she smirks, and I quirk my eyebrow at her. "It was a good start, Outlaw. How's the shoulder feeling?"

Unable to hold in my smile at her concern, I roll my right shoulder. "Surprisingly good. The athletic trainers here are top tier."

"Well, that's good to hear."

My body warms at her not dismissing me. I grin and ask, "Where are G and Lottie?"

"So about that..." The girls all let out a collective giggle. "We may have gotten Lottie a little drunk during the tailgate, so she was done for by half time. Greyson said rain check on the party."

I shake my head, smiling, because I can picture sweet Lottie giving Greyson a run for his money right about now. A memory of the four of us on my boat in the summer creeps in, with Berkley in a pink bikini, lounging at the helm. Fuck, I'd give anything to have that moment back.

I reach out, barely running my finger across the hem of Berkley's crop top before I stop myself. "I like the shirt."

Eyes narrowed, her scowl is now firmly back in place. "I didn't wear it for you."

I bite my lip to hide my smirk. "No doubt, but that doesn't mean I didn't notice how hot you look in it." I trail my eyes all the way down her body, finding the Air Forces I knew would be there.

A slight blush takes over her face as she tries to say something, but she's interrupted by my other roommates.

Maverick nods at Nola and Graham as they come up behind me. "Y'all ready to celebrate?"

"Is that even a question?" Nola chimes in. "I think that reporter wants to come too." He looks at me and gestures his head back toward the stadium.

"Which reporter?" Mav asks.

He bumps his shoulder into me. "The one who interviewed me and QB after the game."

I roll my eyes at Nola. She was more hands on than normal.

"I think I know which one you're talking about. Pretty sure she fucked our captain last year."

I don't miss the way Berkley swallows, looking away at Maverick's response.

"Well, she isn't welcome. And speaking of that, you all will be nice to Graves tonight." Bellamy gives a chagrin smile, pointing in mine and Cash's direction.

I don't like it, but I answer truthfully for Berkley to hear.

"Man, fuck Graves, but if it's what gets you three to come," I pause and nod toward Berkley and Darby, "then I'll behave."

Speaking of the motherfucking asswipe himself... Carter approaches from the corner of my eye. Not wanting to watch them together, I turn my body swiftly and give a quick good-bye. "See y'all at the house. I'm going to go say hi to my dad before I hit the shower." I don't miss Bellamy taking notice of my pain-stricken face, her eyebrows pinching as she looks at me curiously.

I'm sure in her eyes, I'm the asshole who broke her friend's heart, but she has no idea how broken I've been since that day.

SEVEN

Berkley

The bass vibrates through me, and I sway my hips to the steady beat of "Passionfruit" by Drake that's blasting through the speakers.

I swig the last of my beer and place it on the counter, ready to cut myself off. It's been a long day of drinking, and I don't want to feel like shit for the pool party tomorrow. Glancing at Bell, she raises her shot glass and swigs it back. Clearly, she's more advanced at partying than I am.

Although I haven't seen Nate since we first got here, I'm finally relaxing and not trying to spot him in the crowded room.

Bellamy leans into me. "I need another drink! Follow me." She grabs my hand, and we weave ourselves through the crowd. Once we're back in the kitchen, I crack open a Diet Coke as Bell pours herself another mixed drink.

"I still can't believe Darbs overdid it today," I say, chuckling.

"For real, her and Lottie. Out of us all, I thought it would be you who had to bow out early," she teases back with a hip check.

"No way, I'm great at pacing myself," I say as a hiccup escapes, causing us both to break out in full laughter.

I raise my silver can to her red solo, and we cheers. "Love you," I say with a smile. At the same time, Bell's eyes go wide.

Arms wrap around my waist, lips reaching the shell of my ear. "Here you are, gorgeous," Carter says, a slight slur to his tone.

Even though the girls and I only got here about an hour ago, I presume the team has been celebrating their win since they left the stadium.

I spin in his arms and give him a light peck on the cheek. Shifting his mouth so his lips are on mine, he kisses me deeper. We kiss for a few moments, and his hand cups the back of my neck. He's a great kisser; it's actually one of the things I like best about him. I just wish there was still a spark between us when his lips were on mine. The one that began to take off at the end of last semester, but unfortunately, I feel as if the flame has been doused in water. As his hands reach for my ass, that my cut-offs give him easy access too, I pull back.

He's never made such attempts to kiss or be all over each other publicly. I wonder if it's the liquor I'm smelling that's fueling such boldness, or it's the fact that Nate is here too.

It's awkward being in this position with him. Bellamy and some of his friends are all around us, witnessing Carter trying to paw at me, and I'm not having it.

"Alright, settle down, killer," I say as I try to create some distance between us.

"Aw, come on, babe. I've missed you," he says, attempting to pull me close once more.

"Carter, stop," I say, a little firmer this time. Hopefully, he'll pick up how uncomfortable he's making me feel.

His hands fly up in defense. "Geez, sorry. Was just trying to get a little love from my girl."

There he goes again, dropping the "my girl" thing.

"Now is not the time. Besides, you're clearly drunk."

His eyes flare with anger at my words.

"Not the time... What the hell, B? It's never the right time, is it? Ever since fucking Outlaw got here, you've barely even touched me. Is that why? Is he the reason?"

"If you'd like to talk like an adult, we can have this conversation at another time... Now is *not* it," I grind out through clenched teeth.

"Oh yes, of course, must always be on your terms..." He rolls his eyes.

Placing my hands on my hips, I'm over this. "I suggest you go grab some water and sober up before you say something you'll regret."

"Whatever, why don't you go find Nate and tell him all about how I'm the asshole now. It's exactly what he's waiting for anyway."

I shake my head. "Can you just fucking stop? This has nothing to do with him, and everything to do with your behavior right now. So cut the shit and walk away." Well, mostly nothing to do with him...

He grabs another beer out of the bin and storms off without another word.

With a huff, I spin back to Bellamy, who unfortunately had to witness that shitshow. I roll my eyes as I sip the Diet Coke in my cup. "Ugh, drunk Carter is so not it," Bell says with a wince as she throws back another drink.

"You're telling me," I scoff.

I'm beyond pissed now. I don't even want to be here.

Bell eyes me for a minute before putting her arm around me. "You good?"

The expression firmly plastered on my face is answer enough. "I think I'm going to head home."

She lets out a sigh of disappointment.

"I'm sorry, babe, but there's no way I'm recovering from this mood. Not here, at least."

"Alright, I'll walk you back," Bell says. "Let me just tell the guys I'm leaving."

"You don't have to—"

She cuts me off. "I will not let you walk home by yourself after a day full of drinking."

"Please, stay. Honestly, it's okay. You're having fun, no need to leave."

She levels me with a stare before turning away from me.

Bellamy disappears out the back door to where some of the guys are as I stay in place, still stewing from that interaction with Carter. When she returns a few minutes later, Nate trails behind her.

I try my best not to drool at how good he looks. And after the game he played today, too, I swear he catches me staring.

Well, at least he didn't witness what just went down with Carter and me. But instead of joining the party, he continues to follow Bell to where I'm standing.

At just his nearness, my body tenses like it's preparing for his touch. Like it hasn't been without him for years now.

But I school my features, cross my arms over my chest, and brace for what happens next.

NATE

The back door opens, and like every other time tonight, I glance from where I'm sitting beside Cash to see if it's Berkley.

Instead, it's Bellamy who appears to be upset.

"What's wrong, Bella?" Cash asks, immediately standing up.

Bella, huh?

She waves him off. "I'm good." Rolling her eyes, she huffs, "I should have just told y'all to ban Carter from the house. Now he's ruined our night, so I'm going to walk Berk home."

That has me out of my chair. "What did he do?"

"Chill, stalker boy. She's fine. They just got into an argument. Probably over you."

Over me?

"Stalker?" Cash asks with a pinched brow.

"Your friend likes to leave little letters on *my friend's* doorstep. AKA *my* doorstep," she chides.

I wish I knew what Berkley truly thought of my letters...

She keeps talking to Cash. "I just wanted to tell y'all bye. You're picking me up in the morning, right?"

"Like always," he responds, his eyes lingering on hers.

"Okay, come at eight instead of nine, so we can be back for the pool party."

"I'll be there," Cash mumbles, all while my mind is coming up with an idea that has my feet following the fiery redhead.

"Hold up. If you want to stay, I can walk her home."

When she pauses, I think she's considering it, but she opens our back door. "You'd like that, wouldn't you?" she says over her shoulder, continuing into the house.

"Let's go, lady," Bellamy says to my beautifully pissed-off girl.

"Bellamy wants to stay. I'll walk you home," I rush out.

Berkley looks a little stunned by my sudden appearance, her eyes widening.

"I did not say that," Bellamy growls at me, crossing her arms.

"I don't need either of you to walk me... It's only a couple minutes away, and Darby is there. So, she'll call the hounds if I don't show up." She takes a few steps, and her body sways from the alcohol she's likely been drinking all day.

"Not funny," I say, grabbing her arm as she tries to head for the door.

"Nate, there you are." Berkley and I both turn to see a blonde I dodged earlier when I first got to the party. "I wondered where you went. Want to be my partner in beer pong?"

"He was actually just about to walk me home." Berkley slips her hand into mine, and fuck, it still fits so perfectly.

There she is. Claim me, baby. I'm yours.

Thank you, random girl... You just helped me out more than you know.

I catch the way Bellamy raises her eyebrows at Berkley as the other girl walks away.

"Let's get you home, BB," I say, gently pulling her toward the door, not wanting to lose the chance to be alone with her.

As soon as the door shuts, she rips her hand from mine. "I see blondes are still your type."

"You jealous, baby?"

"No! And don't call me that," she shouts and scares the shit out of me when she almost falls down the front stairs. I grab her arm just in time, steadying her.

"Okay, drunkie, keep telling yourself that." I link my arm into hers, and she doesn't fight me as we start walking to her place.

We move in silence for the first couple of minutes. So many things are on the tip of my tongue, but there's too much alcohol involved tonight to breach anything I'd want to.

There is one pressing question that doesn't require sobriety, though. "What happened with Graves tonight?"

Narrowing her eyes, she gives me nothing. "None of your damn business."

"You're right," I say, holding up my free hand, signaling I'll back off the topic.

Berkley shakes her head, and after another minute of silence, she surprises me. "Being this close to you is so confusing… Your damn letters are even more confusing."

I don't respond immediately, trying to articulate what I want to say, but she continues before I do. "Did you really write that letter two years ago?"

I nod, closing my eyes at the memory. I was such an emotional mess back then.

"I know none of it makes any sense, but I didn't just leave that day and move on. My world spun around you—every game, every accomplishment, every day, every minute had been about you since we met. I thought I was doing the right thing back then, but it never felt right." I stop my steps, turning her, so our bodies are almost touching, and it takes everything in me not to pull her into me. Tipping her chin up, I dip my head down so my eyes bore into hers. "*I* haven't felt right since that day. And now I'm here, having to face the feelings that never went away, and I'm confused, too, BB."

Her eyes fill with emotion, and she looks at my lips before she lets out a sigh and steps back.

"I don't even know what to say, Nate. I've probably had too much to drink for this conversation."

"I know. We don't have to talk about it." Releasing a breath, I link my arm back into hers and walk up the steps to her apartment.

"You did really good today." She gives me my first genuine smile tonight. "I'm still pissed at you, but I loved watching you play again."

I smirk, reveling in that admission. "I was showing off for you."

"Psshh, and every other girl there." She rolls her eyes.

"Nah."

We stop in front of her door, and I find myself wishing the walk was farther.

I think of something to keep her talking. "I heard you saw my dad. He was so happy to see you."

"It was really good to see him too. I think the bartender had a crush on him. She couldn't stop talking about how handsome and young he looked." She giggles at the memory.

"I'll have to tell him that. He could probably use the ego boost right about now."

My statement makes her ponder something by the way her eyebrows furrow, and I wonder if she knows.

"I was kinda surprised your mom wasn't with him. I just assumed she wasn't at The Wolfpack on Friday, but I noticed she wasn't in the stands earlier either."

And if I have anything to do with it, she won't be at any this season. The thought of her coming makes me so angry; I know it would ruin a game day for me.

"All those fights they used to have turned out to have some validity, and my dad finally asked for a divorce."

Gasping, she covers her mouth. "Oh Nate, I had no idea." *So, she definitely doesn't know.*

"How is Willow? I feel so bad I've only talked to her briefly…" she pauses before admitting, "It was just too hard."

"Trust me, I get it. And she's doing okay. She's living with Dad full time, and ever since she turned eighteen, she's been taking her anger out on Mom under the tattoo gun. She officially has more ink than me."

That earns another look of surprise. "Wow, really?"

I nod.

"Speaking of ink…" She gently runs her finger along the outer part of my forearm over a tentacle, and goosebumps scatter all over from her touch.

Did she see all of it? I don't think she did.

"I like the octopus. It made me think of that field trip we went on."

"Oh yeah...the one that you let me finger you on the bus during the ride back to school."

Berkley blushes, smacking my arm. "Nathan!" She stumbles into her front door, and I'm reminded of the alcohol running through her system. I want to ask her so badly why she doesn't go home, but I know now isn't the right time. Plus, we are two days away from her most dreaded day of the year.

I put my hands up, shrugging. "It's a good memory. Why do you think I got it on my right arm?" Fuck, my dick is hardening, just remembering how wet and eager she always was for me.

Berkley levels me with a stare. "Stop it," she says weakly, and I don't miss the way her pupils dilate, hopefully recalling the memory as well.

Her so-called current boyfriend was in the seat in front of us with another teammate, and she had to bury her face in my neck to drown out her moans as she came.

"Are you coming to the pool party tomorrow, or is your post-game-day tradition still to lay around and eat cereal all day?"

"Not even Cinnamon Toast Crunch could keep me from seeing you in a bikini… It's been too damn long."

A little smirk she tries to hide pulls at her glossy lips, and she playfully rolls her eyes. "You are in for a treat…"

Her door opens, surprising us both, and a sleepy Darby stands in the darkness. "Bellamy called because you weren't answering. She wanted to make sure your stalker hadn't kidnapped you."

We both chuckle at Bellamy's choice of words.

"Nah. I may be obsessed, but I'd never take her against her will."

Berkley gives her roommate a reassuring smile. "I'm fine. I'll be right in, Darbs."

She turns back to me, a look in her eyes I can't quite place. "Thanks for walking me home. See you tomorrow."

"I'll be the one staring," I wink.

"Good. Bellamy bought me a new swimsuit…just to torture you," she says simply, patting me on the chest and walking inside.

My belly dips, and I bite my lip, imagining the perfect kind of torment I'm in for tomorrow.

EIGHT

Nate

"Is he almost here?" Nola asks, pacing the floor. "We could just walk, ya know. It's, like, five minutes on foot."

Maverick glances at his phone. "He said he was two minutes away. He dropped Bellamy off and grabbed some ice for the cooler."

Graham pushes Nola onto the couch, halting his pacing. "And fuck that. Didn't you play in the same game I did yesterday and stay up till dawn? Why the hell would we want to walk with a full cooler?"

Nola flips him off. "Sorry, I forgot I'm dealing with you, old man."

I can't help but laugh at their bullshit.

"Fuck you. I'm only two years older than you." Then he turns, narrowing his eyes on me. "And I don't know what you're laughing at; I'm technically not even a year older than you."

"Well, I can run circles around both of you, so let's all shut up and get ready for him to be here."

I'm met with a bunch of sarcastic grunts and, yeah, right about the same time, we hear Cash's Chevy pull up.

We walk out to meet him, and when he hops out, letting his tailgate down for us, I see a version of him I haven't met yet.

"Damn, cowboy," I whistle.

"What's up?" He smirks, tipping his hat like a fucking movie star.

Cash reaches back into his truck, pulling out two casserole dishes. "Gigi sent food for us to warm up for Sunday dinner so Nola could enjoy his first win and not have to cook for us incapables after the pool party."

We're all happy to hear this. I haven't eaten Gigi's cooking yet, but I have never had someone's grandma's food that wasn't good. Even though Nola loves testing out his chef skills on us, he seems equally excited about Gigi Leblanc's casserole dishes.

"Hurry up and change." His brother rushes him.

"Chill, the girls aren't even down there yet. Give me two minutes," he says and hurries inside.

"So, he really is part cowboy?" I tease Maverick. I know they mentioned their dad having a ranch nearby, but I guess I never pictured Cash in a Stetson, Levi's, and work boots.

Maverick chuckles. "Yeah, we were raised on a horse ranch." He nods to the sticker on the back of the Silverado... Cane Creek Ranch. "Cash enjoys that shit, and I can ride a horse... but I was born to play in the NHL and live in a big city."

I can totally see that. The Leblanc twins may look similar in the face, but it's apparent they've tried their best to be their own person. Cash has his hair grown out just long enough that it curls under his ears, as well as an impressive mustache to top off his cowboy look. Mav, on the other hand, has a buzz cut and is covered in tattoos, giving him a polar opposite look. However different they might appear or act, they are a force in the hockey rink. From the clips I've seen, neither of them is scared to spend time in the penalty box, especially if someone fucks with the other. I'm excited to see them play in person when their season officially starts.

"That's him and Bellamy's thing. They both still have their own horses that live at the ranch, so they go every Sunday morning to ride."

Interesting. Am I the only one who sees more to them than they lead on? She and Maverick talk shit to each other like I do with my little sister. But Bellamy and Cash have a completely different tension when they are in the same room. Maybe I'm totally off, but either way, it's none of my business.

A few minutes later, we're loaded up, heading the short distance to the girls' apartment complex.

Excitement vibrates through me. I feel like she let her guard down an inch with me last night.

The party was still going when I got home, but I went to my room and came twice. Once to the memory of me fingering her in the backseat of that bus and the second time to the thought of her in a bikini.

Even with the loud music still thumping in the background, I passed out after that. But I still woke up this morning with her on my mind and my hard cock in my hand. I strategically picked my swim trunks today because I know I'll be walking around with a hard-on from the minute I see her.

When we pull up, I notice a lot of the football team is already in the pool and sand volleyball court area.

Fuck, I hope Graves doesn't come today. I don't trust my behavior if I see him with her.

Graham and I grab the cooler together, walking toward the gate. "Hey, look, I'm trying my best." I stop walking, and he follows suit. "But keep me in check today if Graves comes. Just don't let me do anything stupid."

He winks at me. "I got you, QB. But honestly, he was so fucked up last night, he'll probably be sleeping it off all day."

I can only fucking hope.

We're immediately swarmed by our teammates, still on a high from our opener yesterday.

Two red-shirt freshmen grab our cooler from us. The second it's out of my hand, Big John, my enormous center, picks me up.

"The king has arrived!" he shouts, and the pool erupts in cheers. I look around the crowd, not finding who I really came here to see.

She's probably still getting ready...finalizing the personal hell she's about to put me through.

Shaking off the thought, I lift my right hand, touching my middle and ring finger to my thumb, but leaving my pointer and pinky in the air to make the wolf sign to the crowd. "Who's ready to beat Georgia next week?"

Wolf howls echo out around me, and that's when I see *her*.

The crowd parts for her and her roommates as Big John puts me down on my feet. My knees almost buckle at the sight of her.

No cover-up on. Diet Coke can in her hand. Her best friends beside her.

The sexiest little body in the smallest bikini I've ever seen her wear. Triangles that barely cover up the rosy nipples underneath. Her blonde hair is up in a messy bun, and black sunglasses cover her pretty eyes. Eyes that match the blue bathing suit she's wearing. The exact same shade she wore the first day I talked to her, and there's no doubt that was calculated.

I see the little smirk on her face before she turns, heading toward one of the corner tables in the pool area. And that's when my body physically shudders.

I put my knuckle in my mouth, biting down the groan that threatens to unleash.

Her bubble butt is on full display in the thong bottoms. My cock jolts in my pants, unable to stop myself from picturing how she used to let me slide the thin fabric to the side and fuck her wherever we were.

Bless you, Bellamy Clark, and whatever company designed this bathing suit. I need to take my latest Gatorade sponsorship money and buy her one in every color.

Then I notice half my teammates watching her and likely imagining the same thing. If she was still mine, they'd know better than to look at her like that. Unable to control myself, I make my way across to where they are setting up.

I sneak up behind her, letting my breath skate over her neck, "Congrats, BB, I'm in physical pain."

She jumps, eyes meeting mine. "Shit, you scared me, Nate."

I let my hand rest on her hip, and surprisingly, she doesn't push me away.

She turns toward me, snapping her top straps, making her tits bounce. "Figured you love the color."

Fuck me, I'm as hard as a field post.

"I more than love it…"

Completely fucking tortured was right.

I can't stop the memories from flooding straight to my cock.

"I'm so horny, Nate, please," Berkley begs as she keeps grinding her bathing suit clad ass onto my unbelievably hard cock from where I sit on the captain bench of my boat.

"Baby, you're literally killing me. Let's just leave the crowd and find a spot out in the middle of the water."

She bites her lip, shaking her head and pushing her ass into me again. She's so fucking hot.

"I don't want to leave. It's fun." She waves out to the crowd of our friends, all partying on one of the little sand bars. "Shit Shoals," as it's known to the locals.

"Wow." by Post Malone starts playing through Graham's dad's boat that's anchored beside me.

Berkley leans up, pulling her bathing suit bottoms over, giving me glimpse of her wet pussy, more brazen than I've ever seen her. My cock throbs against my stomach, and I glance down and see the head almost pushing out of the top of my shorts. Berkley sees its too. "No one is paying attention. Let me sit on him, baby," she says, rubbing her thumb over the head of my dick, loosening the string on my swim trunks.

"Fuck it." I turn her toward the steering wheel again, freeing my cock but leaving my shorts up. Pushing her bathing suit bottoms over a little more, I run my fingers through her wetness.

"Nate, please," she moans, pushing herself down onto my fingers. "I've never wanted you inside of me so bad before in my life."

She's dripping.

I continue holding her bathing suit to the side and pull her down, guiding her onto my waiting cock with my free hand. "That's it, BB, sit on him. Take him deep into this needy pussy."

And that she does, moving in tandem with the beat to the music. We both lose sight of everyone around us, too desperate for one another.

"What's up, stalker boy?" Bellamy interrupts the sexy memory, and Darby chuckles from beside her.

"Hey. I have to say, you have incredible taste." My eyes don't leave Berkley, and I wonder if she ever thinks about how bad we had it for each other. "Also, this bikini is doing nothing but adding to my stalker cravings, just FYI."

Bellamy lets out a laugh. "Smooth, QB," she retorts over her shoulder before walking away, Darby at her side.

"Yo, come play water volleyball," Graham calls out from the corner of the pool closest to us.

"You in?" I ask Berkley.

She shrugs like she's willing to appease me, but she isn't thrilled about it.

"I call Berkley on my team," I shout back before turning to her again.

"What better way to torture me than jumping around in the pool in this tiny bikini?"

She rolls her eyes. "You have a point."

A few minutes into the game, some of our neighbors who play on the basketball team join in.

"I think it's time for me to bow out. Almost everyone out here

is at least a foot taller than me. I can barely jump in four feet."
Berkley pouts, and she's so fucking cute.

"Want to get on my shoulders?" I offer.

"I'll pass," she says, but stays in the pool, not giving up yet.

"Fine." I shrug as an idea forms in my mind. "Graham, set
her up," I call out and look to Berkley. "Just trust me."

A couple of plays go by before Graham gets a good pass on
the second ball and is able to set Berkley up toward the net. I
swoop in behind her, lifting her as she jumps, giving her
leverage to hit the ball powerfully. Which she does perfectly. I
have to force myself to pry my hands from her tight little
curves when the play is over.

Her excitement is contagious when she turns around,
high-fiving Graham, and then me. That's when I notice a
little nip slip. *Fuck me.* I gently pull her into me and fix
her top. My thumb accidentally brushes over her nipple
in the process, and she looks up at me with lust-filled
eyes.

"Nate, what the hell?" she whisper-hisses.

"Sorry, BB, that itty-bitty bikini slid a little too far to the left."
I try making light of the situation, not wanting her to feel
embarrassed.

She immediately shifts her eyes to her chest, and I glance over
at Graham, who's turned toward our other teammates.

"It's all good now. I promise."

"Did anyone else see?"

"I don't think so." *I'll fucking kill them.*

"You can't touch me like that," she murmurs and makes her
way out of the pool.

"I genuinely didn't mean to." I follow after her, waving off Graham, who calls after both of us.

She sits down at the table they put their stuff at earlier. "I don't even mean that." Shaking her head, she nods to her breast. "I just mean in general."

Heat fills my veins at the thought of who can touch her that way. "Why, because of him?" I snarl and sit down beside her, moving my chair as close as possible.

"What?" Her head rears back as she looks at me. "No, Nate, because of you. It's too much."

Her honesty shocks me.

"It feels too good, and I shouldn't want it." She whispers the last part, and I wonder if she even meant to say it out loud. "It's just too much."

Please want it, baby. I want it so bad. All of it.

"Is it too much to tell you I have imaginary conversations with you every day? I lean in closer, lowering my tone, "How about the fact I jerked off twice last night to thoughts of you?"

She narrows her eyes, trying to hide her desire. "Oh yeah…? "

"You got exactly what you wanted… I've been hard since the second I saw you in this bikini today." I gently run my thumb across her exposed hip bone. "And I can't stop the obsessive memories that keep flashing in my mind of me sliding your bathing suit to the side and slipping into your wet pussy."

She gasps, putting her hand on her forehead. I see her nipples pebble under the blue material barely containing her chest. Unable to keep my hands off of her, I trace my finger over the strap of her bathing suit, from her collarbone disappearing behind her neck. Goosebumps erupt all over her flesh. She's turned on, no matter what she says.

A determined look takes over her face when her eyes meet mine again. They are a darker shade of blue I could get lost in. "I'd give almost anything to sit on your lap and let you slide your big dick into me, right here in front of everyone. No one even knowing how deep inside of me you are." My heart nearly pounds out of my chest as she leans in for the kill, her lips just a breath away. "But I'd give even more to go back to two years ago and not have a shattered heart and soul because of you, Outlaw."

And with that, she stands, leaving me in a mess of being both turned on and heartbroken.

NINE

Berkley

There's a peace that settles over me as we all sit around the guys' massive table, eating the dinner Gigi made for us. Whenever our Sunday schedules align, we all come to The Wolves Den and eat together. This is Nola's first official year living here, but he has deemed himself the main chef of the house, and from what I hear, he's a phenomenal cook. We usually all take turns cooking and buying unless Gigi blesses us with one of her nine-by-thirteen Pyrex dishes of goodness.

When I found out Nate was living here, I wasn't sure if I'd still come to these dinners. They're a more intimate setting than parties.

Now my issue isn't coming here; it's keeping my damn eyes and thoughts off of him. It's really hard, especially when I can feel his eyes on me from across the table. I know he sat there on purpose, so every time I look up from my plate, it would be his stupidly handsome face I'd see.

He looked so fucking hot today. His massive chest on full display, his tattoo hugging one of his sculpted arms perfectly.

And let's not forget about how his swim trunks were just the chef's kiss. Accentuating his strong thighs and ass. Ugh!

It's infuriating to be so turned on by someone, yet also hating them with every fiber of your being.

"Man, Gigi Leblanc can cook. This lasagna is delicious," Nola praises for what seems like the third time since we started. He squeezes Maverick's shoulder enthusiastically.

"Yeah, when she heard it was superstar's favorite, she knew it would be the perfect meal to celebrate the big win," Mav says, pointing his fork in Nate's direction, before turning his attention back to Nola. "I have orders to find out your favorite home cooked meal because she says you're next."

Nola smiles excitedly and takes another bite.

"Thanks, guys. You didn't have to go through all that trouble. Shit, Graham, I'm surprised you even remembered it was my fav," Nate says, directing his focus to Graham, who's sitting to my right.

Graham not-so-subtly tilts his head in my direction. "Might've had a little help."

Nate sets his gaze on me and I know my cheeks are probably as red as can be under his attention.

"Way to blow up my spot," I whisper to Graham through tight lips.

"Like he really thought I remembered he loved lasagna..." Graham chastises me, then shovels another forkful into his mouth.

My phone vibrates on my lap, and I peer down to see a notification from Carter. I internally roll my eyes before swiping open the message.

CARTER

I'm sorry I missed today. Hope you didn't have too much fun without me. Send me a pic of you, so I have something to think of later 😔

Anger simmers in my belly. So he's not going to contact me all day, then he's going to act like last night didn't happen. WTF?

ME

We had a great time today. At the wolves den now for dinner. We will talk later. We still need to discuss what went down last night.

I know mentioning the den would be a sore subject for him, but fuck that. He was acting like a spoiled child last night, so he deserves to suffer a little.

CARTER

Ah, I see how it is. Yup, we'll talk later.

I watch as the three dots appear and disappear multiple times before giving up on the conversation and focusing back on my friends. Frustration bubbles just below the surface, though.

Bellamy leans in, noticing the change in my demeanor. "You good?"

"Yeah, Carter finally texted… He seems pissed I'm here," I answer truthfully. I keep my voice down, so the rest of the group doesn't hear.

"Whatever. He deserves to be brought down a peg or two. Especially after last night. He was being a dick."

"Yeah, you're telling me. Let's just drop it for now. I don't want him to ruin my day," I say, and she does without questioning me further.

That's another thing I love about this girl. She'll always have my back, no matter how reckless my decisions may be. She's there for me. Darby would be in my corner too, but she had a team bonding thing tonight and had to skip out on dinner.

We all chip in to clear the table; Bell and I are on kitchen duty this week, so I'm stationed at the sink, loading the dishwasher while she puts away the leftovers.

I feel his presence behind me before he even speaks. "I'll meet you all outside."

Peeking over my shoulder at him, his nearness catching me a little off guard.

"I have to call Willow back; she's called twice already today," Nate replies to my wordless question.

I turn to him. "Is everything alright?" I ask, unsure if something might be wrong.

"She's fine... Save me a spot?" he says with his mouth mere inches from my ear while his fingers make contact with my hip, and sensation floods my core yet again. Just like it did early today at the pool. Between his hands on me during the game and his whispered filthy words, I was a slut for his attention. Clenching my thighs together more than several times. I fight with all that I have not to lean back into him. I can't give in so easily after all this time.

But how easy it would be...

I clear my throat and those thoughts. "Ugh, yeah, sure. Prob won't be here too late; Bell has an early Monday class."

I swear I feel his body shift just a smidge closer before he's gone, and I release the breath I didn't know I was holding.

Fuck, did I want him to kiss me? To touch me more?

"Ladies, hurry up, we have the firepit going for some s'mores," Mav yells from the back door. That helps us pick up our speed, and we finish in no time, then head out to the back deck.

I've always loved hanging out back here. The view they have of the mountains from the fire pit area is breathtaking, especially with the late summer sunset painting the sky.

Bell and I share a bench, while Mav, Cash, Graham, and Nola sit in their Adirondack chairs. I'm not going to lie and say I'm not disappointed Nate went upstairs instead of joining us out here. *But what does that say about me? Am I weak for thinking that?*

I'm lost in the flames of the fire when I smell the smoke from the joint Bell just lit up. She passes it my way, and I gladly accept the reprieve the high will give my racing mind.

I'm about to pass it back when Mav reaches for it. As I go to pull it away, a handsome grin spreads across his face.

"Chill, B, it's no longer tested for. I'm allowed," he chuckles.

I look to Bellamy for confirmation, like she's their keeper. She just nods with a go-ahead look on her face.

Nola and Graham both decline since they're in season, swearing they'll participate when it's over, but Cash, Mav, Bell, and I all take turns passing it along.

Once we're done, we turn our attention to the s'mores construction. This is quite the comic relief… It seems the higher the individual, the crazier their concoctions. I think Mav had the winning combination with his Oreo peanut butter cup. My favorite out of the bunch, for sure, was using a Rolo instead of a Hersey's bar.

I make an extra s'more, deciding I'll bring it up to Nate and make sure everything is okay with Willow. I know this isn't a good idea, especially since I'm trying to keep my distance, but I ignore that voice as I get up and walk inside, deliberately avoiding Bellamy's gaze as I go. Letting the weed make the decisions for me, light and easygoing, nothing to be concerned about.

My knuckles wrap gently on his bedroom door, and I wait patiently for him to answer. I knock again after my first attempt goes unanswered. No answer.

Did he fall asleep?

The door is unlocked when I test it, and I open it just a crack to peek inside. My senses are immediately overwhelmed by his scent. Subconsciously, I take a deep inhale. God, he's always smelled so good.

Spotting Nate at his desk, I notice he has his headphones on and didn't hear me knocking. So I make my way across the room, sliding the s'more onto his desk in front of him, careful not to make a mess of the journal he's writing in.

He slips off his headphones, and his million-dollar smile spreads across his face when he sees me.

"Sorry, I was about to come back down..." He looks from me to the s'more. "Aw, thank you. This looks delicious," he says, wasting no time and taking a bite.

"Wait, was there caramel in that?"

I smile shyly, knowing that's another one of his favorites. "Yeah, out of all the combinations, I thought the Rolo was the best."

"Fucking delicious. Good call."

"Is Willow okay?" I ask, my voice full of concern. Knowing what I know now about his parents, I regret not staying in touch with her.

"Yeah, I assumed it was something about my mom, but really, she just wanted an update on life after my first win..." He swallows, then adds, "And you."

I stand there staring at him, taking in the sight of his shirtless chest for the second time today. Except this time, I'm not surrounded by a crowd of people. It's just him and me... alone.

Closing my eyes, I try to steel my resolve. Why do I keep putting myself in this position?

Because you want to.

"Thank you for today," Nate says, causing my eyes to pop open.

"For what?"

"For allowing us to have fun and for my lasagna," he winks.

I chuckle and roll my eyes. "I had a good time today. And for the record, Graham asked me what your favorite was."

"And you could have said beef stew..."

"But you hate beef stew," I reply, crinkling my nose as he stands up from his chair. Putting himself in dangerously close range to my racing heart.

"Exactly," he whispers, tilting my chin to look him in the eyes. "That's why I said thank you."

"Well, I guess you're welcome... It was no big deal." I try my best to make it seem like it was nothing with my casual tone. But when Graham had texted me the question, there wasn't a doubt in my mind what I would say.

"It was to me," he says, his chin sinking down to his chest. And that's when, just over his shoulder, I spot something hanging on the inside of his closet door. My belly swoops.

No way.

I walk around him in disbelief as I approach the mounted collage. The one I made for him. My fingers trace over the photos as the memories come flooding in. Our love and happiness pictured in every photo has my heart hammering. He kept it...

Spinning around, I'm startled by Nate's close proximity to me. He reaches for my hip and pulls me in closer. And I don't resist. His forehead rests on mine as we stand in comfortable silence.

"I've looked at those photos every day," he admits, pulling back and brushing a wild strand of hair out of my face.

My breath stutters, and before I know what I'm doing, I'm leaning up on my tiptoes and gently coasting my lips across his. His fingers tighten as I deepen the kiss for only a moment. My body melts at the feel of his lips on mine. Knowing this isn't right, knowing I can't handle being hurt by him again, I stop myself from taking this any further. This is all too fucking confusing.

Placing my hand on his chest, I push away slowly. "Goodnight, Nate," I say, then turn and walk out of the room before I dig myself an even deeper hole.

As soon as I'm out of his room, I lean against the wall outside of his closed door, catching my breath. My fingers trace over my lips that still tingle from touching his after all this time.

I close my eyes and silently berate my decisions. I'm not sure if I'm more pissed at myself for what I've done, or for the fact that I want to do it again.

TEN

Nate

Gently placing the vase of pink roses down beside the apartment door, I slip the letter I wrote her last night in between the stems.

I stand there staring at her door, wishing I could hold her through the tears I know she'll shed today. Tears I'd give anything to kiss away.

Lifting my fist, I consider knocking, but remind myself she wouldn't want that. Even though she kissed me last night, the look of regret on her face as she pulled away keeps playing on repeat in my mind. But so does the way her lips felt on mine. *So fucking right.*

Suddenly, the door is opening, and Berkley stands in front of me. Sporting puffy eyes and a shocked expression as she looks between me and the roses.

"You remembered?" she barely gets out as a sob rips through her, and she covers her mouth.

I instinctively pull her into me. Her head fits perfectly under my chin, just like it used to.

"I'm so sorry, BB." My heart breaks at the way her body shudders against mine.

A few minutes go by before she settles down. Squatting beside us, she picks up the flowers. After smelling them, a small smile spreads across her pretty face. "Her favorite scent and her favorite color. Thank you again." She hesitates, then asks, "I was going to go on a run to clear my head, but how about a walk instead?"

"Sure," I say, way too eagerly.

"Let me put these inside."

I nod and wait by her door until she rejoins me, and we start our walk in silence. The memory of the first year we spent together on the anniversary of her mother's death plays out in my thoughts as we make our way toward Ridgeway Park.

Berkley immediately grabs the rope I toss her as I coast up beside the dock. My buoys gently bounce into the small pier as she reaches for my hand and hops in.

The sad look on my sweet girl's face almost breaks me. I knew today would be hard for her. Her bereavement counselor told her that "the firsts" are always the toughest.

I want to make today the best day I can for her. Full of all the things her mom loves. I was honored when Berkley asked me to take her to Shackleford Banks, one of the smaller islands off Nori Beach, to scatter part of her mom's ashes.

As I get the boat back in the canal, she immediately throws her arms around me. I keep one hand on the wheel and squeeze her as tight as I can with the other.

"How was breakfast, baby?" I ask. She and her dad had a special break-

fast this morning, just the two of them. I invited him to come on the boat, but he told Berkley he would rather have some alone time.

"It was good. My dad made waffles for the first time in over a year because they were her fave," she sniffles. "He said she wouldn't want us to live on this earth without chocolate waffles."

I pull her in between me and the steering wheel, resting my chin on top of her head. One hand on the wheel, the other on her hip. Wanting her to feel the love I have for her, wanting to be the shoulder she leans on during times like this. It breaks my heart that at only sixteen, she's honoring her mother on the one-year anniversary of her death instead of going to the mall or having a mother-daughter day.

"I'll feed you chocolate waffles any time you want." *I gently squeeze her side, where I know she's ticklish.*

"Oh yeah?" *she giggles, swatting my hand away.*

"Yep, they may be L'eggo my Eggo brand until I figure it out."

That gets a smile from my girl, and I bend down gently, kissing her neck. "Speaking of favorite foods...go peek in the cooler before we pick up speed."

She eyes me curiously. "What are you up to?"

I shrug and nod for her to go check it out.

Slowly walking up to the head of the boat, she opens the cooler and lets out a little gasp.

"Nate..." *Berkley picks the pink roses up from the top of the cooler, tears in her eyes.* "How did you know?"

"I listen, baby...every time you talk. I hold on to every word."

I live and breathe for the smile she gives me. Even on days like today, I just stare at her in awe. The way I love her is so much bigger than I ever understood to be possible.

"Keep looking," I beam with pride, happy to bring a little sunshine to my girl on such a tough day.

"Oh my gosh, is that a key lime pie from Friendly's market? Annnd their five-bean salsa dip?" she asks, rummaging through the cooler that I stocked from one of the local markets. It's a favorite for tourists and locals alike. Berkley and I go there often, and she talks about her mom always stopping there when they'd come to see her aunt before she passed.

"Yep, and I have the chips under the seat. I thought we could have a picnic with a few more of her favorite things."

The sadness that was staining her face earlier is starting to fade away.

Walking back to me, she says softly, *"Have I ever told you how amazing you are?"*

"Only during certain times, I don't think are appropriate to speak of right now."

She laughs at that. *"Well, that too, but seriously, thank you…"* Berkley leans up on her tiptoes to kiss me, and I feel it deep in my bones. *"Thank you for being you, Nathan Outlaw."*

"Thank you for letting me be here."

I pull her back in between my legs. *"Hang on, baby. Let's go find your mom the perfect spot."*

We drive out into the ocean and around to the quieter side of the island until Berkley points out a spot. *"I think this is perfect."*

She helps me anchor the boat just like she has many times this summer before we hop out and make our way to the shore.

A wide smile spreads across Berkley's face as she takes in the area. *"She'd love it. You can see the horses' hoofprints in the sand just up the beach."*

I give her a reassuring smile and pass her the ashes she's been keeping in a small silk pouch.

"Wish your dad could have come; it's such a beautiful day."

"I hate the thought of him being alone, but a part of me knows I wouldn't be able to grieve and embrace the moment the way I want to if he was here. I'd be so worried about his feelings, I wouldn't take time to focus on my own. It's something counseling has pointed out and something I'm working on. It's just hard when I'm all he has."

My heart sinks for her, for them both. I'm not super close with my mom, but I couldn't imagine losing her so suddenly the way they did.

"All you can do is take it one day at a time." I reach for her hand, intertwining our fingers. "Your mom will always be with you. She's watching over us right now. Eying up all my snacks," I say, trying to ease her mind and she gives me a gentle smile, squeezing my hand.

"Now let's honor your mama the way you want to, the way she would love."

Her confession is the first to break the silence.

"These last two years have been even harder than the first few."

My heart sinks at her words. She nods for me to follow her over to the bench at the edge of the trail that looks perfectly out onto the mountains surrounding us.

"The happy life I was under the illusion my mom lived was just that... An illusion. I found out the sickening truth Christmas break, freshmen year."

The hairs on the back of my neck standup... *Does she know?*

"What do you mean?"

"One thing that always gave me peace was feeling like my mom had a happy life before she left this earth. In my mind, she lived a fairy tale until her last breath."

I close my eyes. This was a major driving force behind our break up. I never wanted her to lose that vision of her mother.

In this moment, I don't try to fill the silence because of my own discomfort; I just simply listen.

"The day after Christmas, almost two years ago, a man came to our apartment, beating on the door."

Was it my dad? No, he wouldn't have done that to Berkley.

"Do you remember the grief counselor I was seeing once a month in high school, Angela?"

I nod, recalling how helpful that was for her back then.

"Well…it was Angela's husband, claiming my father was having a full-blown affair with her."

My eyes widen. I didn't see that coming.

"Yep. But at first, I believed my dad when he said it was all bullshit, and her husband just didn't like how close she had become with my dad and me." She pauses, almost like she's reflecting back on that conversation. "That was the first lie of many."

"So I went and stayed with my Aunt Judy for a few days. On New Year's Eve, one of her and Mom's best friends stayed up late drinking champagne on her enclosed patio. I guess they thought I couldn't hear them through the screen door, or they were blitzed and didn't realize how loud they were being, but I overheard a conversation that changed my life and the way I will see my father forever."

Fuck, here we go. My stomach sours.

"They basically said the accusations were true and of no surprise to them, as my father had affairs repeatedly during their marriage, one of which was the reason they moved away from Nori Beach when I was ten. My aunt even speculated that my dad didn't come back so that I could be close to her since I didn't have my mom anymore, but actually with hopes of rekindling an old flame with a woman who was still married."

I think I may vomit.

"Fuck." I shake my head, trying to process and consider how to handle this situation. "So, this is why you don't go back to Nori? Do you ever talk to him?"

"No, he tries, but now he's living with Angela, and I just have absolutely no desire to see or talk to him. That may be harsh, but I really don't care."

Living with Angela explains a lot.

"I don't think it's harsh at all. Fuck him. He's ruined too many good things." And I mean that with every fiber of my soul, especially after hearing all this.

She looks at me curiously, and I wait for the questions, wanting to tell her everything. Originally, I had no intention of even bringing this up today because of how tough I know this day is for her.

But would it be another lie by omission if I don't?

She stands abruptly, seeming to shake off her emotion. "Let's head back. I'm sure you have stuff to do."

Wordlessly, I follow her, even though football and school are the least of my concerns at this moment.

"How did you know I don't go back to Nori Beach anymore?"

I look away sheepishly. "Bellamy may be onto something with the stalker nickname. I actually drove by the apartment multiple times over the past couple of years, but I just assumed it wasn't meant to be for me to see you. And then my dad told me he heard you never go back."

"You came looking for me?"

I nod, and she doesn't respond. Likely processing how fucking confusing my actions are. I don't blame her.

Again, we walk in silence until we get back to her door, so many things still left unsaid.

"Can I ask you one thing, Nate?" She turns her body toward mine in front of her door, her blue gaze connecting with mine.

"Anything," I whisper.

"How long did it take you to regret it?"

I feel like Regret is my middle name after everything she just told me...

Tucking a piece of hair behind her ear, I rest my hand on her cheek. "I regretted it before I even did it."

I remember lying in her bed that morning after barely sleeping a wink. I felt so hopeless, so angry, so out of control.

Tears fill her eyes again, and I am teleported back to that day.

Her head shakes in exasperation as she throws her hands up. "Then why?"

Grabbing her hands, I try to plead with her, growing more anxious by the second. "BB, I don't want to do this today, of all days."

"Don't give me that shit, Nate. Today of all days... I need this! I deserve to know!"

I rake my hands through the longer strands of my hair and blow out a breath.

Relenting, I nod, heart pounding in my ears. "Can I come in?"

She looks down at her Apple watch, then back at me. "Yeah, they should both be in class by now."

Berkley unlocks the door with a shaky hand, and I follow in behind her. I'm not sure who's more on edge.

The door opens into the kitchen, where I notice the pink roses sitting in their vase. It's cozy and feminine, the exact way I envisioned where she would live. She walks over to the couch, moving the plush light pink pillows over slightly for us to sit. Then she turns to me, and I know there's no more avoiding this conversation.

I swallow roughly, trying to control my emotions before I begin.

"It all started about five days before we broke up."

Her eyebrows furrow, and I take a deep breath to center myself once more.

"During one of my parents' fights, I overheard my dad say something to my mom I couldn't quite process at first."

"What?" she immediately asks.

"He said…" I wish I could go back and tell her all this two years ago.

Walking in the back door of the house, I immediately stop in my tracks at the screaming coming from the kitchen.

My dad's angry words echo down the hallway. "This is un-fucking believable. I can't believe you're seeing him again. After everything." I hear what sounds like his hand slamming against the countertop. "Especially not even considering your son in all of this. You are even more selfish than I realized."

With more sadness in his words, my dad speaks again. "Fucking hell, Jane. Did you really not think about that? He loves that girl so much."

I hear a huff, then my mom sneers. "They're just kids, Brian. Don't give me a guilt trip."

"Get out of my fucking house!" My dad yells.

Not wanting to see either of them, I sneak back out the way I came in.

Berkley's eyes trace my face as her brain works through what I'm telling her.

"I contemplated asking my dad for days, but I was almost too scared to know the answer. But then, the morning after the pool party, there was no denying my assumptions." I shake my head, wishing I could erase the memory from my mind. "I walked out to the kitchen, knowing you'd need a big glass of water when you woke up, but unfortunately, something caught my eye on your back patio…"

"My mom and your dad in an undeniable romantic embrace."

My gut churns just like it did that morning when I laid back down in bed beside her. I hate the shocked look on Berkley's face as the realization hits her.

She gasps. "Your mom was the reason we moved from Nori Beach to begin with, wasn't she?"

I nod. "According to my dad, who I confronted right before I left for school, their affair had spanned over several years."

"Oh my god." She leans forward, putting her face in her hands.

"I'm so sorry. I should have told you, but I was scared. I felt like I would still lose you, and on top of that, the idea of the fairy tale you thought your parents had would be shattered, along with the respect you had for your father." I want to hold her, but I know she needs some space.

"You should have. They ruined her, they ruined us." Her voice rises with every word. "I FUCKING hate them."

"I do too." The whisper sounds as painful as all this feels.

She looks up at me, and I hate the tears in her eyes are because of me. "I remember how off you were that week. I just assumed it was nerves over us being long distance."

Shaking my head vigorously, I respond truthfully. "I was a coward that morning, using that as an excuse, but I thought I was doing the right thing for you." I take her hand in mine. "I knew your dad was so important to you after losing your mom, and I didn't want to ruin the image you had of the man you loved so much. But even more than that, I didn't want to ruin the happy image you had of your mother's life before her aneurysm. And I felt like if we were together and I hid it from you, that would be the ultimate betrayal."

I'd give anything to go back and rethink that decision that changed the trajectory of both our lives.

Berkley starts sobbing, and I drop to my knees in front of where she sits on the couch, pulling her into me. I didn't think my heart could break any more after losing her, but seeing her like this is killing me.

"I'm so, so sorry, baby. Just never forget your mom had the greatest love ever... Her love for you." I lift her chin, tears welling in my own eyes at her stricken face. "And take it from someone who loves you and has been loved by you, it's the best thing she could have ever experienced."

Her chin wobbles, but she slings her arms around me. We hold each other like this for several minutes before she sits back.

Then she puts her face back in her hands. "I'm sorry. It's so much to process. I'm livid, but I'm also hurt. I feel like they took so much from *her*. So much from us."

"The day I left for college, I spewed venom in my mom's direction, and I haven't spoken a word to her since."

"Does Willow know?"

I shake my head. "She doesn't know it was your dad, but she knows about the affair. She still speaks to my mom at times, but our family is a mess."

"All because of my dad."

"It was just as much her fault. They are both selfish."

She exhales a shaky breath. "I feel sick... This is too much. I think I need to lay down."

I hate them even more in this moment.

"Can I get you something?" I ask, not wanting to leave her like this.

She shakes her head.

"Please let me do something, BB?"

She lies down, and I barely hear the words she whispers, "Hold me, Nate."

Wanting nothing more, I do as she says. Berkley fits her head under my chin like she always used to do, and I place a gentle kiss to her blonde hair.

Everything feels better with her in my arms, even if just for a little while.

A couple of hours later, I wake up, Berkley still asleep on my lap. Pulling my phone out of my pocket, I realize the meeting to watch game film with my quarterback coach was supposed to start thirty minutes ago.

Gently sitting up, I text him back, letting him know I'll miss the film because something came up. I really don't care about the repercussions. Berkley is more important than anything, even football.

I take my time looking her over, wishing I could take every bit of sadness from her heart and replace it with nothing but happiness. It's so hard knowing that everything we went through was for nothing because her father hurt her anyway, showing his true colors.

And I hurt her too.

The creak of the front door opening startles me, and in walks Bellamy, who slightly jerks back when she sees me sitting there.

But in true Bellamy fashion, she quickly adjusts and hits me with the snark. "Damn, stalker boy, you're taking this thing to a whole new level. Staring while she sleeps."

Berkley wakes up at the sound of her best friend's voice, looking between us with a dazed expression.

"Good, sleeping beauty is up." She blows Berkley a kiss. "Darby is on her way back. We have massages and pedicures booked at the Grove Park Inn this afternoon."

"What?" Don't you guys have class?" Her voice is still thick from her nap.

"Psshh. Did you really think we were going to let you sit in here all day by yourself?" She clears her throat. "Or with your crazy stalker... He was a plot twist I didn't see coming."

We both chuckle at that as Bellamy walks down the hallway.

"I'll get out of your hair. Can we talk again soon?"

She nods, searching my eyes. "Part of me feels like our conversation earlier was a dream."

I give her a gentle smile. "I wish it was, and that I could rewind time to two years ago."

Berkley just stares at me until she finally whispers, "Me too," and my heart soars at that admission.

But her next words quickly take the wind out of my sails. "But unfortunately, no matter whose fault it is, we can't."

I swallow my emotions down. "I know."

"But I would like to talk some more, too." She stands up, and I take that as my cue to leave.

Okay, I'll take that. What did I expect? It's been two years, and I just unloaded a shit ton that she hasn't even had time to digest yet. Plus, she has a boyfriend.

I make my way toward her front door, not wanting to push my luck today. "Have fun with your girls."

"Thank you. And good luck with Georgia this weekend. If you play like you did this past Saturday, you'll get the W, no problem," Berkley smiles, opening the door for me.

"Thanks," I say, pulling her into a hug, and thankfully, she complies. "I hope I didn't make today worse."

"I needed it to truly start my healing process."

"Well, just remember what I said about her knowing her greatest love in you."

With watery eyes, she smiles genuinely. "Thanks, Outlaw."

"Of course, BB," I say, walking out the door, even though the last thing I want to do is leave her.

I don't know where we go from here; I just know she's the only thing I want.

ELEVEN

Berkley

"I needed this today," I say as I lounge in the sauna next to Darby and Bellamy, begging my brain to calm down and enjoy the serenity. But my emotions are clawing their way out.

"Honestly, I don't know what I would've done without you two." My eyes well with tears as an overwhelming wave of pain and gratitude floods me. I think they know this, but I don't just mean today…but more importantly, these past two years.

"Aw, babe, we love you," Bellamy smiles, and Darby gently squeezes my arm. I see the emotion shining in both my best friends' eyes as they watch me closely, likely unsure of what to say. At twenty years old, not many people know how to handle death. But sometimes it's not about what you say; it's about just listening and letting that person pour out all their hurt.

Nate is a natural empath; even at sixteen years old, he somehow knew exactly what I needed. When I saw him at my door today, I can't explain what I felt.

Relieved. Loved. Seen.

"I hope today helps ease your mind, even if just for a little bit," Bellamy says, and I see the way her nostrils flare, trying to hold in her own tears.

I smile through my emotion, reaching out to squeeze each of their hands. Thankful to know such true friendships.

So far, today has already been a whirlwind. Even though I've yearned for real answers from Nate, I wasn't prepared for what they would actually be. Strangely, I feel a bit more at peace knowing the truth, but that doesn't mean I'm not pissed about being kept in the dark. My heart breaks for my mom and what the truths he revealed today did to her at the time. And if I'm being honest, I hurt for Nate, too. I've spent so much time being angry with him that I never considered blaming anyone but him. I'm still frustrated with the situation in general, but now I'm so damn confused. There's a small voice in the back of my consciousness, telling me how selfless of an act it was. If anyone besides my therapist knew my struggles over my mother's death, it's Nate. The fact he tried to preserve her memory for me sends a pang straight through my heart.

But was he just going to let me go forever? Did he think I'd never find out?

So many questions. And then the way he's been with me since arriving in Mountain Ridge just confuses me further.

We sit in comfortable silence as we let the soothing music surround us, but my thoughts have my anxiety spiraling.

"What's everyone's weekend plans?" Bell asks, and I'm thankful for the distraction.

"Jackie told me she'll be home this weekend, so I'm going to head out Friday after my morning class," Darby says with a dreamy smile on her face.

"I'm babysitting Friday and at The Wolfpack Saturday night," I reply.

"Aw, man, the boys said they're going to drive to Georgia for the game this weekend since it's their last chance at catching an away game before hockey gets into full swing. I was going to see if either of you wanted to come."

"Sorry, boo, I need to work this weekend." But I'm tempted to call out. For a reason I'm not willing to admit, I want to go to that game more than I probably should.

"Sorry, you're on your own. Who else is going?" Darby asks.

"Mav, Cash, and I think that was it…" Bell says.

"Tori isn't going?" I ask, knowing Bellamy's disdain for Tori runs deep.

"Hell no! That's why I was all about going with them," she quips.

Even though she always brushes it off when we try to bring it up, there's a stark difference in her relationship with her stepbrothers. And I have a strong feeling that even if Tori wasn't the most annoying chick in the world, Bellamy simply wouldn't like her because she's Cash's girlfriend.

"Well, enjoy the peace then," Darby laughs, and she's not wrong. Tori is a lot. She's loud, quite obnoxious, and very over the top…and not in a good way. Her actions are usually very deliberate and a way to seek out the wrong kind of attention. However, if I saw the way my boyfriend looked at his stepsister, I'd probably be insecure too.

Bellamy stands up, mouth hanging open and panting. "I'm getting hot as hell. Let's go out into the little comfy area and wait for our massage therapists. Please."

Darby laughs at her sudden dramatics. "Sure, since you said please."

"Are we going to discuss the fact that I found you in Nathan Outlaw's lap?" Bellamy asks, clearing her throat, as we nestle up in a private area of the women's lounge.

I swat at her arm, where she sits beside me on the plush couch. "You make it sound pervy when you say it like that."

"Only questioning what I walked in on." She puts her hands up, but the teasing smile on her face makes me laugh.

"He brought me flowers today, not just any flowers, but my mom's favorite. Then we went for a walk…"

I proceed to fill the girls in on what Nate revealed to me. Unloading it all, from when I moved away to how dodgy Nate was acting before the night we broke up. Every gritty detail of my father's indiscretions.

Once I'm done, both of them stare at me with their mouths open.

"Holy shit," Darby says.

"Well, that certainly explains a lot," Bellamy says, handing us both a bottle of water from the mini cooler in the lounge. I think his behavior since he's been here has confused my best friends as much as it has me.

"What now?" Darby asks as she takes a swig.

"It was a hell of a lot to take in, and honestly, I don't even know…" It's the truth, of course, because I really don't know what to do with this information. I'm pissed he didn't tell me. Deep down, I know he was trying to protect me, but it was something we could have worked through. Something we could have faced together. Instead, he chose to keep me in the dark, and I've been suffering the loss ever since. But if I'm being honest with myself, I think my real resentment lies with my dad and his mom. Not only for putting Nate in that position, but for hurting my mom the way they did. There's no excuse for my dad's continued adultery, and I'm not sure I can ever get over that.

"Can't say I blame you. That's a lot to unload," Bellamy says as our masseuses enter the room to collect us.

Darby squeezes my shoulder. "Whatever you decide or need to vent about, we're here for you."

I smile at them both, then follow my masseuse to my room. I'm hoping I can shut my mind off enough to relax and enjoy my massage. Not sure that's happening today, though.

———

I lie on my bed, staring at my phone and avoiding my dad's calls. Thankfully, he doesn't call me much, but I guess a day like today gets to whatever conscious he has left. But after what Nate confirmed earlier, I'm considering blocking his number.

And then there's the text that Carter sent an hour ago.

CARTER

> Hey beautiful, decide what you'd like to have for dinner, and I'll pick it up after practice. We can watch any movie you choose... I promise I won't argue. I'm thinking of you today.

I know I need to respond. It's not fair to leave him in limbo, but he's not good at this stuff, and I don't think I have the energy to fake it for him. Wiping the residue from the honey barbecue chips I've been eating off on the old t-shirt I'm wearing, I text him back. I'm in full slob fest tonight, and I don't want anyone to see me like this.

ME

Hey you! Can we grab breakfast tomorrow or Friday before you leave instead? I'm sorry. I have a headache and planning to crash soon.

Then I go into my call log and delete my dad's calls, not wanting to see them in my recent history for my own mental health.

My finger hovers over Nate's number in my contact list. I never could bring myself to delete it permanently. His name looks so formal, Nathan Outlaw. I guess that was one of my tactics back then to make him seem less than what he was to me.

The boy who broke my soul.

The boy I loved, even when I wished I could stop.

I scroll down to find another number I haven't called in a long time. Someone who at one point was like a little sister to me, and even though I regret it now, at the time, it just hurt too much to stay in close contact with her. Part of me wonders if she even wants to hear from me, but I push the doubt away.

The phone picks up, and I hear rustling. "Is this real life?" Willow's voice sounds through the line, somehow the exact same but also so different. *Older.*

Unable to hold in a laugh before responding, I say, "Some days, I'm not sure anymore, babe."

"Fuck, it is you. That same sweet voice." This time, she nearly whispers, like she's trying to decide if this actually is real.

"Excuse me, missy. When did you start using *fuck* in your vocabulary?"

Now it's her turn to let out a raspy laugh. "The day I realized life was full of no fucks to be given."

I fake a gasp. "My little spitfire turned into a full-on rebel, huh?"

"Total anarchist. And B, I hate to tell you, but I'm not little Willow anymore."

"Unless you grew a ton since the last picture I saw of you, I'm sure I've still got you by a couple inches," I tease, trying to picture her now; she was always gorgeous. I can only imagine her now, with her big blue eyes, probably a sleek jawline like her brother, and sexy tattoos on her sun-kissed skin.

"Maybe if you'd update your social media, I'd know a little something. Your brother also said you have more ink than him."

"Social media isn't for true rebels, babe." I can almost see her smirk.

"Also, all I really heard there was that you talked to my brother. Tell me about that..."

I feel a blush creep onto my face at her comment.

"I mean, he did show up at my school like an asshole."

"Funny how that worked out, right?"

I huff a laugh. "I've been thinking the same thing. But I'm tolerating him."

"Same."

A pregnant silence stretches between us. "How are you, Will? Truly?"

She lets out a little grunt. "I'm ok. Getting there."

"I'm sorry to hear about your parents," I say gently, trying to broach the subject.

"It's for the best. I just want my dad to be happy."

"Well, he's already the eye candy of my place of employment." I leave out the part about my one co-worker I officially never want to talk to again after she told me she'd give anything for the father and son duo to tag team her.

"Fuck, great, so he's definitely not allowed to visit me next year."

I can't help but laugh again, until it hits me what she had just said. "Wait, are you coming here?"

"Yep! Well, the dean said I should be a shoo-in. I'm hoping to get my early acceptance soon."

I sit up, reaching for the Diet Coke that's sitting beside the empty taco takeout box on my bedside table.

"I'm so excited to hear that. You should come visit and stay with me so you don't have to stay with all those stinky boys."

Briefly, I think about how fun it would be to have her stay with me, Bellamy, and Darby for our last year here if she does get in. Then, an onslaught of what ifs flit through my brain, and most of them involve Nate.

"Bet! I'm actually coming for the next home game."

An idea comes to my mind. "Do you still like to sing?"

"Of course," she sing-songs back to me.

I giggle. "The girls and I love Karaoke Thursdays at my work. You should totally come up a day early and go with us to that, then crash at our place."

"It's a fuck yes for me. I'll be there."

Smiling to myself, I shake my head. "You're a hellion…but geez, I've missed you so much. I feel like we have so much to catch up on. I need to know grown-up Willow."

"Ditto, babe. I've discovered I don't really like people anymore, just FYI."

She has me cracking up. "Well, I promise you, you'll like my people."

"Speaking of your people, who's better, my brother or Graves?"

I choke on air at her bluntness. "Shut up. You did not just ask me that."

An evil giggle bursts from her. "Actually, I have a feeling I know the answer, and I don't want to know the details. I heard enough through the thin walls of our house when I was, like, fourteen."

My stomach hurts from laughing. This conversation is exactly what I needed to end this day.

"You're awful."

I hear what sounds like a door open before Willow says, "Dad just got home with takeout."

"Okay, go eat. Thanks for taking my call."

"Thanks for calling me, Berkley. I've really missed you in my life."

Her fun, easy-going tone fades, and I hear a bit of the fifteen-year-old girl who was devastated when she found out her brother and I had broken up.

"I've missed you more than you know. I'm sorry, babe."

"Nothing to be sorry about, B. Bye, babe." And then she's gone.

My desire to call Nate is even greater after talking to Willow, but I stop myself.

I do something I said I'd never do, though. Finding his name for a second time, I unblock his number.

Unwanted excitement thrums through me, and I know this is a dangerous game I'm playing with my heart, but I can't seem to stop.

TWELVE

Berkley

A steady tingling at my core signals how close I am already. Nate's encouraging moans have me picking up the speed of my hips.

"Fuck, BB, you feel so good. Rubbing that needy pussy of yours all over my cock," he says through a groan, tightening his grip on my hips as I grind on him in the back seat of his truck. I could barely contain myself; I practically ripped his clothes off as soon as we closed the doors.

Seeing his sun-tanned skin glisten with sweat at the end of today's practice made me ache to lick every inch of him.

"Please. I need you inside of me," I beg, kissing him hard. His fingers tangle in my hair at the nape of my neck. He tugs just enough, and I let out a feral moan.

"God, you drive me crazy when you're desperate for me. I can feel how wet you are through your soaked panties."

"So desperate," I pant as I continue to use the fly of his jeans to my advantage. My lips trail kisses up his neck, and I swear I might come just from rubbing on him.

He lifts my hips enough that he can undo his zipper and slides them *down, freeing his thick cock. Within seconds, I remove my thong and lift my skirt.*

I hover over him, his eyes locked on mine, and my heart flutters.

"Ride me, baby. Show me how badly you needed it."

Easing my way onto him, I relish the slow stretch as he fills me. Our heavy breaths blend with the low bass of the song streaming through the speakers.

"Fuuuck," I whimper and lean in to kiss him. Our tongues tangle as I slowly begin to rock my hips.

"You feel like heaven," Nate says as his hands grip my hips once more. I steady myself, using his strong shoulders as he begins to take over and thrusts up into me. I swear I lose my breath the instant his thick cock hits that perfect spot.

"Oh... Yesss. That's it, babe, right there," I moan when his hips maintain a relentless speed that has me on edge within minutes.

"Come for me, gorgeous." His hands abandon my hips and cup my cheeks, his hazel eyes locking onto mine. He's so fucking perfect... My whole body clenches, and I fall into bliss, crying out his name.

"I love you so damn much, BB."

"I love you, to—"

I wake up, gasping for air. What the hell was that?

My racing heart and aching pussy know damn well what that was.

Ugh. I audibly groan, flip over, and yell into my pillow.

He's slowly consuming my every thought, and I don't know how much more I can take before I break.

Clearly, my body is ready... But is my heart?

The chime of a text message shakes me from my internal battle.

CARTER

My morning workout ran a little over, so I'll be a few min late. See you soon B.

ME

No worries, leaving my place in a few.

Damn, I never oversleep, and according to my clock, I should have been dressed and out the door five minutes ago.

Hopping out of bed, I rush to get ready. I take the quickest cold shower known to man, but even the cool water can't calm my heated skin. Every swipe of the washcloth has my body begging to be touched, and not by my own hands.

Shit, how am I supposed to sit through a breakfast with another man after that?

Guess there's only one way to find out.

I practically run from the parking lot to the café, knowing I'm already late and he'll be waiting for me. As soon as I walk through the doors, I spot him sitting in a booth in the back. His big frame is hard to miss.

Carter's face lights up with a smile when I approach. He stands and kisses me, wrapping his arms around my waist. I should be melting in his embrace, but instead, my mind flits to my dream in the backseat of a familiar pickup.

"This is exactly what I needed before we head out," he says, still sporting a goofy grin as we sit down.

"Aw, glad I could be of service," I tease, trying to keep things light. "That means you owe me a big play in Georgia."

"Anything for you, B." He grabs my hand across the table and squeezes it gently. His touch is comforting, friendly even…but not the one I'm subconsciously craving.

We take a few minutes to look over the menu, but considering this is one of my favorite places to eat off campus, I already know what I'm ordering.

The waiter comes and takes our orders and delivers us drinks. A look of confusion must cross my face because Carter informs me that he ordered my coffee just how I like it, since I was running a little behind.

"That was sweet of you. Thank you."

He stares at me for a few moments, a nervous look taking over his usually cool persona. Releasing a breath, his hand grabs at the hair at the back of his neck. "Uh, listen. I'm not sure how to do this. So, I'm just going to come out and say it," he starts, and I sit up straighter.

"I'm sorry for the way I acted this weekend. I was an asshole, and I hope you can forgive me. I know this week was a tough one for you, and then me being an asshole didn't help."

"Thank you for apologizing. I appreciate it." And I mean what I say. It takes a lot for someone to admit when they are wrong, so I welcome his honesty. But what gets me is that I haven't thought about our fight last weekend. This further proves how clouded my brain has been lately.

"It's just—I've been so worried about this ever since he showed up," he says, his hands tightly wound together in front of him on the table. "I saw the way you used to be with him, and you've never given me that…"

My stomach tenses as I go to speak, but he continues. "I know... I know, we aren't like that. But shit, B, I really want you to give me a chance here."

He lets out another long breath just as our food arrives at the table, effectively pausing whatever else he was about to confess. Can't say I'm not thankful for the reprieve. I really don't know what to say... I don't want to hurt him, but he also needs to remember I wasn't looking for a boyfriend when we first started hooking up.

"Shit, I'm sorry for unloading all this on you right now. I'm sure it's the last thing you need this week. I know that might be selfish of me, but I just had to get it off my chest."

I try my best to hide my wince. In all actuality, I feel like the selfish one, considering I can't come to terms with what I really want.

"Thank you for being honest with me." My mind flits to Nate and the honesty he finally gave me this week.

Focus on the man in front of you, B.

"I'm sorry I have never been able to promise you more, Carter; if I could, I would." For the first time ever, I internally question if I want him to give me the easy out here. But, like so much other shit in my life... I just don't know.

I do know my mind is clouded because of Nate, but even when I was trying to give it my all with Carter, I still wasn't able to.

He smiles, trying to hide his disappointment, and I hate myself a little more. "That's okay, babe. I'll hold out for the possibility of one day."

I force a smile onto my face, even though deep down, I know that isn't the response I was hoping for.

He points his fork to my plate. "Now eat up. I have to be on the bus in a couple of hours."

Unfortunately, my appetite went out the window with my ability to speak my feelings.

"Hello, earth to Berkley."

The sound of Marie's voice has me snapping to. "Shit, sorry, I zoned out there for a minute."

"Not to worry, girl. Was that regular salt or Tajin on the rim of the jalapeño margarita for table eight?"

"Tajin, please," I answer after double-checking my order pad. Which is unusual for me, because I don't typically need to write anything down, but tonight, my brain is complete and utter mush.

After my late breakfast with Carter, I immediately went for a run, hoping the fresh air would clear my thoughts and help me think straight. Unfortunately for me, it didn't work, so I was left to stew all through my two-hour-long afternoon special education seminar.

"You okay, girl?" Marie asks before continuing with my order.

"Yeah, just a lot on my mind this week. I'm good, though," I say with as much conviction as possible. I escape to the office for a moment to collect myself.

My heart aches for what Carter confessed earlier today. Am I at fault for leading him on more than I should have? Knowing my heart was never there for the taking in the first place. I thought I made that clear enough to him from the moment we took it a step further, but apparently not. I wonder if, in another life, I could see myself with Carter. He's handsome and sweet in his own way, but when his lips are on mine…it's not the earth-shattering, all-consuming feeling. The feeling I know existed because I've experienced it before, just not with him.

I unloaded a bit of my conversation on Bellamy when she caught me after my run, and she, too, didn't know what to say. Which is quite surprising, considering she's one of the best advice-givers I know. However, she's a lot less *I hate Nate* these days, and a lot more *I wish I had a hot stalker who's obsessed with me.*

Everyone seems to be at a loss for words about my situation when all I need is some sound advice to help me navigate it all.

I swipe at the lone tear trickling down my cheek.

It's times like these that I miss my mom the most. How badly I wish I could pick up the phone and call her. I know that in a crisis, she would have dropped everything and come to visit me. We would have gorged ourselves on snacks and talked until the wee hours of the morning. She would know what I should do…and without her guidance, I feel so lost.

I take a deep breath, knowing I need to get back out on the floor. The silly pictures of Phil, Tiffany, and the kids that are glued to the back of the door bring a smile to my face. The sight of them makes me think of how Nate had the collage I made for him hanging on the inside of his closet door. Unwanted butterflies swarm inside me at the thought—just one more confusing revelation since Nate's been back.

A thought that has been pushing its way into the forefront of my mind since Wednesday has me pulling my phone from my apron. Even though I know it will do nothing to ease my confusion, I can't seem to stop myself from what I do next.

ME

> Hope the bus ride to Georgia is smooth. I know how those South Carolina roads are.

NATE

...

The three dots of his response pop up immediately, and I wait with bated breath for the message to come through.

THIRTEEN

Nate

BB

Hope the bus ride to Georgia is smooth. I
know how those South Carolina roads are.

H oly Shit. Am I seeing things?

I look over to Graham for some affirmation, but he has
his Beats on, eyes closed, and head leaned back against the
seat.

Focusing back on the text, I scroll up and see the hundred
before, from me to her, that went unanswered.

I'll take any type of progress when it comes to her, and something about this feels huge.

ME

I'm about to ask Graham to pinch me. Am I
dreaming right now?

BB

Don't be so dramatic 💀

Seeing her name on my phone again reminds me of the excitement I felt as a teen when she first texted me. It's even more special now. It gives me a sliver of hope that's she's thinking of me and intentionally reaching out without me initiating.

> ME
>
> Nah babe, no drama here. Just living on cloud nine right now.
>
> ME
>
> As for this shitty ride. You're too late. I think I have a concussion from the number of times my head has hit the window.

I can't help but look up to the middle of the bus to see if Carter is texting too, and it kills me, knowing he has every right to be talking to her. But somehow, I also feel no remorse for kissing his girlfriend the other night or falling asleep with her in my arms a few days ago. I have no problem being that guy in this scenario. This isn't a contest; this is the love of my life who I let others' bad decisions affect. I won't let her go completely unless she asks me to. Unless she tells me that he's who she really wants, and even then, I may put up a fight.

So yeah, fuck bro code. He ain't my brother anyway. He hasn't been my friend since I got the starting quarterback position in our eighth-grade year on the middle school team. The jealousy ate him alive, and I knew the days of him being my buddy were gone.

> BB
>
> Welp, maybe it will knock some sense into you.
>
> ME
>
> If it doesn't, I'm sure Georgia's linebacker, Solomon, will. Have you seen that dude?

BB

Yeah, more QB sacks than most of their defensive ends. But you're quick, and you have a tough o-line.

ME

True. But I'd be even faster if you were going to be there.

BB

Heavy on the charm today, huh?

ME

Always for you, BB.

BB

I'll be watching. What are Dad's manifestations for this week?

ME

Five touchdowns, and two drives that get our kicker close enough for field goals. At least two of those touchdowns will be passes to Nola. He thinks this one will be a closer game since they have the home-field advantage.

BB

Sounds like a good game.

BB

You got this.

ME

Can I tell you something?

BB

It depends...

ME

Maverick told me they were coming and Bellamy too. My heart sank when they said you weren't coming with them.

I know even if she came, I wouldn't be the only one she'd be coming to watch. But just having her there is all I care about. The rest will work itself out.

> **BB**
> Sorry, I have to work.

> **ME**
> Tell Phil... Outlaw said you need the night off.

> **BB**
> I have no doubt he would prob give it to me, but I'm covering someone's shift this weekend.

I don't want to push it, so I let it go. I have no right to demand things from her, and I'm semi-reasonable enough to know that.

Opening my photo gallery, I smile at the happy, beautiful girl looking back at me. Briefly, I wonder if she kept any of our pictures. Doubtful. Unlike me, who has a whole album dedicated to her in my phone and a closet door that haunts me daily.

> **ME**
> Can I tell you something else?

> **BB**
> I have a feeling even if I said no, you'd still tell me.

> **ME**
> I'd give anything to look in the stands and see this again...

> **ME**
> [Picture message]

The picture is of her in the stands, wearing one of my practice jerseys on my senior night. The sports photographer at our school captured it perfectly, of her right after I ran a touchdown in from the 20-yard line.

> **BB**
>
> Oh geez, I haven't seen that in forever. I look so young and innocent... And happy.

My chest constricts at the thought I damaged that happiness.

> **ME**
>
> You're still young. And let's be honest, you weren't innocent then either. Do you remember what we did afterward...in my truck?

The thought has me adjusting my cock in my pants. Berkley and I could never keep our hands off each other. She doesn't respond immediately, and I torture myself by glancing up in Graves's direction again. This time, he has his phone up to his ear. It fucking guts me that it's probably her on the other end. I imagine going up there, ripping his phone from his ear, and throwing a Hail Mary out the window.

A few minutes later, she responds

> **BB**
>
> I remember.

The next day, we beat Georgia 40 to 28. Five touchdowns, three with two-point conversions, one with an extra point from Pike, and one we didn't quite get the extra points across the line on. The only prediction of my dad's that was off was the field goals; we managed to put our kicker in position for one in a fourth down, which Pike kicked beautifully. Nola scored three of our five touchdowns, turning the buzz about his abilities up even further. And I only got my block knocked twice by Solomon, so I'll take that as a win.

Now, the guys have convinced me to sneak out of the hotel and go to a house party. Apparently, our linebacker, Williams, has a cousin in a sorority here. It sounds like an awful idea, but I know I'll just sit in my bedroom and wait for Berkley to text me if not. I get in the Uber with Nola, Graham, and Maverick. Cash and Bellamy decided they didn't want to go. Checking my phone for what feels like the hundredth time tonight, I scroll to the last messages between us.

BB

Good game, Outlaw. Brian's predictions are almost so spot on it's scary.

ME

Thanks, BB. Yeah, I'm starting to think he's got a magic ball or some shit.

BB

How's your head? Solomon is a beast, huh?

ME

Nah, barely felt it.

BB

I'm sure, tough guy.

ME

What you doing tonight?

BB

Working the late shift. I'll be here with the drunkies all night.

ME

I know the guys said we're holding off on Sunday dinner since we'll all be driving back from Georgia, but I'm free once we get home if you are.

She still hasn't responded to that. I'm trying to convince myself that it's because she's busy at work and not avoiding gently letting me down.

We arrive at the Delta Phi Epsilon house that's already thumping with people and music. Supposedly, no Georgia football players will be here, even though I find it hard to believe since this is a big campus.

Most of my teammates are talking to girls or playing drinking games. I'm standing beside the pong table, babysitting my beer, watching Graham and Nola flirt with two sorority girls. I've kindly avoided all the flirty whispers and little touches throughout the party. No part of me even wants to entertain another woman.

Almost worse than a flirty Georgia college girl, Carter Graves walks up beside me. I bite my tongue from saying something smart. I'm not sure how he's going to play this since he typically just avoids me altogether.

He looks out toward the pool behind the pong table. "This party reminds me of the summer before college. The party at Berk's place."

I grind my teeth, remembering the way his hands were on her that night. The visions of them coming to fruition make me want to vomit and break his nose at the same time.

"I knew that night you'd break her heart. And I knew I'd be there for her."

I tilt my head, looking him straight in the eyes, heeding a warning.

"You don't know what the fuck you're talking about. And I'd tread lightly if I were you."

"No, Outlaw, you should tread lightly. She's mine now. I heard how chummy y'all were at the pool party on Sunday when I conveniently wasn't there."

I push my finger into his chest. "There's your first mistake, Graves; she isn't yours."

He pushes my finger away, and I let him, knowing I can't put my hands on him here, of all places. It would jeopardize my whole team. And he knows that, too, which is why he approached me.

"Well, that isn't what she told me at breakfast yesterday or on the phone earlier. She made sure I knew exactly how she felt about me before I left."

His words slice through me. I try to school my features, not wanting to give him the satisfaction, but just picturing her and him after everything from this past week feels like a knife digging into my chest.

"How long did it take you to make your move freshman year?" I ask him, partly curious, partly to act unaffected by his previous words.

He raises an eyebrow with a slick smirk that I want to knock off his face. "We hung out before she moved to Mountain Ridge."

My response is instant. "Bullshit. You left not long after me for football."

His smirk turns into a smug smile, and I hate that I showed my emotion. "Yeah, but I drove home almost every weekend until school started. She needed a friend from the broken heart you left her with, and I was happy to oblige. Happy to help her forget *you*."

I crack my knuckles, begging my rational brain not to punch him. I want him bleeding at my fucking feet.

"But she never forgot me," I retort, and he tries to hide it, but I see the anger from the truth of my statement as it flashes over his face. I take a threatening step toward him, and I see Graham move from behind the pong table.

"You can try to convince yourself that she has, but you know who she sees when she closes her eyes," I whisper in his ear.

"Woah, woah, come here, Outlaw," Graham says, dragging my ass away.

I comply, not saying a word as he questions me about the altercation. Just running Graves's words over and over in my head as my fists clench tighter and tighter.

"I'll call myself an Uber; you stay with Nola and Mav. I'm good," I finally say as we get to the front of the house.

"You sure?" he asks, concern marring his face.

I nod.

"That bullshit between you two has got to stop."

"Don't," I warn, trying my best to hold my shit together.

Happy to help her forget you.

Graham doesn't say another word; just stands with me until my Uber comes.

I know I shouldn't, but I can't fucking help it.

ME

> So, you moved onto Graves before you even left for Mountain Ridge, huh?

Fuck, I'm pressing my fucking luck, but for some reason, I need her to confirm it or, even better, tell me it's bullshit.

But just like my earlier text, this one goes unanswered.

THE HOWLER

Mountain Ridge University

Volume 20-09

ANOTHER 'W' FOR THE WOLVES...

Happy Sunday! It's another win for the Wolves. And from what we heard the guys enjoyed some Georgia peaches afterwards.

Apparently, even the opposing team's sorority girls couldn't resist Nathan Outlaw. Can you blame them, though?

FOURTEEN

Nate

I roll my eyes at the latest Howler Report. I know it's all in good fun, but I hate the thought of Berkley reading that shit. I'll have to deal with that in the NFL, but I thought I had a couple more years before worrying about rumors with no truth behind them.

Flashing the headline to Graham, he chuckles from his seat beside me, shaking his head. "Let's hope Coach doesn't see that."

Shit I didn't even think about that. My head is still reeling from last night, that I didn't even think about the fact Coach would have our asses if he knew we snuck out of the hotel.

From the furthest seat away from Graves, I lean my head against the travel pillow I packed. I slept like shit last night, waking up every few hours to see if Berkley had texted me back. Even though I still have no chill when it comes to looking at my phone every few minutes. Especially when right before the bus took off, she texted me, totally ignoring my last message, only responding to the one before that.

> **BB**
> I'm working again tonight.

I keep staring at it, trying to decipher how to respond. A huge part of me wants to ask her if she's just going to ignore my other text, but the smarter side of my brain knows if I push her, she'll shut me out.

Another thirty minutes into the ride, my phone vibrates in my hand. My heart rate spikes when I see it's her.

> **BB**
> Heard you didn't ride back with the guys to the hotel last night. Hope those Georgia peaches were worth it.

Fucking Bellamy.

But I also like the thought of her being jealous. It means she still cares.

> **BB**
> And yes, even though it's none of your fucking business, we did hang out in Nori a few times after you left.

I feel the continental breakfast from the hotel climbing back up my esophagus at the image.

> **ME**
> Good to know I was that easy to move on from.

> **BB**
> No comment on your Georgia peach?

> **ME**
> I didn't ride with the guys because I was already back at the hotel.

ME

ALONE!

ME

There is only one woman I want.

I see the bubbles start and stop over and over for a few minutes.

BB

But that wasn't always the case, was it, Nate?

ME

What's that supposed to mean?

BB

I may have blocked you, but I still saw things. Even when I wasn't trying... I saw all the girls you were pictured with your freshmen year. You telling me you didn't fuck any of them?

I hate the thought of her seeing those pictures and imagining that. In all reality, it wasn't like that at all. It didn't happen until the end of my freshmen year when football wasn't occupying my time and it was taking everything in me to not call her and tell her everything about her sorry ass father.

ME

I won't lie to you, Berkley. It's no excuse, but I was so fucked up over you, and in my mind, I had to attempt to move on.

ME

News flash... It didn't fucking work.

Trust me, if I could go back, there would be no one but her. I wish I could erase everyone before her and after her. They all meant nothing. I couldn't tell you one thing about them. That probably makes it more fucked up, but it's the truth.

BB

> Well, congrats. Those images are what pushed me into Carter's bed.

I hate myself even more than I thought possible. But the vision of them sends me into a fit of anger, and I'm thankful Graham is in between me and the aisle leading to Graves.

ME

> Oh, don't worry, he told me all about it last night. Including your little Friday morning fun with him. I guess everything from this past week didn't mean shit to you.

BB

> I don't owe you anything, Nathan.

ME

> You may be right. But don't act like you've been sitting here heartbroken when you moved on within weeks. With someone like him nonetheless.

BB

> You have no fucking clue what you're talking about.

ME

> Then explain it to me. Let me see you tonight.

BB

> Get fucked.

BB

> And not literally...or maybe I'll hear about it on the Howler report tomorrow too.

Fuck this. I have avoided doing this to her, but I know exactly where I'm going when I get home.

I'm used to funneling my nervous energy into fuel as the quarterback of a division one school. But I'm not used to the nerves that cloud my mind as I walk into The Wolfpack on Sunday afternoon, wondering if I'm making this whole situation worse by ambushing her.

The hostess greets me, "Hi there, just one?"

Debating on how I should play this, I go with using my armor first.

Her boss.

"Is Phil available?" I ask, pretending to look for him, but really, I'm seeking out my favorite petite blonde.

"He's actually cooking tonight. But let me tell him it's you and see if he can step away."

I'm still not quite used to people just automatically knowing who I am.

"Let him know I have something for his son. Just really quick."

She nods, giving me a smile before heading to the back. I let my eyes roam the busy restaurant, but there's still no sign of Berkley.

Did she lie about being here? She doesn't owe me anything, so why lie...? Maybe she's out on the enclosed patio area.

My eyes stay trained in that direction, not wanting to miss her, until I see Phil coming from the back.

"Outlaw, what's up man?" He shakes my hand. "Great game yesterday. Hell of a start to the season."

"Thank you. I appreciate it." Pulling the tickets out of my pocket, I hand them over. "I brought your little guy something."

After our first win, I spoke to our family ticket liaison and worked out a four pack for Phil and his family. I was planning on dropping it by one day next week, but I knew this was the perfect excuse to show up at Berkley's job after our argument earlier.

A huge smile spreads across his face when he sees the tickets. "Holy shit, this is like right behind you guys."

I smile, his excitement contagious. "Yes, and I got you four. I wasn't sure how big your family was, but I can try to get more if needed."

He pats my shoulder. "This is perfect. My wife is more into basketball, plus our sitter likes to go to the games, so I'll probably go with our three older kiddos." With a bright smile, he looks at the tickets again. "Man, thank you so much."

"I was happy to do it."

"We are super short-staffed tonight. I'm actually cooking and my wife is behind the bar." I take the chance to look around, and there's still no sign of Berkley.

I wave him off. "No worries, get back to it." He shakes my hand, and I know if I don't ask now, I'll lose the chance. "Hey, is um, Berkley working tonight?"

He looks a little surprised at first. "Are you friends with Berkley? I'm going to get that little shit for gatekeeping."

I laugh at that, but swallow roughly. "Yeah." For some reason, just calling her my friend out loud hurts to say. "She's my friend, and I thought she was going to be here tonight."

"Berkley's keeping our kids from burning down the house tonight." He shrugs. "They like her more anyway."

Disappointment floods me, but if I'm being honest with

myself, this wasn't my best idea. It's way too busy to bombard her with a conversation.

"You'll have to ask her which job she prefers?" he chuckles to himself. "One is way less stressful than the other, in my humble opinion."

Realizing I need to respond, I come up with something quick. "No problem, I just wanted to drop something off to her too, but I'll shoot her a text and just take it by her place later."

Phil smirks at me like he just had the best idea ever. "Our house is two blocks over on the corner of Dogwood and Glendale if you want to drop in. Take these with you." He raises his finger in the air, pointing to the west, and I don't hesitate at his offer when he passes the tickets back to me. "Jack Jack's going to freak."

Phil's the real MVP here.

Reminding myself to play it cool, I smile. "Perfect. What's the house number?"

"You aren't Berkley's stalker, right?" he asks, and I can tell he is teasing.

If he only knew. Hopefully, he never talks to Bellamy.

"Depends on who you ask," I joke, but before he can retract his offer, I say, "We're both from Nori Beach. No stalker."

Just a guy hoping for a second chance after the biggest fuckup of his life.

"Oh yeah, I saw that on ESPN."

Someone calling his name frantically from the back snaps him out of our conversation.

"Alright, gotta go. Thanks again." He turns over his shoulder and rushes out, "We'll be there next weekend. Stop by sometime this week and dinner is on me."

"House number?" I call out.

"5361."

"Have a good one, Phil."

With renewed nerves and excitement, I head out the door and down Dogwood Street.

Laughter and squeals of fun filter out the open windows as I approach the front door of the two-story white house. I smile at the sound, remembering the time I tagged along with her to babysit my cousins in Nori Beach. That was the night she told me she wanted to be an elementary school teacher. At seventeen years old, when I was thinking about nothing but her and football, she had told me that she wanted to make a difference in children's lives, whether it was teaching them something or simply showing them love. I think I fell even more in love with her that night. She made me want to strive for something more than just being a football player.

I knock on the door, wondering if Phil gave them a heads-up I was coming.

Feet thudding through the house is the last thing I hear before the door is snatched open, and a young, wide-eyed girl stands in front of me, gawking.

I give her a friendly smile, but before I can tell her who I am, I hear Berkley yell from somewhere upstairs, "Don't open that door, Josie. Wait for me."

The girl, or Josie, shrugs and yells back, "That hot new quarterback is here!"

Lord have mercy.

"What!?" Berkley hollers back, followed by three pairs of feet clomping down the steps, heading our way.

She rounds the corner, a cute redheaded toddler on her hip and two more kids close behind. My stomach dips at the sight of her. Her blonde hair pulled up on top of her head, and there's no makeup on her gorgeous face. I always loved her like this.

Berkley's surprised expression quickly morphs into one with narrowed eyes and pursed lips.

I smirk at her, and that's when the young boy runs up, standing beside his older sister. "Is this for real right now?"

"You are, like, my brother's idol," Josie says, at the same time Berkley speaks up again to ask, "What are you doing here, Outlaw?"

Digging into my pocket, I pull out the set of four tickets and squat so I'm at eye level with Jack. "You're Jack, right?"

He gasps and nods enthusiastically. "How'd you know?"

"Your dad sent me. I went to The Wolfpack to give him these." I hold the tickets out for him to see.

Berkley steps up, peering over Josie's shoulder, and that's when I spot the little guy attached to her leg as well. It's obvious these kids love her.

Trust me, little dude, I get it.

"Oh my gosh! This is frickin' awesome!" he screeches.

"Jack, don't say frickin'," Berkley reminds him, but there's a small smile on her face.

"Oops," he shrugs.

"Can my sister come too? She can throw a football almost as good as you." He smiles proudly at his big sister, and it's adorable.

"Yep. I got you guys four tickets, but I told your dad I can get more if I need to."

"Bruh, this is the best day ever," he says, tugging on his sister's arm, and she rolls her eyes at him playfully.

I laugh. I can tell this kid is a handful.

"Berkley, will you be there?" he looks up at her, adoration shining in his eyes.

Looking at the tickets, she ruffles his hair. "Yep…but it looks like you have even better seats than me."

Jack's smile beams from her to me.

"Thank you." He gives me the wolf sign, and I do it back.

The youngest girl in Berkley's arms lets out a howl, and I officially love this family.

"Be right back," Jack says after handing the tickets to Berkley for safe keeping.

"Do you guys know each other?" Josie asks, looking between Berkley and me.

Berkley says, "Kind of," at the same time, I say, "Yep, since we were sixteen years old."

Raising my eyebrow at her, I keep it PG because I notice the way Josie is watching us closely.

"Hey, QB, do you have a few minutes to spare?" Jack appears back in the doorway with a football cradled in his arms.

Nodding, I give him a smile. "Yeah, buddy."

Berkley's eyes widen, but before she can shut down the idea, I say, "Only for a few minutes, though."

"Perfect." He starts walking down the hall, waving for me to follow. "Come on, we have more room in the backyard."

I motion for his big sister to lead the way. "You too. I gotta see this arm of yours."

Berkley stands there with her mouth agape, probably pissed that I've now invaded another part of her life.

I reach my hand out for the quiet little guy wrapped around Berkley's leg. It takes him a minute, but he finally relents.

Tapping Berkley's non-toddler-carrying hip, I say, "Come on, BB. After all, I really came here to see you."

"Okay, so little dude wasn't lying about your arm," I say, impressed with Josie's spiral.

She smiles proudly. "Thanks."

"You ever thought about playing?" I ask curiously; there still may not be enough, but more and more opportunities for females in football are popping up throughout the states.

Josie shakes her head. "No, it's the same season as volleyball. So I already know when I can try out for the middle school team, I would rather play volleyball."

"That's cool," I say, watching Berkley pretend to tackle the toddler who's running with the ball. Her loose bun falls, and I'm captivated watching her pull the scrunchie from her hair and slide it onto her wrist, letting her long strands cascade down her back.

"Do you look at every girl the way you look at Berkley?"

Damn, this kid is preceptive as hell.

Chuckling, I smirk. "Nope, just her," I respond, right as the littlest girl runs my way, and I scoop her up. At first, I worry she'll freak out from the stranger-danger, but she immediately giggles.

Berkley watches us with a genuine smile on her face, and Josie joins in with tickling her little sister.

"Can we have our ice cream now?" the one who doesn't let Berkley out of his sight asks, and I get the sense maybe he's a bit overstimulated.

"Sure, bud. Why don't all of you go in and wash up," Berkley says, rubbing his back.

Josie grabs the youngest from me and leads her siblings inside.

"I'm going to walk Nate around the front to tell him bye and thank you."

That's my cue. *Damn, I was hoping for an ice cream sundae too.*

Jack runs back to me, giving me a fist-bump and thanking me again for the tickets.

"See you on Saturday, Nate," Josie calls back over her shoulder.

"I'll look for you guys."

Instead of taking me back through the house, Berkley waves for me to follow her through a small gate that leads from the backyard to the front.

"That was sweet of you. I know they've been before, but never not in the nosebleeds, so this is going to be so special for them."

"It feels good to be able to do it. I had the idea after Phil told me how much of a fan his son is."

"I thought you said you were really here to see me?" she asks, and her voice is so steady, I can't tell if she's calling me out because she wants to catch me in a lie, or because she's disappointed if that isn't the reason.

We stop at the edge of their front sidewalk. "After the way we left things earlier, I wanted to see you in person, so the tickets were the perfect excuse to show up at your job. It just worked out even better when Phil offered to let me drop them off here for Jack."

"I typically don't question his parenting skills, but thank God, you aren't an ax murder." She rolls her eyes, and I see through her tough exterior. The smirk on her lips tells me she likes that I'm here. She likes that I took the time to seek her out.

I shrug. "Kinda hard to be an ax murder and the quarterback of the local college...plus, I told him we were friends."

She side-eyes me. "Great, as if I don't get tired of hearing about you already. Now I'll get twenty-one questions from my boss."

"What are you going to tell him?" I gently nudge her side. She pops the scrunchie against her wrist, and it takes me back to our teens when I would steal her hair ties to wear them on my wrist, staking my claim.

"That you're the dumb jock who made me fall in love with you, the boy I very willingly gave my virginity to, who treated me like the queen I am, until one day you broke my heart, even though you believed you were doing the right thing. Does that sum it up?"

Well, fuck. That hurts.

"Or you could tell him, I'm the love of your life, groveling for one more chance."

The front door swings open, interrupting the moment. "Are you guys going to kiss or what?" Jack yells and then slams the door. Movement in the front window catches our attention. Josie and her three younger brothers all have their faces pressed against the glass, watching our exchange.

A laugh bursts from me as Berkley lets out an exasperated huff and covers her face.

"They are hella cute. Is Jack about the age you want to teach?"

Her facial expression softens again, and she nods. "Yep, he's in second grade. I'm focusing on early education."

I smile, happy to hear her dreams are coming true. "Just the way you are with them shows how perfect of a fit that will be with you." I nod to the house. "And Josie really looks up to you. That was super obvious."

"I think Josie, like every other girl in Mountain Ridge, has a crush on you, Outlaw." She playfully jabs me in the stomach, and I feel it down to my toes.

I would kill to truly feel her hands on me.

I move closer and tuck a piece of hair behind her ear. "Well, there's only one I want, and I'm not so sure how she's feeling about me these days." Picking her hand up in mine, I gently slide the scrunchie off her wrist and onto mine before she even realizes what I'm doing.

Berkley gasps. "Hey, that's my favorite!"

I shrug, searching her eyes. "Come on…for old times' sake."

Again, she fights her smile, shaking her head at me.

A loud crash comes from inside, and Berkley immediately turns to head up the front porch. Josie yells from somewhere inside that everything is fine, but Berkley doesn't stop.

I rush out, "When can I see you again, BB?"

She stops, possibly considering her words before she turns around. "Give me a few days, Nate. I'm trying to work through some things in my head. Just get through this weekend. You have another big game ahead."

Understanding, I nod, trying not to let my disappointment show. "I know you have to go, but I want to make sure you believed me earlier. That report was bullshit. I didn't even look at another girl this weekend. I stared at my phone, waiting for a text from you most of the time."

She stares at me for a few beats before whispering, "I believe you." Then she twists the knob on the door, leaving me with a softly spoken, "Have a good night, Nathan."

I stand there for a few minutes after she disappears through the door, contemplating when it's appropriate to text her again.

Smiling to myself, I walk down the sidewalk.

I'll give her a few hours.

FIFTEEN

Nate

I see someone unblocked me on socials

BB

Yeah, kinda regretting that at the moment,
though.

ME

Damn, already?

BB

Remember her?

A picture comes through of me and two girls I was tagged
with my freshmen year. I immediately realize why this
particular picture bothers her.

ME

Yes, I know what you're thinking, but it wasn't
like that.

BB

Yeah, ok.

> **ME**
> I'm serious, Berkley. I never touched her.

Honestly, seeing Nikki at Texas Tech made me sick to my stomach. She was so insignificant, but her presence served as a constant reminder of the night that everything spiraled between Berkley and me.

> **BB**
> Clearly, based on this picture.

> **ME**
> You know what I mean. Never more than a friendly hug.

> **BB**
> I'm trying here, Nate. Trying to believe everything you tell me. Trying to remind myself of the ways you've shown me you care since you've been back, but then I see shit like this. And my mind is racing. It's just hard for me to believe a girl who you happened to meet the night we broke up has you tagged in multiple pictures, and nothing ever went down between you two.

> **ME**
> Where are you? Can we meet up so I can explain? I promise it's not what it seems.

> **BB**
> I'm going to class.

Fuck. If she only knew. Part of me contemplates showing her more of my thoughts I wrote in my playbook during that first year, wondering if the rawness would help her process or make things worse. This is all so fucked up, and it's my damn fault.

ME

> I know it seems sus. And she did seek me out. I was initially nice to her since I had met her before, and I felt obligated to be kind. But if you notice, the pictures stop fairly early into the first semester.

ME

> The first night she came on to me, I passed it off as her being drunk. The second time, I told her it would never happen between us and to keep her hands off me. She never tried again.

I was a total dick to her, if I'm being honest.

ME

> We still have so much to talk about. I want to answer anything running through your mind.

Her silent treatment unsettles me enough that I find myself searching back through the first journal my dad gave me.

Rereading the entry makes my gut churn and briefly takes me back to a headspace I don't want to be in again. I contemplate ripping it out and leaving it on Berkley's doorstep, but I'm not sure it will have the effect I want it to.

"I hope we have this weather for Saturday's game," Graham says as we take our food out into the courtyard.

"Me too." The campus really is something beautiful, especially this time of year as the leaves start to change. We don't usually have time to relax like normal college kids on campus, but Coach told us to take an extra hour today for ourselves in preparation for our home game in a few days.

When Graham asked if I wanted to eat with him, I knew I could use the distraction after my last text to Berkley went unanswered.

"You good?" Graham asks, examining me in a way only he does.

Glancing at the UTZ bag of chips I bought myself for a taste of nostalgia, I nod. "Yeah, brother." Not wanting to unload my shitty mood on him, I lie. "How about you? Lots of chatter about who's going to pick you up in the draft."

He sets his sandwich down and smiles at me. "It's surreal, ya know."

I can only imagine what that feeling will be like for myself after next year.

"If you could go anywhere, who would be your first pick?"

"The kid in me says The Commanders. You remember how obsessed I was with them."

I smirk, because I do. We used to talk so much shit to each other.

"But honestly, I think I could really help build something with The New Orleans Phantoms. I like their style a lot, and I think they're building a dynasty down there," he shrugs. "But we'll see how the combine goes in February."

Patting him on the shoulder, I say, "Middle school us would be fucking proud."

He chuckles. "Fuck yeah, they would."

Across the lawn, blonde braids grab my attention, and the pit in my stomach grows into a gaping hole at the sight of Berkley smiling up at Carter.

"Speaking of middle school," I growl, resting my elbows on the table as I bury my face in my palms. But because I'm a glutton for punishment, I look in their direction again, right as she throws her head back, laughing.

What hurts the most is I know this isn't for show. I have stupidly convinced myself that the other times I've seen them together have been part of her ploy to torture me. Apparently, *delusional* is my middle name. Because I know that smile and this is her being naturally happy in her element with him. And I feel physical pain watching them together.

She smiles when he tugs on one of her braids, and I'm almost certain my heart is bleeding into my throat. I'll choke on it at any minute.

"Breathe, dude," Graham says gently, placing his hand on my shoulder, and I do my best to listen, but I can't take my eyes off them.

There's no way he loves her the way I do. Maybe I didn't make the right decision two years ago, but without a doubt, I did what I did because I love her, not for any other reason.

"Stop thinking what you're thinking." Graham turns his attention away from there.

"How can I not, Graham?" I trace my finger across the soft velvet scrunchie on my wrist, using it as a reminder of the progress I've made with Berkley.

I'm a selfish fuck, but I want to be the one making her smile, taking her to lunch, holding her at night. Not him or anyone else.

Finally breaking my view of them, I look at Graham. "Imagine loving a girl more than anything. More than football, more than yourself. And then picture you have to break up with her because some bullshit your parents created, and now you find out it didn't protect her from the pain like you assumed it would, and you're back in the same town, but she's dating a guy who's hated you over some dumb shit since middle school. A guy whose eyes always lingered on her a little too long when you were dating."

Graham's expression morphs into one of surprise. "Ya know, that's the most you have ever shared with me about you and Berkley's situation?"

I do know this, and now that Berkley knows, I don't have a problem telling him everything, but not right now, not when I can barely control myself from walking across this courtyard.

"I'm not going to ask you to elaborate, but I am going to tell you what you're seeing over there isn't what you think."

My gaze flits back in that direction. Berkley tosses a piece of food up in the air and Carter tries to catch it, making them both laugh. They look pretty fucking chummy to me.

"You forget, I used to make her laugh like that. I used to be the one she gave that attention to." My hands shake as I grab my Gatorade to take a sip, trying to calm my nerves down.

"No, you forget I was there for that. And I've seen this relationship she has with Carter since the beginning too. Trust me, he has always wanted her more than she wants him. They were truly just friends for a long time, and what you are seeing right now is them as friends."

I don't want him to be anything to her.

"Well, I fucking hate it."

"I get that, but you can't just come in here and expect her to drop everything for you after all the shit y'all have been through. Give the girl some time." He pauses, looking back at her before back to me. "I have a strong feeling she'll find her way back to you."

His words ease the turmoil brewing inside of me. Only slightly.

"I know you're right, that she needs time and space. It's just hard for me. Now that we've talked about everything, it's hard for me not to want it all to go back to how it was, because I've never stopped loving her."

He rolls his lips like he's contemplating his next words. "Take a closer look at them."

My stomach twists, scared of what I may see this time, but I do as he asks. They each sit on separate benches, seemingly eating their own lunches now.

I focus back on Graham.

"If that was the Berkley I witnessed in love, she'd be on the same exact bench as him, barely giving each other any room. Literally feeding each other, whispering words in between bites. And don't forget the unforgettable PDA you two always put us all through. Neither of you could keep your hands or your eyes off each other."

I watch them for a few minutes, letting his words settle. A renewed hope stirs inside of me, and I stand, grabbing the bag of chips off the table.

"Oh fuck, that wasn't your invitation to go do anything," Graham says with wide eyes, grabbing my arm.

"I'll play nice." I shake out of his grasp, but I hear his big frame shift out of the picnic table and follow me.

My long strides take me across the courtyard faster than I can think this through.

A surprised Berkley meets my stare.

"What's up, Outlaw?" Graves tries to act casual, but I hear the bite in his tone.

"Looked like you two were having a *friendly* lunch, didn't seem like we were interrupting anything," I retort as Graham walks up.

And I'm going to punt your ass right back into the friend-zone.

"I was craving this flavor so bad..." I open the bag and pop one in my mouth, savoring it. "Mmmm," I moan at the taste, and I don't miss the way Graves's eyes zero in on my hair tie-clad wrist.

Take a long, hard look, motherfucker.

I set the bag of chips down in front of Berkley, smirking when she looks up at me. "But since it's your fave, I'll share."

The look in her eyes tells me, if we were alone, she would give me a piece of her mind, but she's treading lightly with Carter and me in close proximity.

"Thank you," she mumbles.

"You guys enjoy the rest of your lunch," Graham, ever the peacemaker, says, squeezing my shoulder.

Only because I don't want to piss her off more, I relent.

"Have a good day, BB." I wink and follow Graham back across the courtyard.

A FEW HOURS LATER

BB

Your little stunt at lunch wasn't necessary.

ME

What? I was just being sweet. Did you enjoy the chips?

BB

Yes, thank you, but I'm serious. I told you I needed time.

ME

I'm trying, BB.

BB

I am too.

Sixteen

Berkley

CARTER

Have fun with the girls tonight. Sad I can't make it... I have an incredible voice.

ME

Oh, is that so?

CARTER

Yes, the voice of an angel... you're truly missing out.

ME

Haha! Thanks, we'll somehow have to survive without you.

CARTER

Please try your best.

I stifle a laugh before putting my phone down and picking my curling iron back up. Carter has jokes, and hanging out with him yesterday felt good, refreshing even, like it used to be before we complicated things with sex. But spending an innocently casual afternoon with him helped me further realize that's all we will ever be, and I need to stop playing games. It's not fair, especially when I know he'll patiently wait for the day for me to offer more, and that day will never come. Carter and I are friends and will remain that way... hopefully.

WILLOW

Be there in 10! So excited.

Shit, I need to hurry my ass up. I wanted to be fully ready by the time Willow got here so I could give her all my attention. Karaoke night starts at eight, and if you want to get a good time slot for singing, you need to get there on time.

"Willow will be here in ten!" I yell through the apartment, hoping Bellamy and Darbs can hear me from their rooms.

Darby peeks her head into my room a few moments later. "I just finished making strawberry margaritas. Do you want one?" I notice the extra glass she has in her hand, just as Bellamy walks up, grabs the extra drink, and delivers it to my desk.

"Of course she does. No one turns down a margarita," She laughs, and we all join her.

"Perfect, thank you," I say, raising it up. We air cheers and take our sips.

"Oh, that's dangerously delicious. Tastes like some bad decisions will be made tonight," Bellamy teases with a wink.

Darby rolls her eyes. "Please don't forget it's Thursday."

"Uh huh, *thirsty* Thursday, my friend."

A knock on the front door has me up and out of my seat in an instant. I'm so frickin' excited to see Willow; it's been way too long.

Throwing open the door, I don't even give her a second to say hello before I wrap my arms around her and pull her into me. Her short frame barely making it past my chest.

She chuckles from where I have her head trapped against me, and my eyes well up with tears. It's crazy how close we used to be…and the fact that my stupid father's actions took away my relationship with her as well. After several more moments, I release her, swiping away my loose tear.

"Shit, I told myself I wasn't going to cry," Willow says, wiping away her own.

"Okay, that's all for tonight," I tease as I dry my own eyes, and we both laugh.

Darby and Bellamy appear a few seconds later, Bellamy with a drink in her hand for Willow.

"So glad to finally meet you. I'm Bellamy, and this is Darby."

"Thank you for letting me stay here."

"Anytime," the two of them say in unison.

"You're so frickin' cute… Are you single?"

Willow nods, and a small smirk spreads across her face.

"Oohh, the guys are going to eat you up!" Bellamy praises, grabbing onto Willow and walking her away from the front door. I laugh and grab her bag from just outside the entrance. I was so wrapped up in seeing her that we never actually made it into the apartment.

"Yeah, there will be none of that. Thank you very much," I chastise, following behind them.

"Oh, you hush. Let us have some fun. Now, are you into athletes, or…" Darby questions as she sits on the couch on the other side of her.

Willow's big smile lights up her face, clear blue eyes sparkling, and I take in the sight of her. She's absolutely gorgeous. Her dyed black hair is in a fun, carefree, messy bun. Her tank top and cut-offs showcase an impressive scattering of tattoos all over. I can't help but smile. If she's going to attend this school next year, Nate is going to have one hell of a time keeping his teammates away.

She fits in perfectly with my girls, and I can't wait for all of them to hear her sing at karaoke. Tonight's going to be so much fun, not to mention a much-needed mental break.

"Wooooo!" I cheer as Willow finishes singing "Valerie" by Amy Winehouse. She really is a great singer, so it doesn't surprise me one bit that she crushed it. Our table floods her with praises as soon as she sits down next to me.

"Damn, girl, you have some pipes," Bellamy says as she raises her glass in Willow's direction, then takes a sip.

"Why, thank you," Willow blushes. "Okay, who's next?" She looks around our table that was just joined by half of the women's basketball team. Directing her attention to me, she asks, "You ready for a solo?"

I bite my lip, turning to Bellamy.

"What about you, Bell?"

"I'm tapped out after that N'sync "Bye, Bye, Bye," you guys dragged me up there to do."

Willow slaps her hands against the table playfully. "Geez… anyone else?"

"I wrote my name down," Maverick says from across the table. Cash scoffs, and Mav elbows his twin in the side. The boys decided to join us at the last minute. Since their house-mates were taking it easy tonight, they figured they might as well have as much fun as possible before they're in full-blown training season.

"Oh, and what did you decide to grace us with, Rick?" Bellamy teases Mav with the stupid nickname she gifted him.

"Psshh, you'll have to wait and see, *Amy*," he smirks a devilish grin.

"I think Shay is up soon," Darby says playfully, slapping her teammate's shoulders. Shay shrinks into her seat when all of our gazes flit in her direction.

"Oh, come on, it's not bad. I promise. After the first one, you'll be fine." Bellamy's encouraging words do nothing to help Shay's mortification.

"Captain here lost a bet, and now she has to serenade us all," Darby smirks.

"I'm sure your voice isn't that bad. There're far worse out there," Willow says, just in time for the current singer to attempt a high note and fail miserably.

"She has a great voice. She just hates being put on the spot like this," Maverick says, and all of us look to him, even Shay. "I've heard you sing before, Little Moore. Don't act like I haven't," he teases.

Bellamy gives me a side-eye, and I know she'll have some tea for me later.

Willow quirks her eyebrow and focuses back on Shay. "Aren't you, like, the best basketball player at this school? You'd think you'd be used to being in the spotlight."

"Ha, one would think. But our darling girl only likes to sing in the showers or when she thinks no one can hear her. I think she has an amazing voice, so I made her a bet…and she lost, and now we're here." Darby fills us in on why Shay looks like she could quite literally melt to the floor at any moment.

"Ugh, don't remind me!" Shay whines and hides behind her hands.

"I feel like I need to know what this bet was for," Bellamy laughs, and Darby winks at her.

Several acts come and go, before Shay's name is called. I watch as the beautiful, tall blonde takes a steadying breath, downs the shot in front of her, then heads to the makeshift stage.

The screen loads behind Shay, and I see "Shallow" by Lady Gaga and Bradley Cooper pop up. Knowing this song is a duet, I look around to see if she has a partner to sing with. Before I know what's happening, Maverick stands and rushes to the stage. The familiar strumming of the sad guitar fills the room, the spotlight illuminating Shay's surprised face as Mav settles on the stool next to her. He takes his microphone just in time to sing his first note.

Our table stares in awe as the two of them serenade us all with their phenomenal vocals. No joke, they sound so good together, I even get goosebumps on my arms.

"Holy Hannah, the chemistry between the two of them is hot!" Willow says as they hit the crescendo.

I'm unable to take my eyes away. "For real."

"Crazier thing is…they're not together," Darby adds to our mini conversation but keeps her eyes on the stage.

"Is there a reason? Because damn, they should be," Willow says, her gaze still on the duo.

Cash decides to join our conversation. "Well, for one, her dad is our head coach. Plus, she's dating our neighbor, Jordan Andrews."

"Who's a total hottie and happens to be the captain of the men's basketball team," Bellamy chimes in.

"Oh damn..." Willow says, and I stifle a laugh. She took the words right out of my mouth. Staring at the two of them, you can feel the tension. It's so thick, it seems as if you can reach out and grab hold of it. One I'm much too familiar with these days.

When their song finishes, our table immediately stands up and gives them a standing ovation. Shay's cheeks flood with crimson red as Mav throws his inked arm around her shoulder and walks her back to our table.

"I'm not sure what that was...but I think I just got pregnant," Bellamy teases, fanning herself when the two sit down.

"Don't tease like that. I'm not ready to be an auntie." I slap her arm, and we both laugh.

Maverick's eyes hold Shay's stare until Darby's words break through their trance.

"See, I told you, you could do it!" Darby cheers.

Shay nods in Maverick's direction. "Thanks to this guy... Jack of all trades."

She smiles at him, and he winks. "My pleasure, darlin'."

"Hey, I'm going to grab a bucket of beer from Marie... You guys want anything else?" Bellamy asks as she pushes her chair out from the table.

"I pre-ordered some munchies with her earlier. Can you have her send it through?" I say, knowing Bellamy has just as good of a relationship with The Wolfpack bartender as I do with how often she comes to visit me at work.

We give her our requests, and as she's about to leave, Cash stands and follows her to the bar. He's been quiet tonight. Something has definitely been off between the two of them this past week, and I'm not quite sure what it is…

Our food arrives, and our table breaks off into small conversations as we snack and listen to some really good and some really bad singing.

After a particularly awesome "Tennessee Whiskey" rendition by an unfamiliar face in Greek letters, the karaoke host announces a fifteen-minute break, and I turn my attention to Willow. Tonight has been fun, but not ideal for catching up.

She smiles at me and grabs my hand. "I'm so happy you called me."

My heart aches at how many times my fingers hovered over her name. But the thought of seeing and speaking to her was just as painful. I wasn't strong enough to handle that.

"I'm so sorry—" I start to apologize, but she places her finger over my lips.

"Please don't apologize. I get it… Trust me. I wouldn't have been able to either."

"Thank you." I squeeze her hand, still in mine, admiring the scattered tattoos that trail up to her fingers.

"Your brother wasn't lying when he said you had more than him. They look good on you."

"I guess you can say they have been my form of therapy. I started drawing them first, then decided to give them a permanent home on my skin."

"You drew these?" I ask as I grab her arm and pull it closer to get a better look.

She laughs at me, but points to various ones on her arms. "Some of them, not all."

"They're stunning."

"Yeah, Nate even let me help with the design of the locket."

My face must look puzzled, because Willows takes on an 'oh shit, you don't know' look.

"Will…" I say, encouraging her to explain.

She puts her hands up in defense. "I'm not saying shit if you don't know about it yet. All I'm going to say is take a look at the inside of his wrist. You'll see."

"Really, you aren't going to tell me?" I tease, unable to ignore the thrill that runs through me.

"If you haven't seen it yet, then you're not there yet, B."

"You're being cryptic…"

She seals her lips and throws away the key, and I roll my eyes.

What could possibly be in that tattoo that I haven't seen yet…?

Maverick and Cash drop us girls off at our apartment, and we can hear them laugh at us as we stumble and giggle out of the Tahoe. Not sure if bracing yourself with another wobbling human is a great idea to help keep your own balance.

"What's the deal with you and the Riley Green lookalike?" Willow asks Bellamy as we wave goodbye to the guys watching us walk through the parking lot.

"Your guess is as good as mine," she huffs.

"Well, he seemed pretty adamant about Tennessee-Whiskey-singing-dude keeping his hands off you tonight." Willow raises her eyebrows suggestively.

"Yeah...well, he's a stupidly confusing gorgeous pain in my ass."

"I'd be confused too if I was in love with my stepsister," a tipsy Darby chimes in, and Bellamy smacks her arm as she looks back, likely to see if the guys are paying attention.

Willow gasps. "Wait, the twins are your stepbrothers?"

Bellamy does something she never does and blushes as she nods.

"No shame, babe. I'd let them tag team me in a heartbeat, stepbrothers or not."

"Geez, Willow," I sputter, and we all laugh.

"But for real...your brother would kill you."

She just shrugs like the little rebel she is, and I link my arm through hers and laugh some more.

"Ya know..." Darby says, squinting at the two of us. "You two could totally pass for sisters."

"Aww, you guys totally could!" Bellamy agrees.

"Ah, I wish. Maybe if she decides to give my brother another chance..." Willow trails off, leaning her head on my shoulder as we wobble our way down the hallway. I peek at her, and she's giving me major puppy dog eyes. The thought has my heart thumping.

"Oh, will you stop that." I swat at her, unable to hide the big smile on my face. "I don't know who's worse, you or him."

"A girl can wish," she winks.

We finally make it to our door, and we all squeal in excitement at the surprise package that's awaiting us.

Speaking of Nathan Outlaw. This has his name written all over it, and a rush of butterflies takes over my insides at the realization.

Not only is there a case of Diet Coke, but there are candy bars, one being Snickers, of course, bags of chips, and four Gatorades. A note peeks out of the top of one of the bags, and that confirms who these goodies are from.

After dropping off our snacks in the kitchen, I take out the note and smile.

> Wish I could have been there tonight...but I'm glad you got to hang with Will. She missed you. Hope the snacks help with the hangover. I know how you get, so there's a Snickers in there for you, too.

What am I supposed to do with you, Nathan Outlaw?

SEVENTEEN

Berkley

Good Game, 2!

NATE

Thanks BB. That last touchdown was for you.

ME

Well, I won't tell Jack. I saw them after the game, and they were still so hyped up over you tossing them the ball when you scored. You made it so special for them.

NATE

Their excitement was motivation for me. I loved seeing them all so happy.

NATE

And you too, don't think I missed you jumping up and down after I scored.

ME

Chill... I ride hard for my Wolves. Don't flatter yourself.

NATE

Please refrain from using "ride hard" in a text to me. I'm not a strong enough man for that.

ME

Remember, I love to torture you.

NATE

Oh, don't I know it, baby.

NATE

Speaking of, I was looking for you after the game, but the guys said you and the girls headed back to get ready.

ME

Yeah, we're going to Alchemy tonight. You going?

NATE

I am now.

"I feel like I'm going to have to cut someone's dick off tonight with the way these guys are looking at you two," Darby says loudly as we walk past a group of men who shamelessly check us out.

"We want to make 'em sweat. Especially a few in particular," Bellamy says, bumping her hip into mine. We're both wearing strapless body con dresses. She paired hers with short cowgirl boots that fit her vibe perfectly. Of course, I went for comfort in my Air Force Shadows, adding a little height to my small frame.

Raising my eyebrow at her, I ask, "Something you want to share with the audience? Who are you trying to make sweat?"

She playfully rolls her eyes. "Every single one of them, babe."

But somehow, I think she has a brown-eyed, hockey-playing cowboy in mind.

"Okay, sis. If that's the lie we're telling," I smirk.

"You really want to go there..." Quirking her eyebrow, she gives me a knowing look.

Darby laughs and shakes her head. "Before I call both your asses out, let's go get a drink."

"And Berkley, please don't forget again and hand the bartender your real ID."

I throw my hands up. "Ugh, I'm never going to live that down. It was spring break, and I was already hammered."

Only a few more months until I'm legally twenty-one and don't have to worry about it anymore.

We opt for shots so we can dance without spilling drinks on each other. After downing them, Bellamy notices the guys over in the VIP section. Nate and all his roommates are surrounded by a bunch of football players. I watch on as several groups of girls are let into the section as well.

Darby starts that way, but I grab her arm and nod toward the dance floor. "Let's dance."

She looks surprised at first, but then she says, "Oh, that's right, gotta make them sweat."

Bellamy and I giggle and head to the dance floor just in time for Sabrina Carpenter's "Espresso" to come on.

We dance and sway, singing along, but my eyes keep finding their way back to the VIP area. I see a girl I recognize as a Zeta whisper something in Nate's ear, and hot prickles scatter across my body.

He smiles but shakes his head, slinging his arm around Nola's neck. Nola gives the brunette his signature playboy smile; then he grabs her hand and heads out to the dance floor. The satisfaction I feel from witnessing what seemed like Nate turning her down floods me with renewed confidence, along with a need I've been ignoring.

A few songs later, Nola spots us and ditches his dance partner. The song changes to "Yeah Glo!" by GloRilla when he joins our little circle. Bellamy and Nola get in each other's faces, having a rap off. Bellamy is always guaranteed to know the lyrics to any popular rap or country song; it's why she makes a fun karaoke partner, since she doesn't even have to read the screen. Her red hair sways down her back as she bops her head to the beat.

Strong arms wrap around me from behind, catching me off guard. He smells good, but it isn't the scent I crave or the touch I ache for. Turning around, I smile up at Carter. "Hi."

He leans in to kiss me, and I turn my head in time for him to kiss my cheek.

The frown on his face brings on the guilt I've been feeling so much lately. I need to own my shit and tell him the truth, point blank, instead of gently trying to move him back into the friend-zone. It isn't fair to him.

"Oh, it's like that," he huffs, and I smell the alcohol on his breath.

Part of me wishes I could just snap my fingers, and we could go back to freshmen year, when we were just friends before things got complicated.

"Come on, let's dance," I say, turning back around as the song changes again, wanting to keep things light. Seemingly satisfied, his hands rest on my swaying hips. I can officially admit to myself something about having his hands on me in the same room as Nate feels extremely wrong. No matter what my heart may feel, I remind myself I belong to no one. I haven't made any promises to either of them.

I just need to relax and try to have a good time. Rocking to the beat, I let my body move to the music as I watch all my friends have fun around me.

Carter pulls me into him, and I feel him harden against me. Not wanting to give him the wrong impression tonight, I put some space between our bodies. My eyes flit over to the VIP section, but I don't see Nate.

My attention must linger over the area for too long, because Carter interrupts me, "You're looking for him, aren't you?" he asks, biting my ear. "You know we haven't fucked in what feels like forever. Hell, you barely even let me kiss you anymore. He's right, isn't he?"

With my heart now pounding harder, I ask, "What are you talking about?" I take his hand, dragging him away from the crowd around us.

"Never mind. Let's get out of here." He grabs my hips, pulling me into him again. "I miss you."

I shake my head, feeling uneasy. "No, I'm here with my friends, Carter. I can't leave right now." I'm using a cop-out, and it's obvious. This conversation is evidence enough I need to end things with him officially.

"Can't, or won't?"

I flinch at the bite in his question. "Both."

"I bet if I were him, you wouldn't be saying that. You think I'm stupid? You think I didn't see what he was flaunting on his wrist yesterday?"

"Carter..." I swallow, trying to find the right words; the last thing I want to do is hurt him. "I'm sorry, I'm not trying to hurt you. But I think…"

"Don't fucking say it, Berkley." He jerks his arm out of my grasp. "You know what…fuck this shit."

His reaction twists my stomach as I call out after him, "This is why I never promised you anything, Carter. I didn't want it to ruin our friendship."

He salutes me and walks away.

Ay, ay, captain, but don't be a fucking dick.

I rejoin the girls, no Nola in sight anymore.

"You okay?" they both ask me.

I nod reassuringly as a sense of relief washes over me. "Yeah, it's my fault. I should have womaned up a while ago and told him how I was feeling. It was stupid and selfish of me not to."

"Don't beat yourself up, babe. You've had a confusing couple of weeks and, honestly, if Carter actually thought y'all had a chance at being more than friends with benefits, he was delu-lu," Bellamy says, grabbing my arms and moving my body with hers.

"I agree, B. I know your kind heart, but just remember you never promised him anything else. Now have fun and let yourself have whatever or whoever you truly want. No matter how wrong you may think it is or how scared you are. Take it from me, life is too short to worry about all that and not be with who you want to be with." Darby slings her arm around my shoulders, swaying with Bellamy and me.

I let both their words ease my guilt. After all the revelations over the past few weeks and the way my heart and body still feel, I know there's no reason to keep denying myself something I want so badly.

Letting the peace of that self-awareness calm me, I give them both a big smile, suddenly feeling more like myself than I have in a long time. "I love y'all! Let's dance and then cause some chaos in the VIP section."

"Bet!" Bellamy gives me a shit-eating grin.

Several songs later, Darby nudges me, and I look up, seeing Nola leading the literal pack of wolves over to us.

My belly dips, and my toes tingle when my eyes meet Nate's. He's so fucking hot it's ridiculous. Willow's words play on repeat as my gaze drifts to the sleeve on his right arm. I have the urge to find out exactly what she meant the other night, and I don't want to wait any longer.

"Where's the rest of your dress?" I hear Cash growl under his breath to Bellamy, and I smirk.

Make him sweat, sis.

Bellamy rolls her eyes and keeps dancing with Darby, but I see the smug grin she tries to hide from the way he watches her.

"Is the coast clear?" Whispered words flutter across my neck, and my core clenches at his closeness.

"What coast?"

"The one where your boyfriend, or whatever he is, was hovering around?"

"He isn't my boyfriend, never was." I spin around to face him.

His hazel eyes darken as he steps a bit closer. "Does he know that?"

"Yes." My voice breathier than just moments before.

"Good. I don't give a flying fuck, but I don't want you to feel bad."

"Feel bad about what?"

He licks his thumb, rubbing it across his bottom lip, and all I can think about is how good that mouth would feel between my legs. I'm so turned on, I almost miss when he says, "When I kiss you later."

Wetness floods between my legs, but I tilt my head, playing it cool. "Very presumptuous of you, don't ya think."

He closes whatever space was left between us. "You telling me you don't want it as bad as I do?"

It's hard to breathe; all the air has been sucked out of this club.

"Come on," he says, putting his hand on the small of my back and nodding toward the group. "We came out here to get y'all." His touch burns through my dress, and I feel like I'm going crazy with need.

Nate's hand never leaves its place on my back as we enter the VIP section, and I'm ridiculously close to begging him to put his hands somewhere else.

NATE

Dancing with Berkley feels like old times. The feeling of her body against mine consumes me. Every slide of her ass, every laugh, every gentle touch drives me fucking wild.

I'm harder than I've ever been, and I keep having to think of the time a dirty jock strap was being thrown around the locker room and hit me right in the face to stop myself from coming in my pants.

Not sure how much longer that's going to work with the way her ass keeps rutting into me.

"BB, you're going to have to stop that," I growl through Berkley's blonde hair into her ear. "You forget I know what your ass looks like when I'm hitting it from this angle, and right now, I'm trying my best not to think about that."

She bites her lip, looking over my shoulder, purposefully grinding into my cock. I don't miss the way her eyes roll back before she closes them.

"I know you remember, too," I whisper.

Giving me a break, she turns around and dances in front of me against Bellamy, but never takes her blue eyes off mine. Then she leans closer, her lips just barely touching my ear, "I remember *everything*."

My hands find her hips, and I smile. Her admittance has my insides flip-flopping, especially when she was denying that just a few weeks ago.

God, this feels good; it feels like *us*.

She bounces between Bellamy and Darby, each time making her way back to me. I love seeing her have fun like this. When we were younger, I would literally sit and watch her do anything. As long as she had a smile on her face, I was content.

"I can't take my eyes off you," I whisper the next time she steps in front of me, swaying her hips.

She surprises me, turning and slinging her arms around my neck. The smirk on her pretty face makes my knees weak.

"That was the goal, Outlaw."

"Oh yeah?"

Biting that damn lip again, she nods toward the small alcove in the back of the VIP section. "I want to see something."

She moves her hand down, slipping it into mine, where it fits so effortlessly. My heart races like she's asking me to jump off a cliff with her.

I'd dive headfirst if she asked me to.

Once we've made our way over, I purposefully sit first so I can pull her onto my lap. Her hands fall to my chest as she looks down at me. "What did you want to see, BB?"

"A truth for a truth?" she asks, trailing her finger down my tattooed arm.

I swallow, not sure where this is going, but I nod anyway. I'm ready to give anything to her.

"Why did Willow say I needed to take a closer look at the locket on your tattoo?"

Dammit, Will.

Without hesitation, I twist my arm so my forearm is facing up. Berkley trails her fingertip over the inked skin there.

She gasps, pushing to stand between my legs and picking up my arm like she's trying to make sure she's seeing it correctly.

Her eyes blink rapidly, and I see the emotion pouring into them. "When did you get this?"

"Spring semester of freshmen year over several sessions."

She closes her eyes, head shaking. "I just don't understand."

I pull her back onto my lap and kiss the lone tear that slips onto her cheek. "You were burned into my very core, and when I wasn't with you, I felt you here." I press her hand into my chest, right over my heart. "So, it only made sense to have a piece of you where I could see it any time."

"In my journal that day, I wrote: In another life, I'd come back as an octopus, and you'd be the treasure I'd find and keep forever." Berkley clenches my shirt like she's not only holding on to me, but to every word I'm speaking.

"Maybe it's cheesy, but I meant it, and in some weird, alternative universe, it gave me peace."

"This is too much, Nathan." She sniffs as her delicate finger finds her initials etched into the locket the octopus has tangled in his tentacle. "This whole time, I'd convinced myself you were living your best life with no second thought about me, but that wasn't the case at all, was it?"

Shaking my head, I assure her, "Not for one second." I push her hair to the side, exposing her neck.

"Now, can I get my truth?"

She nods, her clear blue eyes shining brightly from emotion.

I kiss the corner of her mouth and whisper, "Who do you see when you close your eyes? Not right now, but at the end of a long day before you fall asleep?"

She encases my face in her hands and answers without a second of hesitation. "You, always you."

And then her mouth is searing into mine, taking my breath away. Her glossy lips linger, and it takes everything in me not to deepen the kiss, but I let her lead. Unlike the other week in my room, this kiss isn't rushed.

Her lips trail down my jaw, and when she gets to my neck, her tongue licks along my rapidly beating pulse.

"Fuck, BB."

"I'd like that too," she smiles against me, throwing her leg over my lap and straddling me. My hands find either side of her thighs, loving the skin-to-skin connection of my palms on her bare legs.

"Baby, be careful. I can make that happen right now," I growl, grinding up into her. Her lips find their way back to my mouth, and her hand cups my hard cock through my pants. We both swallow each other's moans at the contact.

God, this woman is my weakness. Emotion clogs my throat at the fact she's in my arms, kissing me like this again.

Berkley runs her hands through my hair, tugging my head back. As she drags her lips back to my throat, my hands roam her body. She moans and nips at my ear, and I dip my head down, trailing my tongue across the top of her cleavage, unable to get enough of her.

"Touch me," she whimpers. My hands are all over her body, but I know what she's asking. I briefly glance over her shoulder; all our friends are just a few yards away but in their own world.

My hand slides across the soft skin of her inner thigh until it disappears under her dress, finding her silk panties are damp. "Fuck, you are so wet, BB," I groan into her mouth, tangling my tongue with hers as she palms my cock again. I swallow her moan, sliding one finger into her soaked pussy. "Words can't even describe how much I've missed this."

"I wish I could see your cock right now. Just the feel of you…" She squeezes me, and we both whimper, "Fuck, I forgot how thick you are."

Her praise has my dick throbbing even harder, and I can't control the way I'm rutting up into her; I'm so consumed with lust, I block everything else out.

She watches me as I reach into my own pants, adjusting my cock; I'm so hard, the top of it sticks out of the waistband, resting heavily against my stomach. Berkley bites her lip at the sight and swipes her thumb across its head, making me shiver. Her pussy clenches around my fingers as she touches me.

"I've missed this needy pussy."

"Nate..." She pulls my head to hers, eyes locking onto mine. "Tell me you've thought of this as much as I have over the last few weeks."

"Baby, I have thought about this every day since the last time I touched you."

Her eyes roll back in her head, and she rides my hand harder. The thought of us being in public is apparently the last thing on either of our minds.

She braces my shoulders, legs shuddering and tightening around my hips. "Nate, oh fuck. I'm coming. I'm coming." Her head falls forward, and I know there's no stopping my own orgasm as it rips through me. As her pussy spasms around my finger, my body turns molten hot. Our moans mix together, and I buck up into her uncontrollably until ropes of cum are spilling between us.

When her breathing regulates, she immediately looks down. My finger's still inside her, and my cum is sticky on my stomach and shirt.

"Holy shit, did you come?" she moans again at the realization, rolling her hips.

I nod, and she clenches on my fingers. "That's so fucking hot, Nate."

"You make me lose my fucking mind."

Then she's swiping her two fingers through my cum and bringing it to her lips. My dick twitches back to life at the sight. "I didn't think you could be any sexier, BB," I groan, languidly moving my finger in and out of her pussy.

"I'm not lying when I say I would sit on your cock right here and now," she whispers in my ear, still riding my hand.

But unfortunately, I see a wide-eyed Graham walking up to us. "Incoming," I whisper to her, grabbing her hip to slow her motions.

He's holding up his phone as he says, "Yo, your sister said she tried you and Berk and couldn't get y'all, but she's just leaving her friend's place, heading here." He pauses as he looks us over briefly, then glances down and clears his throat. "I see now that y'all are...umm, a little busy. But anyway, I told her where to find us."

Berkley buries her head into my neck, and I can feel her laughing.

"Thanks, man," I call out as he heads back toward the group. I realize we've now attracted the attention of a smirking Bellamy, too.

"He's gone," I say, and even though it's the last thing I want to do, I pull my finger from inside her.

"Now it's my turn." Slipping my finger between my lips, I savor the taste. "Sweet as I remember," I hum, and she watches me with a look of lust.

"Come home with me after?" I ask.

A smile takes over her face, and she nods.

Fuck yes.

BERKLEY

"You little slut," Bellamy whispers playfully in my ear.

I smile proudly, because I'm pretty sure I just had the hottest orgasm of my life, and he didn't even put his dick in me.

"I'm going home with him, just so you know."

"Good for you, babe. I wish I had a hot stalker to fuck me good at the end of the night." She pauses, grabbing my arm. "He is good, right?"

I smirk, giggling. "The best."

"What are you two conspiring about over here?" Nola asks. "Ways to kill Nate and Cash?"

"What makes you think I care about what Cash does?"

"You reallyyy wanna go there?"

"Whatevs, playboy. What are you doing anyway?" she pretends to look at her imaginary watch. "By this time, you've normally picked your flavor of the night and ditched all of us."

Nola chuckles. "You're right. It's about that time." He shakes his head. "Man, I met this girl last night who has me all kinds of twisted up today."

Bellamy smacks his arm. "Oh fuck, do tell?"

"Not much to tell. She doesn't go here. I didn't even get her number, but I find myself comparing everyone tonight to her, and they are all falling short."

"Shit... Nola finally got knocked on his ass," I tease.

"Nah, I'm sure I'll be over it by tomorrow," he laughs, but it's not his normal confident one.

"Graham, on the other hand, looks like he's really into that chick." I nod in his direction.

"Leblanc ain't letting nobody lock his ass down with the draft coming up… Not all of us are like loverboy over there." He nudges his shoulder toward Nate, who's watching me from the VIP railing, where he stands beside Maverick, who can't seem to stop texting tonight.

My eyes trail to the bottom of his shirt, which was thankfully white, so it just looks like he spilled some of his drink on himself. Nate bites his lip, trying to hold in the smile, most likely knowing exactly what I'm thinking about.

Focusing back on Nola's statement, I ask, "Oh yeah, what's up with loverboy?" I can't help but want to know everyone's take on it.

"Completely obsessed with this little blonde cutie… You know her?" he teases.

I feel myself blushing. "Touché."

"So y'all were pretty in love once upon a time, huh?"

Bellamy chuckles.

"Yeah, you could say that," I smile, looking at Nate.

I'm starting to think neither one of us ever stopped.

"There's Willow." Bellamy waves to the much smaller but equally gorgeous Outlaw walking into the VIP.

She immediately hugs her brother, and I smile at their exchange.

"Nola, close your mouth," Bellamy teases. "I know she's hot as sin, but Nate will not approve of your playboy ways when it comes to his baby sis."

Nola looks from Bellamy to me, confusion all over his face.

"Wait, that's Nate's little sister? The one still in high school?"

I nod. "Yep. She's most likely coming here next year."

He watches closely as Nate introduces her to Maverick and drags his hand down his face like he's awestruck over Willow. *It's cute seeing him like this.*

My focus drifts from them to Nate. The smile on his face and the look of promise in his eyes have my stomach dipping and clenching all at once.

Knowing Willow will be in good hands, and we'll see her again in the morning, I mouth to Nate, "Can we go?"

He nods without pause.

I've missed this man more than I let myself admit until tonight, and now I want him to consume every part of me again.

Eighteen

Berkley

Nate opens the door to his ensuite bathroom. "Make yourself at home. I'm going to go warm us up some Hot Pockets for old times' sake. Pizza or ham and cheese?"

I side-eye him playfully. "What do you think?"

He smiles and tugs his cum-coated shirt off, throwing it in the dirty clothes and answers, "Ham and cheese."

Biting my lip at the sight of his broad shoulders and ripped body, I nod and close the door behind me. Even with two years apart, it's amazing how much we still remember about each other.

I use the bathroom and wash the smudged mascara off my face. My panties are soaked from the club, so I slip them off and lay them on the side of his tub. There's no way I was keeping them on for long anyway with how needy I'm feeling.

Looking at myself in the mirror, I still can't believe what we did in the club earlier. It was so fucking hot and the fact he came in his pants gave me a confidence I didn't even know I was lacking.

But as I step out of the bathroom, I find myself nervous with anticipation. I slide my Air Forces off beside his football bag. Something catches my eye, and I bend down to examine what appears to be my scrunchie he stole the other day when he showed up at Phil and Tiffany's. He has it tied to his bag like a trophy, and I would be lying if I said I didn't love it. When he took it from me, it brought back so many memories. Sixteen-year-old me loved being the center of his world.

I hear the microwave beeping downstairs, and I contemplate going down there with him, but a journal on his desk captures my attention next. I don't even attempt to justify me invading his privacy. I immediately snoop, knowing this must be where the letters he has left me come from. I open the page to where the ribbon is placed.

Freshmen Year- May 7th

Last night felt so wrong. I've never wanted to take back a night in my life so bad.

Well, maybe one other, but the truth would have eventually come out, ruining us anyway.

I thought it would be different. I thought I'd feel relief or satisfaction, at the very least. Instead, I feel fucking ashamed and disgusted. I tried staying present in the moment and enjoying the touch of someone other than my own hand for the first time in almost a year.

In the beginning, the alcohol was enough to take over my senses, but I'll never forget the

moment her brown eyes opened, and they weren't
blue. It hit me like a tidal wave.

So, I closed my eyes and pictured her.
Blue eyes, blonde hair, gloss on her lips, my
BB. And when it was over and I opened my
eyes again, reality slapped me in the face.

How am I supposed to do this? All because
two selfish people ruined everything.

I re-read the middle part again, digesting what this entry is referring to. He pictured me when he was with someone else. I don't know whether to be flattered or sick.

"Berkley, let me explain." Nate's voice is suddenly right behind me.

I turn toward him as he sets the food down on his nightstand, rushing over to me as I process what I just read.

"May 7th… Was that your first time after…" I swallow the lump in my throat. "After us?"

He gently rubs the back of his knuckle down my cheek and nods. "First and only."

My eyebrows pinch as I try to process what he's saying. "Like first and only with her?".

With his eyes on mine, he shakes his head. "No, BB."

Realization hits me. "How? Why?"

"After that night, I knew I was nowhere near ready to move on. It wasn't worth it."

"Because you had to think of me?" I find myself inching closer to him, desperately holding on to every word.

He nods, but the concern hasn't left his face. "Does that upset you?"

I bite my lip. "I don't know… In some really fucked up way, I think I like it."

It's hard not to touch him with how he watches me. I can also admit to myself that while reading that was hard, the woman inside of me who's absolutely feral for Nathan Outlaw loves that he couldn't get off without thinking of me.

Reaching between him, I tug the waistband of his pants, bringing him flush against me. His hands find my hips as I speak. "I know how sexual of a man you are, Nate. What have you been doing the past two years?"

His hazel eyes turn almost black like they were at the club. "Fucking my hand and thinking of you. Hence why I came in my damn pants tonight." Nate moves his right hand around me, gripping my ass. "I'm not exaggerating when I say I was seconds from coming when you were rubbing your ass all over me, but the minute my finger slid into your pussy, I knew there was no controlling it."

I moan, and we both move simultaneously. In the next breath, our lips are colliding. I almost forgot what this was like. Tongues tangling, teeth clashing, skin nipping…an all-consuming kiss.

The type of kiss that only has one way of ending.

He walks us backwards, and we crash down onto his bed, only taking a breath before our lips are searing together again. I straddle him just like I was at the club, my dress riding up over my hips. With my bare pussy grinding into his already hard cock, we both groan into each other's mouths.

Nate looks down between us, and I feel his cock throb against me at the sight.

"What did you do with your thong, needy girl?"

I roll my hips across his hard dick and moan.

"I knew I wouldn't need them for long." Leaning down, I bite his lip. "Plus, they were drenched from earlier."

"I want to see all of you." He leans up, tugging my dress over my head. My breasts bounce free, and if I could bottle up this feeling, I would. He watches me with both familiarity and a renewed appreciation. I've never felt sexier in my life, from just the appreciation on his face.

"You are so beautiful." He closes his eyes for a brief second, like he's committing it to memory.

Shaking his head, this time when he speaks, his voice is full of emotion. "To think I almost lost the privilege of ever seeing this again."

I gently kiss his lips. "Hey, don't do that. Stay with me in this moment."

He runs his thumb over my hip bone. "I'm here, BB. I'm here."

We kiss desperately again, until his fingers move between us, finding my wet center.

"Fuck. I didn't think you could get any more soaked than you were earlier."

Letting my teeth graze the pulse on his neck, I whisper, "This needy pussy wants you inside me so bad."

"Oh yeah?" The confident Nate I know is back, circling his thumb over my swollen clit.

He slips two fingers into me. "Ride my hand," he commands as his free hand roams all over my body. His fingers expertly find my G-spot, like he knows my body better than I do.

I completely lose it when he grips the back of my neck, pulling me down closer, causing my clit to rub against the palm of his hand as his fingers move in and out at the perfect pace. My body shudders, and I call out his name as I come so unexpectedly fast, my vision blurs.

"Fuck yes," he groans, kissing me through my orgasm.

Then he's flipping me over, laying me on my back, and I watch as he frees his cock. My core clenches again as I take him in.

Nate's eyes never leave me. He makes a display of circling his thumb and the two fingers he had inside of me around his shaft, rubbing my arousal on himself. I groan at the sight. He's the sexiest man on this earth, and I'm desperate with a capital 'D' right now.

He gives his cock a squeeze, and his eyes roll back in his head. "Fuck, I'm trying not to come before I get inside of you. I need to feel you, but you are my every fantasy come to life."

His words light me on fire.

"Well then, get inside me, Outlaw," I tell him breathily.

His eyes narrow on me, and then his knee is on the bed, and he's lining his cock up with my pussy. One hand on his thick dick and the other on my waist, he rolls his hips into me, my wetness coating his cock even more.

"Shit, I need to put on a condom. I'm sorry. I'm just so used to—"

He stops himself, but I know what he's thinking. We never used condoms when we were younger.

"Don't use one... Just me and you. I want... No, I need to feel you. I've only ever been bare with you. If you're comfortable with it, it's what I want."

He doesn't even respond; instead, the head of his cock presses against me. With one fluid stroke, he pushes the tip inside, making me whimper. "Oh shit," he moans, closing his eyes and taking a deep breath. He swivels his hips, and it drives me even wilder with lust to feel him fully seated inside of me.

When his eyes open again, he pushes all the way, letting out a guttural moan I feel down to the tips of my toes. My body happily accepts him, like it's been waiting for this moment for far longer than I was willing to admit.

I see a fire in his eyes, unlike anything I've seen before, as he watches himself disappear inside of me. Everything this man does makes me feel so damn special, but especially the way his soul sears into mine, full of adoration, through his hazel lust-filled gaze.

He starts slowly, moving in and out of me with measured strokes, and groans, "You feel unbelievable."

When I meet his stare, his eyes are glistening with unshed tears, and it truly hits me just how prolific this moment is between us. He leans down to kiss me again. "I've missed this so much... Missed you so much."

I swallow thickly. "I've missed this too."

The feeling of him inside of me, his hands and emotional eyes roaming all over my body, and the impending orgasm have me overwhelmed in the best way. Watching Nate move with so much fervor in his eyes is something I don't think I could fully describe if I wanted to.

A bead of sweat from the longer strands on top of his head

drips between my breast, and he licks it, tongue swiping up to my neck, where he leaves a wet kiss. *Fuck, why was that so hot.*

My body is more alive than it's been in two years, and I meet him thrust for thrust, chasing the feeling of ecstasy.

"BB, I'm about to come," Nate sputters.

"I'm close, so close," I moan, feeling just as desperate. "Come inside me."

"You want me to coat the inside of this tight, needy pussy with my cum, baby?" he asks, twisting my nipple, and I'm a goner.

"Oh shit, Nate." I moan, long and low, as my orgasm starts from the base of my spine, and the second I hear the groan rip through him, our eyes lock, and I come harder than I ever have.

My pussy continues to spasm with aftershocks as I come down from the high.

Nate immediately kisses my lips, down to my neck and the top of my chest. The need to touch me, even in his post-orgasmic bliss, makes me feel incredible.

"That was unreal," I say breathlessly

"Like it always was with us," Nate says, standing up and walking into the bathroom. "Were you worried it wouldn't be the same?" he asks when he comes back out with a washcloth and cleans me up.

The sweet gesture takes me back to our first time together. He has always cared for me in a way I took for granted, until I realized that not every guy is like him.

I shake my head and answer honestly, "No, not one bit, but sometimes I wondered if I created an illusion in my head about how good it was between us."

He pulls me in to him, placing his chin on top of my head. "I'm so sorry I ever put those doubts in your mind."

I breathe in his scent. Everything about this night feels so surreal, but one thing I genuinely feel in my bones is that Nate didn't intend to hurt me.

"I know, but I also have come to terms with the fact you did what you felt was best. You aren't the villain in this story, Nate. They are," I whisper, kissing his bare chest.

"Knowing what I know now, if I could go back and change the decision I made that night, I would."

Leaning back, I look him in the eye. "I won't sugarcoat things. Something changed inside my soul that day..." I swallow, my voice thick with emotion. Being in his arms feels like all is finally the way it should be, but I also remember how painful the day he left me was. "And I've built up some major barricades around my heart since then."

I see the pain flash in his eyes at my honesty, but I don't let myself feel guilty. Nate didn't have any intention of hurting me, but I also can't help how I dealt with it.

"I understand. I'll take whatever you give me."

This man. Who am I kidding?

My barricades are more like hazard cones at this point, and he's plowing right through them.

Literally.

I bury my face into his neck, and we hold each other until I think of something I've been wanting to ask him.

"The journal... When did you start that?"

"My dad sent it to me one of my first weeks in Texas. He knew I was going through a lot, so he encouraged me to write it all down to help me work through everything." He lets out a chuckle. "At first, I was a typical teenage boy, skeptical at the idea of keeping a sort of diary. But one day, he said to just pretend it was a playbook. It's only for you to see anyway, so who cares. Now I realize how effective it has been for me. It was the best coping mechanism I could've asked for at the time. Honestly, if we——" He clears his throat. "If I ever have children, I will encourage them to write in a journal from an early age."

The butterflies in my belly multiply at his slip-up.

I smile at him. "I think it's amazing. Your dad is the best."

"He really is." He digs into his nightstand and pulls out a stack of journals.

"This was my first one." He passes one to me, and I sit up, clenching the sheet to my bare chest with one hand and tracing my fingertips over his handwriting with the other.

The Playbook of Nathan Outlaw's Life

"The very first page is about you. Not sure if it's too much tonight, but if you're comfortable with it, take a look." He nods toward the book to encourage me.

Even if it hurts, I want to know. The not knowing and assuming over the past two years has been the hardest part.

I take a deep breath and open the journal.

Freshmen year- August 15th

I finally broke down and tried to call you

today. As I suspected, you blocked me. I can't
say I blame you.

It's so hard when the one person you want
to talk to about something is the one person
you can't for so many reasons.

I keep second guessing if I did the right
thing. What if my mom and your dad end up
together and you end up finding all of it out
either way? What if your image of both of
your parents is ruined by all this? I think the
last piece of my heart will break if that
happens.

I will have lost you and you will have lost
that.

I'm so frustrated with my mom and your
dad. Disgusting, selfish assholes. But I just
keep telling myself I did the right thing. I
would have never wanted to keep that secret
from you, especially while navigating a long-
distance relationship. It would have just put
another hundred miles between us. And these
would have been tainted with lies and betrayal.

My dad thinks I should tell you, but he
doesn't understand that your dad is all you
have. He doesn't understand that you idolized
your parents' love story as a memoir to your
mother.

These are the things that keep me up at night.

I miss you so fucking much, BB. I wish my life was like a DVD, and we could just scratch out the bad part, the part where I saw something that changed the trajectory of our love story.

Nate takes the book from me as I process what I just read. My chest aches for the boy I loved so much, who was silently hurting. The next page he hands me is a date easy to recognize.

My birthday.

Freshmen year- March 26th

Happy Birthday to my BB. Today, you turn 19. If you had asked me how I would be spending your birthday a year ago, it definitely wouldn't have been drunk in my room, avoiding reality.

I saw pictures... Graham said y'all celebrated a day early. He won't really tell me anything else.

I saw Carter Graves in your pictures. I'm pretending he's just a familiar face from back home, that there's nothing more to his arm around you. The alternative would gut me.

You look happy in the pictures with the girls you're hanging out with now. I know you blocked me, but since Graham was tagged, I was able to see. I loved seeing your genuine smile. In some fucked-up way, it brought me peace today.

I hope you feel your mom's love today; I know she'd be so proud of you.

I'm pretty fucked up, BB, but I'm trying to get back to the old Nate.

I'm just not so sure I know who I am without you anymore.

Happy Birthday to the most beautiful girl in the world. Speaking of the most beautiful girl... Did you know the beach wasn't the first day I saw you?

It's true. I don't know why I never told you this before. But I saw you on the boardwalk a couple of days before. You had on a purple sundress, and I literally ran into a pole and got ice cream all over myself, watching you smile at people as you walked down the boardwalk. I wanted to talk to you so badly that day, but I looked like an idiot with chocolate ice cream all over me. I searched for two days until I found you lying on the beach in that sexy blue bikini. Nothing was stopping me that day from talking to you.

244 | L.A. Shaw

> Sometimes, I wonder if you regret giving me
> a chance.

I let out a deep sigh, just staring at the page for another moment. My stomach sours at the torment in his words.

Shaking my head and trying my best to keep my tears at bay, I tell him, "Nate, I would never regret that day. No matter what... I mean that with every fiber of my being. Never."

He gently traces his finger over my exposed thigh. "Thank you for saying that."

"I mean it. Even on my worst days, I never regretted a second of my time with you." We just look at each other for a moment, so much love still between us it's palpable, before I ask, "Can I see one more?"

"You can see them all." He smiles up at me and opens the journal from the bottom of the stack, flipping through the book until he finds the entry he's looking for and passes it to me.

> April 25th- Sophomore Year
>
> It's official, I'm going to Mountain Ridge.
> I've known it since the moment they asked me.
> They have one thing that Alabama and Florida
> don't, and she makes the decision easy.
>
> I'm hoping this is fate's way of kicking
> me in the ass and giving me one final chance.
> But another part of me is scared to take
> that chance because won't everything we went

through be for nothing if she finds out the truth?

Am I willing to be the person responsible for destroying the image she has of her parents?

I'm as conflicted as I was the day we broke up, but one thing I do know is that I'm not giving up on the chance to be near her again. I'll figure out the rest when I get there.

Let's just hope I don't shatter my heart even more than I already have.

My own heart hammers, and I close my eyes. I can feel his chaotic emotions coming off the page in each of these entries.

We were both in so much pain.

His large hand cups my face. "BB, talk to me."

My mind retraces the words from the first page he ripped out and left on my doorstep when he came to Mountain Ridge. I was so angry with him then, and now I'm seeing all this in a completely different light.

"It just hurts so bad knowing we were both aching for each other."

Maybe if I hadn't blocked him, he would have given in and told me.

"Do you think if I had answered that night when you called, you would have told me?"

He shakes his head. "Don't do that to yourself. None of this was your fault. Do you hear me?"

I nod, resting my forehead against his.

"I'm glad you said yes to MRU's football team," I whisper, because I wouldn't want to go another day not knowing what I know now.

"Me too, baby. Me too." As he smiles at me, I feel it deep in my soul.

Loud noises from downstairs breakthrough our bubble.

"Call of Duty, anyone?" Maverick's voice sing-songs.

"The hellions are home," Nate whispers.

"I'm down," I hear Willow holler back. My expression mirrors Nate's confused one, and then we hear Bellamy and Cash arguing over pizza rolls versus taquitos.

"They must have talked the girls into coming back."

Nate peeks at the time on his phone. "I hope Willow texted Dad and let him know she wasn't going back to the hotel."

"I'm sure she did. Even when she stayed with us girls Thursday, she still texted him to let him know when we all got home." I run my fingers through his hair. "Is it bad if I keep you all to myself up here."

He smirks. "What'd you have in mind, baby?"

Using my thumb to tug his bottom lip down, I whisper, "If I remember correctly, you were really good with this mouth of yours."

He lets out a deep laugh and my pussy clenches at the sexy sound.

"Baby, I'd…"

Bam. Bam. Bam. "Berk, don't forget to use plenty of lube on that pretty little finger of yours."

I gasp, picking up Nate's pillow as I bury my face in a fit of laughter.

"Fuck off, Nola!" Nate yells back, but I hear the smile on his lips before he's laying on top of me, tickling my sides. "See what you started?"

We laugh until he grazes my nipple, and the air immediately shifts again. The lust is back in his eyes, and he bends his head, flattening his tongue and running it from one nipple to the other.

Then he sits up, kneeling between my legs. His hard cock draws my attention until he speaks, "I'm ready to eat, BB."

He sucks in his bottom lip, and I'm pretty sure I stop breathing with anticipation. One gentle swipe of his tongue from the top of my slit to the bottom, and my body bucks off the bed.

That sexy chuckle is back, and with it is a devilish smirk. "Just to make sure you remember correctly..." He slowly licks his top lip like he's savoring the first taste of me. "I'm about to eat this pussy till it's dripping down my chin and you're begging for a break."

My core weeps at his words. Leaning up on my forearms, I spread my legs wider. "Please, Nate, I need a really good reminder."

Nineteen

Nate

My cock bounces between us, completely hard again at the sight of her spread out in front of me.

Everything about tonight has been perfect, and now she's unleashed the beast within me. The one who has been waiting to devour every inch of her for two years now.

Gripping her thighs, I lower my head slowly, licking her from the bottom of her slit to her swollen bud. Her hips buck again, and it drives me insane with lust. "Fuck, I've missed the taste of this needy pussy so much," I groan, and Berkley cusses under her breath.

I take my time, dipping my tongue inside of her and dragging it up, barely giving her clit what she wants before I'm licking her slit again. Over and over, I lick and tease. I close my eyes and savor the taste of her.

She loves to be edged. Until she's ready, and then her clit wants all the attention.

Her fingertips grip my sheets, pulling the corner off the

mattress, and I hump the bed beneath me, needing relief from the sight of her writhing in pure pleasure.

With my chin dripping with her juices, I groan, "You taste so fucking sweet."

I trail my knuckle through her wetness, teasing her more as I watch her come undone for me.

She lets out a low growl when my finger leaves her aching pussy.

"You want more?"

"Yes, I want it all," she moans, gripping the back of my hair and pushing me down.

That's it, BB, take what you want. Take what's yours.

I flatten my tongue on her clit, using the pressure I know she's craving.

The whimpers escaping her mouth have me needing to come so bad I don't even realize I'm rutting into the bed hard enough for it to hit the wall until she asks, "Does your cock need me, baby? Are you going to come before you get inside me again?"

I smirk, and when my eyes meet hers, she's not teasing. No, she's turned on at the thought and the reminder of what happened earlier. I grab my dick, and when I know she's watching me, I give it a lazy stroke.

"Baby, I've come so many times to just the memory of you; if you don't think the sight of you wet and horny beneath me won't have me coming all over these sheets, you're mistaken."

Berkley throws her head back on a whimper, and I see her pussy clench at my words. My tongue flattens against her clit, circling and circling. I can feel her get closer and closer, her body lifting higher and higher off the bed and into my mouth.

I continue stroking her clit with my tongue as she comes undone beneath me. The sight of her has me pressing myself into the mattress again to relieve the ache. "How about instead of coming on my sheets, I come inside of this needy pussy again?" I growl, flipping her over once I know her orgasm has subsided.

"Please," she says, arching her ass as far in the air as she can with her chest flat on my bed.

I stand up, and taking a step back from her, I greedily drink in the view. Fuck, I've jerked off to this ass so many times, I couldn't even attempt to count.

"So pretty, baby," I say through a groan, stroking my cock.

She's so wet, I push inside her easily. Holding on to her hips, I roll my own slowly, because I know she needs a second to adjust to this angle. An indescribable feeling comes over me at the sight of our connection.

I will never get enough of this.

"Spread your cheeks for me," I demand as I pick up my pace.

The sight of her face buried in the mattress and her hands digging harder into her ass with each thrust has that tingling deep down in my belly back and ready to explode.

I lean in, placing my fingers on her clit.

"Oh shit. I'm already about to come again."

Her hands fall forward onto the mattress as she looks over her shoulder. "Come with me, Nate," she moans, and her eyes roll back.

"Look at me while I come deep inside this needy pussy of mine," I growl, and the second I feel her convulse around me, I let go. Her blissed-out baby blues bore into me before she falls forward, and we both come apart. Something similar to a roar pushes past my lips as the overwhelming sensations take over my body.

After my vision clears and my breathing evens out, I kiss her shoulder and slip out of her. "You are mind-blowing. Do you know that?" I ask.

"I was just thinking the same thing about you." She replies smiling, her eyes still closed, her cheek pressed against my bed.

I scoop her up, and she lets out a gasp. "Nate, what are you doing?"

"You need to use the bathroom. Then we are going to take a shower."

"Okay, but I'm dripping all over you." I feel her legs tremble around me.

"Does it look like I am scared of our cum getting on me?"

She laughs lightly, and I kiss her forehead, sitting her down on the toilet. Turning on the shower, I step in, giving her privacy.

I hear the toilet flushing, and then she's joining me, wrapping her arms around my middle and placing a kiss on my back.

An onslaught of emotions burn inside me. Tonight has been surreal, and a huge part of me is scared for it to end.

If I have anything to do with it, it won't.

With my loofa soaped up, I turn around and begin washing her. Sensually rubbing over every inch of her, I revel in the feel of her being so close again. I used to love doing this. Typically, when our hands were on each other, it always turned sexual, but there were times when it was genuinely just for intimacy or, at times, comfort.

"Gah, that feels so good," Berkley moans.

"It reminds me of our outdoor shower back in Nori."

She bites her lip. "I've thought about that shower more than I should probably admit."

When we first started dating, it was an easy place to sneak to for some privacy. We experimented a lot in that little shower, unbeknownst to my parents.

I give her an admission of my own. "I haven't used it since I went to college... I just couldn't without you. Hell, I barely even took the boat out when I was home in the summer. Everything made me think of you and just miss you even more."

She wraps her arms around me, fitting her soapy body against mine, and whispers, "I get it. I literally even changed my toothpaste because it was the one you used. We were so intertwined."

I press a kiss to the top of her hair. "Do you think we can ever find our way back to that?"

My heart thuds powerfully, anticipating what she'll say.

Berkley's quiet for longer than I'd like before she whispers, "I'm not sure we ever fully lost it."

Her words light me up, warming me from the inside out. I know we didn't lose it, not one bit. Now I just have to keep breaking down her walls and show her we can have it all again, maybe even better than the first time.

I maneuver her body under the water, helping her rinse off the soap.

"Can I stay with you tonight?" she asks, and I can hear the vulnerability in her voice.

"If you leave, I'm coming with you," I answer without skipping a beat. There's no way I'm letting her out of my sight after everything that's gone down tonight.

She giggles. "I'm kind of liking these stalker vibes."

Then her eyes widen sightly, like she just remembered something.

"Speaking of that. I can't believe you never told me about seeing me on the boardwalk a few days before we actually met."

I chuckle. "Yeah, I guess my stalking days started long ago."

"Well, it's definitely a turn-on. So, keep it up, Outlaw," she smirks and lifts onto her tiptoes to press a kiss onto my chest.

We finish up in the shower, and I wrap her in a towel before she even steps out, knowing she hates the cold air.

With heavy eyes, she kisses the corner of my mouth, and then languidly deepens it for a moment before pulling back. I see an emotion in her gaze that I don't think she allowed me to see before as she asks, "Can you hold me now?"

I nod, taking her hand in mine as I walk toward my bed. As I dry her body off, my chest aches, because the moment takes me back to the day we broke up. But when I look up at her and find her watching me adoringly, I shake the thought away and remind myself that this is the fresh start we needed.

We settle into bed. Her body perfectly molds into the little spoon position she loves, and I realize this is the most at peace

I've felt in so long. A smile takes over my face as I stare at her, knowing I'll lie like this for hours tonight. Not wanting to miss a second of her.

Berkley's body melts further into me as she whispers, "I think I've missed this the most."

I hold on to her a little tighter. "Me too, BB. Me too."

TWENTY

Berkley

Of course, I would forget to turn off my volume in the middle of my lecture. Thankfully, I'm in one of the last rows, but that doesn't mean I'm not scrambling to find my phone and switch it to silent while also peeking at the screen. Before I left for class today, I texted Nate a picture I knew would drive him crazy. Figured it would be a nice surprise when he returned to the locker room after practice.

My fingers fumble as I swipe open the message.

> NATE
>
> [photo message] He's waiting for you anytime, anyplace, BB.

My mouth drops open at the photo. I have to place my phone face down on my lap in order to school my expression. Holy shit, he's so fucking hot. Peeking at the image again, my eyes roam over his exposed body. From the looks of it, he's in the locker room and just got out of the shower. His large hand is holding his towel against his thick cock, and beads of water grace his tanned chest and abs. I swipe at the corner of my mouth to ensure no drool has formed.

ME

Sir, I am in class. You cannot tease me like this...

NATE

You expect me not to show you how hard you make me? That photo was 😊

I glance up at my professor, who's currently deep diving into an ancient civilizations map, and return my attention to my phone.

ME

Thought you'd like it 😉

NATE

Oh, you're in for it tonight...

ME

Give me your worst... I can take it.

NATE

Fuuuck, you're killing me. I'm rock hard in the locker room. Smiling at my phone like a fool.

NATE

Get back to being studious before I storm into that lecture hall, drag you out, and fuck you in the closest empty room.

Even though I'm sore in all the right places, my body pulses at the thought of being so mischievous with him on campus. Since Saturday, we haven't gone a day without seeing each other. Even if it is really late at night after his practices or my work shifts, we make it our business to be together, and I relish every second I'm in his arms.

ME

Promises, promises.

ME

Actually, that locker room pic unlocked some new fantasies... Think you can make it happen, QB?

NATE

I can make anything happen for you, BB.

ME

I'll see you later 😊

How in the world am I supposed to focus on anything after that? I put my phone away and stare at the large screen in the front of the room. This is my last class of the week, and I'm itching to be done. Only one more hour.

The smell of something delicious hits me as soon as I open the front door to my apartment. I follow my nose into a kitchen, where I find Nate at the stove, sauteing some vegetables.

"Well, this is a welcomed surprise." Walking up to him, I wrap my arms around his midsection. His abs constrict with his chuckle.

"Surprise," he says as he leans down to kiss my forehead.

I eye the ingredients strewn across the counter and realize he's making us tacos for dinner.

"You certainly know the way to a girl's heart... Oooh, please tell me you're making your salsa?" I squeal when I notice the varied peppers and spices.

"Would it be a steak taco night if I didn't?"

"Yassss! I hope you made enough. Darby and Bell are going to devour this."

He laughs. "Yes, that was part of our deal. If they gave us the place until at least midnight, I would make enough for them to eat tomorrow."

"You kicked out my roommates?" I ask incredulously, but I secretly love that he made these plans without me.

"Absolutely… To be honest, they were more than happy to oblige. I think they would have agreed even without the promise of food, but I threw that in to sweeten the deal."

"Well, that was very thoughtful of you. Now, how can I help?"

"You don't have to; I have it all under control," he continues to sauté the veggies, and he looks so damn sexy, I can't help but run my hands over his body.

My fingers trace the defined ridges of his stomach under his shirt. One hand teases a little lower to the waistband of his grey sweats, and he groans.

"Well, if I help…the sooner we'll have dinner, and the sooner I can repay you for this thoughtful surprise of yours."

"When you put it like that, there's the chopping board," he nods, pointing to the setup to his left, and we both laugh.

I organize my station and begin to grate the cheese. "Remember when I tried to make you lasagna that first time?"

"How could I forget? It was the first time I ever had lasagna soup," he jokes.

I pout. "I was trying so hard to impress you… I still can't believe I forgot to buy the noodles."

Gripping my chin, his hazel eyes lock onto mine. My breath is stolen from my lungs at the loving look on his face. "Baby, you could have served me slop, and I would have been impressed by you."

His lips meet mine briefly, then he swats my ass. "Now get back to work. There's no messing around in my kitchen."

"Yes, chef," I swoon.

I quickly get to finishing my task. It's not that I don't want to enjoy the thoughtful meal he prepared for us…it's just that I've been dying to get a taste of this man all day, and tonight, I plan on devouring him.

———

Nate's large hands cup my ass as he lifts me into his arms. "You don't know how much I needed this," he says as he presses me against the wall.

"Rough day?" I ask as I trail kisses along his neck.

"No, BB. This, right here, is what I look forward to most. The moment you're in my arms."

The way this man's words turn me into a puddle will never get old. He's not afraid to express his emotions. It's something I've always loved about him. I should be petrified that the words *love* and *Nate* are in the same sentence so soon, but deep down, I know my love for him never truly disappeared.

I cup his face with my hands and kiss him. Pouring my emotions into every swipe of our tongues, I moan softly when he rubs his thickening cock against my sensitive core.

"I need you," he says, kissing along my jaw.

"You have me."

My response earns me a low, possessive growl, and the next thing I know, I'm being tossed onto my bed.

Nate rips off his shirt, and I sit up to run my hands along his exposed skin, down to the waistband of his sweats. I tug at the strings and slide them down his legs, his erection springing free. He reaches for the hem of my shirt and lifts it over my head, then in one swift move, unhooks and removes my bra.

Licking my lips, I grip onto him and tease his tip with my tongue. Eventually, taking him deeper, he lets out a loud groan of satisfaction.

"You look so damn perfect," he says as I stare up at him from the edge of my bed. Nate's hand goes to the back of my head, where he tangles his fingers into my hair.

The strong hold has me shifting my legs as an ache builds between my thighs. I take him even deeper, and I gag slightly as he hits the back of my throat.

"Open up for me, BB. Let me fuck this gorgeous mouth of yours."

Holy shit, this man.

I relax my throat as much as I can. "That's it, baby. Fuuuck, just like that."

He continues to gently rock his hips in time with my mouth as I stroke and suck his thick cock. My free hand goes to the waist of my leggings, and I shift slightly so I can slide them off, desperate to touch myself.

Nate notices my attempts to remove my pants and pulls out of my mouth with a smirk. "You're a needy little thing tonight, aren't you?" He lifts me from under my arms and slides me up the bed, kneeling between my legs.

"I need you to touch me, fuck me...anything. I'm dying," I pant, unashamed to ask him for what I want.

He pulls off my leggings, then spreads my thighs wide and stares at me. I whimper with need as he trails a knuckle through my wet pussy. Lifting his coated finger, he sucks it into his mouth.

"Baby, you're dripping for me. Look at how eager your pussy is for my cock. Is that what you want?"

"Please, yes," I beg, and he glides the head of his cock through my core, wetting the tip. Wrapping my legs around his torso, I keep him exactly where I need him to be, and he slowly slides himself inside.

I moan when he bottoms out. Filling me completely, I relish the feel of him, of us being tangled up in each other.

His hips rock at a steady pace as I writhe, my hands grasping for anything to hold on to. My headboard hits the walls with loud thumps from his forceful thrusts. The noise pulls me out of the moment, and Nate grabs a pillow from my bed to shove it between the bed and the wall to stop the sound. But then he pauses his thrusts.

I look at him, puzzled, as he reaches above me once again. This time, he comes back with my pink vibrator. The one I definitely forgot to stash away this morning.

He turns the toy on a low speed and places it against my clit. I jolt at the sensation.

"Tell me, BB. Did you use this before or after you sent me that photo today?"

As if trying to fuck the answer out of me, he thrusts again.

"Ahh. Be-before," I pant. My body tenses with overwhelming sensation while Nate lets out a deep groan as my pussy clenches around him.

"Did my girl wake up aching for me?" His hips slam into me relentlessly as he turns the speed up on the toy. Both of us chase the orgasm we know is not far from reach.

"Yes… Fuck, Nate. I was such a needy slut. Desperate to come for you."

He growls once more, and then he lets me have it. His hand covers mine and signals for me to hold on to the toy as he grips both my ankles.

His pounding thrusts fill me completely, and I moan so loud I'm sure every single one of my neighbors hears me.

"I love that you ache for my cock to fill this needy pussy as much as I do."

Slam.

"That *I* make you a needy slut, just for me."

Slam.

My legs begin shaking as I brace for a tidal wave of an orgasm. Gradually building in my toes and spreading throughout my body, the vibrator and his punishing thrusts have me teetering on the edge.

"Fuck yes…come for me, BB."

I moan again, this time so loud that I cover my mouth to stifle the sound. Nate's hand pulls mine away, just as another slips past my lips.

"Let them hear what I do to you… Let them hear how desperate you are to come all over my cock."

And with that, I'm done for. Every limb shakes uncontrollably as I'm hit with wave after wave of sensation.

Nate groans above me. "I'm going to fill this pussy over and over again until you can't think straight."

I mutter unintelligible words as he releases into me. No longer feeling like I'm in my own body, I melt into the bed, and Nate collapses beside me.

He pulls me into him as his lips find mine, and he kisses me deeply. I smile at him, and he gives me a goofy ass smile back. Both of us are unhurried to move or clean up. We're more than happy to stay just as we are…freshly fucked and sated.

An hour and another round later, Nate and I are cuddled up in my bed, watching an episode of *Yellowstone*. My fingers twirl along the octopus's tentacles on his arm. It's become somewhat of a habit now. Especially knowing the significance the tattoo has for both him and me. Our story is forever etched onto his skin.

My phone lights up with a notification, pulling my attention away from the TV.

TIFFANY

> I know it's late, and you might not see this, but I was hoping you could come over and stay with the kids. Phil is slammed at The Wolfpack, and PJ fell; correction, he flew off the back of the couch and landed on the corner of the coffee table. He definitely needs stitches.

"Shit," I curse, abruptly sitting up and throwing my legs over the edge of the bed. My poor, sweet little boy. He must be so scared.

"What's wrong, babe?" The alarm in Nate's tone has me glancing his way.

"Tiffany just texted. PJ flew off the couch, and now he needs stitches, and Phil can't go."

Nate hops out of bed and slips on his sweats. "Come on, let's go."

"Really? You're going to come?"

"Of course. Get some pants on."

> ME
> Be there in 10.

> TIFFANY
> You're a lifesaver.

> ME
> I have Nate with me. Is that okay?

> TIFFANY
> Of course, the kids need the distraction.

I'm dressed in a matter of minutes and were out the door. We jump into Nate's pickup, and he pulls out of the parking lot. Grabbing his hand, I squeeze it gently. "Thank you for coming with me. I'm sorry our date night had to end like this."

He brings our now intertwined hands up to his lips and kisses the back of mine. "Don't worry about me. As long as I'm with you, I'm good."

My heart soars as his words sink in…because I finally let myself believe them. The doubt I have been carrying around for so long is gone, and I know with every fiber of my being that this man loves me. Always has and always will.

In less than a few minutes, we're pulling up outside of the Oakley house, and I'm running up the stairs before Nate gets out of the truck. The front door swings open, and Josie greets me, and her smile widens when I feel Nate approach behind me.

"Hey you, how's PJ?"

"Luckily, he didn't bust his head open," Tiffany says from somewhere in the house.

Josie rolls her eyes. "He literally yelled 'I'm Superman' and leaped off the back of the couch with no plan on where he was landing."

I cover my mouth to stifle the laugh about to break free. Nate's elbow hits my side, and I look up at him. He's biting his lip, trying to contain a smile of his own.

We walk toward the kitchen and find PJ sitting on the island with a cloth pressed to his chin and Tiffany loading up a backpack with supplies to keep them busy while they wait at the hospital.

"Thank you so much for coming. I'm sorry if I interrupted any plans," Tiffany says, eyeing Nate.

"It's perfectly fine. I'm glad he seems to be okay," Nate says, approaching PJ just as Jack appears in the kitchen and comes to give me a hug as he stares, starry-eyed, at Nate.

"Superman, huh?" Nate asks as PJ smiles shyly up at him.

"You should've seen how high I flew," PJ whispers, but Tiffany must overhear, because she quips back, "There will be no more flying attempts in this house, young man."

Her attention flits to mine, and she chuckles, throwing the backpack onto her shoulder. "Words I never thought I would say in my lifetime. Come on, buddy, let's go."

"Stay strong, little man," I say, helping him off the counter.

"So, Gwen is sleeping already, since the kids do have school tomorrow. Don't let them tell you otherwise. I'll keep you posted. Hopefully, it's not too crazy there." I inwardly laugh at Gwen's amazing ability to sleep through basically anything. I guess when you have three older siblings, it's a necessary skill.

"No problem. We're good, don't worry," I say, and Tiffany shuts the door behind them.

"Alright, one show before you two need to get washed up for bed."

"Oh, come on, it's only eight-thirty," Josie whines.

"How about a game?" Jack proposes.

"What do you have in mind, buddy?" Nate asks, following Jack into the living room, where the TV is paused.

"I was playing Mario Kart on the switch. Want to play?" Jack asks.

"Oh, I haven't played this in years," Nate says as he looks at the screen. A calculated expression takes over Jack's face, and I have a feeling about what comes next.

"How about a deal? We challenge you guys to a round of Mario Kart. If we win, Josie and I get to stay up later. If we lose, we'll go to bed with no arguments." I eye Josie and Jack, who both appear to be very confident in this bet, but little do they know, I'm a Mario Kart champion and I will take them down…no doubt.

"Bet," Nate says without even confirming it with me. Probably because he knows how many times I kicked his ass playing this same game.

We settle onto the couch, choose our players, and then it's on.

"Goodnight, buddy. Sweet dreams," I say to Jack when Nate finishes reading him his story. The kids' defeat was a swift and painless one. Jack was extremely impressed with my skills and will now be challenging me way more often, I'm sure. After they washed up, without an argument, Jack asked if Nate could read to him for a little while. How could I say no? Besides, watching them had my heart soaring to new heights.

"Night, Berk. Goodnight, Nate," he says before Nate closes the door. I walk across the hallway and peek my head into Josie's room. She's reading in the dark with a book light on.

"One more chapter, and it's lights out," I say to her.

"Okay, goodnight," she says without raising her eyes from the page.

We creep down the hallway and settle onto the couch, turning on Netflix.

I place a pillow on his lap and make myself comfortable, his arm instinctually laying across my shoulder.

"Thank you for coming along with me tonight."

"Anytime, BB. Glad I was here," he chuckles then adds, "Still can't believe it was PJ who flew off the couch. Seems so out of character for the little guy."

"It's always the quiet ones you have to worry about. Once he warms up to you, that one doesn't stop." I smile knowing how much PJ has flourished over the last two years.

As the ending credits of the movie start, my phone chimes.

TIFFANY

Finishing up in a few. How were they? Hope they didn't give you too much of an issue.

ME

They were perfect, not to worry.

TIFFANY

So the QB, huh?

I chuckle at her text. We've talked over the years about my heartbreak, but never told her he was now here at MRU.

ME

We have a lot to discuss.

TIFFANY

Can't wait! Thanks again, be home in a bit.

"A lot to discuss, huh?" Nate teases, and I hit his arm. "Why are you reading my texts?"

"Just checking to make sure the kid is okay," he smirks.

"Yeah, yeah, likely story. He's fine. They'll be home in a little bit."

Nate glances at the clock, which reads 10:30 p.m. "Good, because I still have plans for you."

My core clenches at the promise.

"Again, Mr. Outlaw? One would think you may have an addiction."

He smiles the megawatt grin of his and leans down to kiss my lips. "You have no idea, baby."

THE HOWLER

Mountain Ridge University

Volume 20-10

PHOTOSHOOT ON CAMPUS

A little birdie told us Gatorade is on campus today, taking pictures of our top athletes for their newest campaign. Inside sources say we're getting an exclusive picture of the hot jocks living in The Wolves Den.

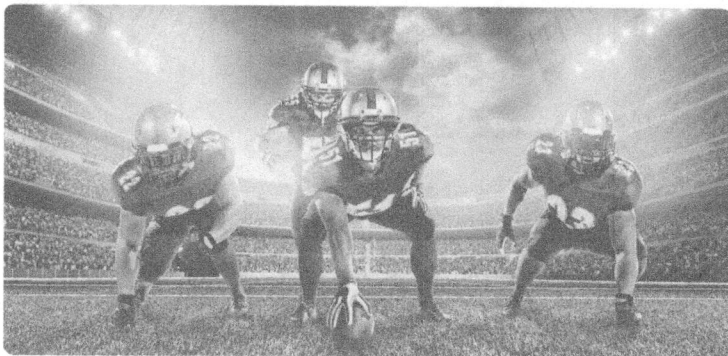

Who are you most excited to see shirtless and swallowing their electrolytes?

TWENTY-ONE

Nate

"Okay, guys, the basketball and hockey teams are heading over from the gym. We'll take a few group shots in front of the sign between the indoor arena and the football stadium. Then we can officially wrap up," the photographer working the Gatorade advertisement calls out over her shoulder as we follow the crew out of the stadium.

It's been fun so far, but it's our bye weekend, and I'm just ready to wrap this up so I can get to Berkley. It was so hard to leave her in the bed this morning. After we finished up babysitting, I stayed over at her place last night, and while I was thankful for an early practice so we could have the rest of the day to chill for once, I missed our morning sex and cuddles.

She's been on my mind all morning, and now that we have a short break, I pull my phone out of my bag to text her.

ME

We should be done in about an hour. Do you want to meet me at the practice facility and go grab some food after?"

BB

> Sounds good. I hate that the shoot was closed. I really wanted to see you swallowing...those electrolytes.

The fucking Howler report.

ME

> I'd rather see you doing the swallowing, baby.

BB

> That can be arranged.

ME

> I was just thinking about you in that little blue bikini you wore to the pool party.

I'm getting hard again thinking about the way it barely covered up her ass and tits.

BB

> Oh yeah, what made you think of that?

ME

> When I saw you in it, I vowed to take the money I make from this sponsorship with Gatorade and buy you one in every color.

BB

> I loved torturing you that day.

ME

> Oh, I know you did. Now I think you owe me for the pain you put me through that day.

BB

> You poor thing.... What could I possibly do to make it up to you?

ME

Put that bikini on tonight and beg me to fuck you in it. Then I will have to buy you a new one after I destroy it.

"Yo." Maverick's voice breaks through the air. He and Cash are leading the winter athlete group heading our way.

They join us in front of the huge Mountain Ridge Athletics sign; to the right of it is the big Wolf monument.

"I can't believe I'm saying this, but knowing we have the rest of today off, the last thing I want to do is party tonight. Anyone down for some Madden and take-out later?" Nola asks, and all four sets of eyes whip to him.

Maverick places the back of his hand on Nola's forehead. "Bro, you sick?"

Nola chuckles, swatting him away. "Whatever… You'll be the first one to park your ass down beside me on that loveseat and put them long fingers to good use."

Mav raises his eyebrow in Nola's direction. "That's right… You know these long fingers work all the magic."

I shake my head, laughing at the two playboy-class clowns of our house.

"Hey, Superstar?" Maverick nods at me with his finger in the air. "Too bad Berkley's finger isn't this long, right?"

I roll my eyes at him, fighting the smirk on my face as I flip him off. My mind flits back to that night and all that sass she was trying to hide behind.

"Let's have a roomie night tonight, and Nate can tell us all about that. That's what Berkley, Bellamy, and Darby do," Graham suggests.

"How do you know?"

"Because one night I tagged along to karaoke night, got drunk as shit thanks to Bellamy, and slept it off on their couch. When I woke up, it was 2 a.m., and they were eating chips and watching some chick flick while talking about their favorite sex positions and the riskiest place they had ever had sex before."

"Shit, I wanna be at that type of roomie hangout," Nola chimes in.

Casually, I nod my chin to Graham. "So what was Berkley's answer?" At the same time, a broody Cash asks, "And what did Bellamy say?"

"Nuh uh… It was part of the sacred girl night. I ain't telling y'all shit." He pretends to zip his mouth shut to further annoy us.

The crew for the shoot interrupts, passing each of us fresh Gatorade bottles.

My eyes meet Graham's playfully. "This ain't over, buddy."

Then our attention is brought back toward the photoshoot by the assistant letting us know our group is up next for positioning.

"Bro, you're staring again," Cash growls at Maverick as we watch on while the basketball teams are placed where they want them for the shoot.

I follow his trail of vision and find him watching the point guard of the men's team with his girlfriend, Shay Moore, the star of the women's team.

"Shut the fuck up, Cash. I know you aren't talking. Do you want me to start calling you out on your shit?"

They often pick on each other, but that's the first time I've seen Maverick have a serious tone, which further proves there's likely some truth to Cash's accusation.

"Okay, boys, we need both the Leblancs behind the basketball players. We're doing winter sports on this side."

Turning around, the photographer walks backward, glancing at Nola, Graham, and me. "We'll get some shots with you three and the twins after the big group, so just hang tight."

We all nod, since we were briefed on this earlier. Gatorade learned that Graham and the twins are cousins, so they contacted them, interested in featuring them in a special shot today. However, one of the writers at The Howler Report told Gatorade that we all lived at The Wolves Den together, so they decided to include all five of us in the extra shoot.

Cash and Maverick make their way over to where she's pointing. I wait for Mav to make a smart comment about how hockey is the most elite winter sport, but instead, he's unnaturally quiet.

I observe Shay, who glances at Maverick before her boyfriend slings his arm around her shoulder and she quickly looks ahead.

I think I just discovered another thing the Leblanc twins have in common with their polar opposite personalities.

They're both pining after girls they can't have.

Thankfully, the main part of the shoot is over within twenty minutes, and the crew dismisses everyone but my roommates and me.

The photoshoot with the guys has been the best part of the whole thing.

We're able to laugh and cut up, just being ourselves.

The photographer shows us one of her favorites of the candid shots on the screen of her camera. Nola's jumping on Graham's back, just like he does every time Graham scores a touchdown. I'm in a squatted position, throwing up the wolf sign, and on the other side of me, the twins are mid secret handshake that they do on the ice.

It strikes me as I look at the smiles on their faces, how close I've gotten with Nola, Cash, and Maverick in a short period of time. And my relationship with Graham has only grown even stronger. He's been there for me at all stages of my life, and I'm forever grateful to him for that. I can't wait to see where the draft takes him after this year.

In Texas, I always felt like such a huge part of me was missing because of Berkley, but I also don't think I had truly found my people until I came here.

"We need to frame that one and put it up in The Wolves Den," I say proudly.

The photographer smiles. "We work with a high-quality printing company, so how about I send you guys some copies."

We all nod, collectively telling her we'd appreciate that.

Once we finish, the guys set a plan in place for a true roomie night. With hockey now in full swing, we're all exhausted and want to take advantage of a no game weekend.

"Okay, but can the girls come too? They always make shit more fun," Nola asks, and I smile, because he's right. And because I don't really want to spend my free Saturday night without my girl.

"They're basically like honorary Wolves Den members," Mav says. Everyone nods in agreement that they should come.

In the next breath, Cash's pinched eyes stare at his phone intently before he snaps his eyes up. "If y'all are riding with me, I need to go."

I should ask him if he's okay, but one thing I've learned with Cash so far is that if he wants to tell you something, he will when he's good and ready.

Tilting my head in the other direction, I tell them, "I'm going to shower in the locker room because Berkley's meeting me."

"Sounds good. We'll see y'all later," Graham says, and they all call out their goodbyes as they follow Cash to his truck.

ME

The facility code is 9653.

BB

I'm in. It's eerily quiet in here. You almost done?

ME

Where are you?

BB

In the hallway by the trainer's room.

ME

Keep walking to the end of the hall. You'll see our locker room entrance.

BB

Okay... here.

ME

Come in.

BB

What if someone else shows up?

ME

Nobody else is here. Trust me, when Coach gives us the rest of the day off, we take advantage of it.

ME

I thought we could fulfill that locker room fantasy. [Picture message]

I hear her footsteps enter the locker room, but I don't move from my seat on the bench. My hand still slowly strokes my hard cock, mirroring the picture I sent her.

A few seconds later, Berkley's eyes meet mine, her gaze bouncing up and down my body.

"Hey, BB." I bite my lip at the sight of her in those tiny cut-off shorts I love so much.

"You started the fun without me," she smirks and walks the few feet to where she's standing in front of my aching cock. Her scent and nearness have the blood pumping between my legs even faster.

Berkley places her hands on my shoulders, and I tilt my head back as she leans down, pressing her lips to mine for a chaste kiss. I try to deepen it, but she pulls back, sliding her fingers through my hair and tugging. "Are you sure no one's coming?"

"Pretty sure," I answer truthfully.

She shrugs, gripping the back of my neck, but surprises me by dropping to her knees between my legs. "That's good enough for me, QB... You ready to slide your dick down my throat?"

Fuck, I love a confident Berkley. "I'm always ready for that."

My ass lifts off the towel-covered bench when her lips meet the head of my cock. The way my fist wraps around my shaft looks like I'm feeding her my cock. That and the sight of her tongue swirling around the tip already has my eyes rolling back.

It's even sexier when she pushes my fist away and wraps not one but two hands around my thickness. Working me up and down with one on top of the other, her mouth focuses on the head.

I moan, "Feels so good, Baby."

She slows her pace, licking the slit and letting her eyes slide up to mine. Mouth open, tongue out, her eyes on mine...driving me absolutely insane. A mixture of love, lust, and extreme possessiveness suddenly overcomes me.

"This perfect mouth belongs to me," I growl.

She moans around me, her nails now digging into my thighs and her mouth moving farther down my shaft. I thrust up into her and she opens wide, allowing herself to take me in deeper. The sound of her gagging around me has my balls tightening up.

I stand, unable to control myself any longer, and grip the back of her head. "Can you handle it?"

She nods, her eyes watering. "You still love choking on my cock, don't you, needy girl?"

Squirming in her spot on the floor, she whimpers *yesss* as she moves her hands down, rubbing her thumb over my taint. Just like I remember her body, she also knows my sensitive spots.

Berkley grips my thighs, so I slow my pace and her lips pop off. The sexy grin on her face has me waiting on bated breath.

"You ready?" she whispers seductively, sucking her middle finger in and out of her mouth. I swallow in anticipation.

I nod and barely recognize my voice, "Get that finger nice and wet for me first."

With her mouth back on my cock, she teases my puckered hole with her wet finger.

"Keep sucking me," I command, thrusting my hips into her. Berkley takes me into the back of her throat at the same time she presses her finger into my ass.

"Oh fuck... fucking... Berkley," I groan with nothing but pleasure.

All the sensations overwhelm me. "Don't stop. Don't stop."

Her finger and mouth move in tandem, bringing me so close to losing it, but it's not till her blue eyes meet mine that I completely lose it.

"I'm coming," I moan from deep in my chest. Ripple after ripple sweeps through me.

With my cock still buried in her throat, I gently caress her hair where I was gripping so tightly just a few moments earlier.

I love you is on the tip of my tongue, but I remind myself she's not ready for that, so instead I say, "Shit, BB, you are too good at that."

The vision of her on her knees in my locker room, swallowing my cum, will be stuck on replay for the next decade, at least.

Her flushed face smiles proudly up at me, and I can tell my girl is horny.

I take Berkley's hands in mine and help her stand. Kissing her deeply, I taste both of us on her lips.

"Now it's your turn," I wink.

TWENTY-TWO

Berkley

Typically, at away games, you don't see many jerseys with the visiting team's colors, but not today. Nate and the Wolves are taking on East Carolina, which happens to be only about an hour from where we grew up.

I've seen many Outlaw jerseys, including a few from Texas Tech, which shows that people are here to see him play because he's special. I knew this when we were teens, and it's even more evident now: He'll be a household name by the time he hits the NFL.

But I smile proudly because no one's jersey is like mine. It's an exclusive, and I can't wait for him to see me in it.

"I wish I didn't have to drive back tonight. This place seems to know how to party," Bellamy says, eyeing a group of students to the right of us who are pulling airplane bottles out of their cowgirl boots.

I laugh. "Yes, but you're doing the right thing. Your mom deserves a nice birthday lunch with you there." I would normally go home with her for a quick trip like that. Cane

Creek Ranch is beautiful, but I'm excited to see the place I used to consider my little slice of heaven.

A look of empathy flashes over her face. "For sure, I wouldn't miss it," she nods and changes the subject. "Plus, I have a busy week ahead. I feel like everything is suddenly due."

"I was feeling the exact same way and a little overwhelmed with coming here this weekend, but...fuck it," I shrug. "You only get the true college experience once."

"True... Well, hopefully, I won't get kicked out of college this week," she huffs.

I stick my neck out in her direction, confused. "And why in the heck would that happen?"

Her nostrils flare. "Because Professor Douglas is demanding I come in during his office hours to discuss a grade appeal."

"He's such a creep... I don't like that one bit," I state through gritted teeth. "Do you want me to go with you? Or get one of the guys to go."

She shakes her head. "No, no. I've already made up my mind. Fuck that dude and his office hours. I'm going to show up in between his lectures to his classroom so I can discuss it with him privately, but in a more open, public setting."

"Smart." I should have known she has a plan. Bellamy always does things the way she wants to, and that's one of the things I admire most about her.

She nudges me. "By the looks of it, I don't think number two is going to be able to warm up because he can't take his eyes off you." Bellamy nods toward the field.

Following her gaze, Nate is smiling up at me. My heart thumps, my belly flutters, and my core clenches at the sight of him on that field.

I blow him a kiss and quickly turn around, pointing to the back of his old practice jersey. Shimmying my butt in his direction, I smile over my shoulder. I love the look of adoration on his face.

Then he does something that he hasn't in so long. My heart skips a few beats, and I swallow down the tears of joy as I lift my hand to mimic his.

His tattooed arm is outstretched in the air and his hand curved, making one side of the heart while my left one does the same.

Who am I kidding? I love Nathan Outlaw with my whole heart.

It's been true since I was sixteen years old. At eighteen, I tried to tamp it down with pain and resentment, but it never went away. And now, it's back like a raging sea, ready to engulf me in its waves.

And in this moment...I want nothing more than to drown in him.

I people watch as I sit in the hotel lobby, waiting on the team to get back. The somber expressions on the Wolves' fans who walk in the door tugs at my heart for Nate. I know even in high school, as the quarterback, he put so much pressure on himself when they'd lose a game. I hate the thought of him beating himself up over his interception in the fourth quarter. If I thought his coach would approve of it, I'd force him in my car and take him home for the night just for the mental reprieve.

Originally, Willow and I were going to hang out with the guys for a bit, and then head back to Nori Beach for the night. I think ever since things have changed between Nate and me, my love for my hometown has resurfaced. It didn't feel right to be so close and not put my toes in the cold sand.

But thirty minutes into the game, when she and her dad were both no shows, I started to worry. Finally, she texted me, telling me something came up and she wasn't feeling so great and that she'd call me later.

It's very unusual for Brian not to come, especially with how close it is, so I'm wondering if they're both sick.

I'm still considering driving the short distance home in the morning. Maybe I can drop them off some food and take a walk on the beach before heading back. I'm sure Nate talked to his dad, so I'll see what he thinks.

A couple of the guys start making their way into the lobby. I search for Nate, hoping the frown I'm almost sure he's sporting from their second half performance will morph into a smile when he sees me.

No sign of Nate yet, but my eyes do land on another familiar pair.

Carter.

He smiles at me, and to my surprise, walks over. He hasn't responded to my text since the club, so I assumed he wanted nothing to do with me. As I stand up, we exchange a friendly hug. "Hi, Berk."

"Hi. Tough game today."

"Yeah…not our best. How ya been?"

"I've been doing really good." I try not to think of Nate because I know the smile on my face will tell it all, and I don't want to hurt Carter that way. "Look…"

"No, no. Don't worry about it, Berkley." Carter holds up his hand, waving me off, not in the mean, dismissive way he did in the club, but more in a *I truly don't owe him an explanation* way, and I appreciate he recognizes that.

"Do I love it?" He shakes his head. "No. But if I'm being honest here, I knew it was coming the moment I heard he was transferring."

I swallow, unsure of what to say back to that.

"I just want you to be happy. And it kinda kills me to say it, but I know he makes you happy."

I smile, nodding as I lean in to give him another hug. "Thank you, Carter."

"No need to thank me, babe," he whispers.

Of course, in that moment, Nate walks up. His eyes bore into mine, causing unease to zip up my spine as I step back from Carter's embrace.

He nods nonchalantly, pointing between Carter and me. "I'll be upstairs when you're done with whatever this is."

NATE

The fucking day just keeps getting better and better.

I walked into my hotel room for only long enough to drop my bag before I'm heading back to the elevator. But when the metal doors split apart, the beautiful blonde I was going back for steps off.

She storms past me, and I expect her to keep going past my room to her own, but she doesn't.

The second the door closes behind us, she throws her hands in the air. "What the heck was that, Nate?"

I walk to the far side of the room before responding.

"That was me hating the sight of you with him." Unable to control myself, I continue, "The guy you've been fucking for the last two years."

Her brow pinches as she exhales heavily. "Well, that's not very fair."

"Yeah, you're probably right, but I can't help how I feel."

She comes closer, grabbing my shoulder and forcing me to look at her.

"He was my friend before he was anything else."

I grit my teeth, trying to remind myself this isn't on her.

"Trust me...he never wanted to just be your friend. He has had his eyes set on you since the day you came to our high school."

"That may be true, but he was my friend when I needed one because I was so fucking broken," she says, pointing at her chest.

"Oh, I know. He told me all about it, remember? That's how I knew you were seeing him before you even left Nori beach that summer. You walked right into his waiting arms, didn't you?"

Again, she's throwing her hands in the air, exasperated with me.

"Seriously, Nate, do you hear yourself right now? You have no fucking clue." She shakes her head furiously.

"Well then, explain it to me, Berkley." The anger in my voice is replaced with pain. "Why him? I would have rather it had been anyone but him."

She takes a deep breath. "It wasn't like that for a long time. We were just friends for almost all of freshmen year before anything else happened."

A shiver runs through my body at the thought of them together. "It kills me knowing he had you like that." I close my eyes before looking at her again. "It literally feels like someone is shoving a knife into my gut at the thought."

Berkley winces. "Trust me, I know the feeling. I felt it almost every day for the first year after you left and even some days after that."

We both have a lot of pain from the past two years, and I was stupid to not address that clearly before now.

"And you know what, Nate? I don't blame you anymore, but I certainly won't be made the bad guy here. I thought you had moved on, and I was barely hanging on, trying desperately to do the same. I'm sorry it was him, and I'm sorry that hurt you, but I trusted him, and to me, that was enough." The emotion in her eyes as she plops down on the hotel bed makes my chest burn with the realization of how much of an asshole I'm being finally breaking through.

"I know, Berkley... Shit, I'm sorry." I hate that I let my attitude from today and my insecurities overcome me.

"Fuck..." I tug on my hair and sit beside her. Surprisingly, she lets me take her hand in mine. "I was so fucking bummed from our loss and my family acting weird today that the one thing I was looking forward to was seeing you up close and in my jersey." I gently run my finger across the hem of my old practice jersey. "But the minute I did, his arms were wrapped around you, and maybe the way I acted was shitty, but it's a whole lot better than what I considered doing in that moment."

A loud knock on the door startles us both, but the panicked voice on the other side has my blood running cold.

TWENTY-THREE

Berkley

A loud banging on the door effectively halts our argument.

"Open up, it's me." Willow's distressed voice sounds through the closed hotel door.

Her unusual tone has us both rushing to the door.

She hurls herself into Nate's arms as soon as the door swings wide. Her face is stained with mascara streaks.

"What happened?" I ask while Nate hugs her tightly. Too concerned with Willow's well-being, I don't notice she isn't alone until Nola slowly shuts the door behind him.

"She—she called me in hysterics, asking if I could bring her up to you," Nola says, concern etched on his face as well.

Nate wraps his arm around Willow and walks over to the bed to sit beside her.

"Will, talk to me. What's going on?" Nate asks and holds her hands in his.

"I'll leave you guys alone. If you need me, call me, okay?" Nola says as he takes a hesitant step toward the door.

And I wonder if I should do the same as my gut churns with thoughts of what could have Willow so upset right now.

"Do you want privacy? I can leave you two to talk," I ask them, and Willow's sad blue eyes meet mine.

"No, stay. You're going to want to hear this, too," Willow says, reaching for my hand. I hear the soft click of the hotel door close, and the anxious energy radiating off Willow fills the air.

"Fuck, Will, you're scaring the shit out of me. What's going on? Are you pregnant or something?"

"God, no. Nothing like that…but it does involve children."

"You're worrying me being so damn cryptic right now." Nate's unease rises to a new level.

"There's so much that happened. I'm trying to figure out how to say it…"

I reach for her hand and squeeze it lightly. "Why don't you start at the beginning? Maybe that will help you get your thoughts straight."

She takes a deep breath, and her eyes linger on mine like she's seeing something in them for the first time. A strange sensation washes over me as she begins talking.

"Okay, well, I was talking to Mom this week. I know nothing good comes out of interacting with that woman; however, I haven't seen her in months, even though she's been making an effort to see me. So I reached out to her, asking if we could get breakfast and then head to the game together to watch you. Well, while I was there at her house, she wanted to give me a tour of her new place. She even showed me a room that was supposedly mine. She asked if I wanted to stay there, that she missed me and wanted me to move back in with her. I told her I wasn't ready for that yet..." She shifts ever-so-slightly, angling her body toward Nate, her hands laced together in her lap. "That I was still hurt by her actions and what she did to Dad and our family. I saw the switch flip inside of her, her mean streak rearing its ugly head. I braced myself for whatever venom she was gonna spew after I turned her down. But I was not prepared for what she actually said..." Willow takes a shaky breath, and I hold mine.

"She said she didn't understand why I wouldn't want to be with my actual parent." Willow pauses, looking between Nate and me expectantly. Before either of us can form a thought, she continues, "I'm pretty sure time froze in that moment..." Tears begin dripping down her face again. "And when I asked her what she meant, she flat out said... She—" It breaks my heart to watch her struggle so badly with what she is trying to tell us. "She said that Daddy wasn't my father." Willow's eyes lock with mine, and her next words don't just stop time, they tilt my whole world upside down. "And when I demanded answers, she told me that *your* dad was my biological father."

The air is sucked out of my lungs like a vacuum. All three of our gazes bounce between each other's.

"Wait, what?" I say, trying to comprehend fully what she just said. "You're my sister?"

Willow curls her lips and starts to cry again, and I wrap my arms around her, letting my own tears fall. Not only for her, but for me...and the loving family I once thought I had. But slowly, that fairy tale has been stripped down piece by piece.

A sister.

Willow is my sister.

"I'm so sorry, Will. I'm sorry I wasn't there for you. I'm speechless as it is right now. I can't imagine hearing those words from that woman's mouth," Nate says, his tone full of anguish.

"You wouldn't have been able to prevent it... I feel like she was holding on to that ammunition, just waiting for the right moment to unload it," she sniffles, then dabs her eyes with a tissue I hand her.

"That fucking bitch. How dare she unleash that on you. Of course, she would use that knowledge as a weapon and not sit you down and have a civilized talk like a parent should. I've known for quite some time I no longer wanted that woman in my life. But after today, after what she did to you... I couldn't care less if I ever see her again," Nate roars his frustration.

"I can't believe this... I mean, I can, knowing their history, but still, I was only three years old. What a piece of shit," I say the last bit more to myself than to them. All this time...I've had a sister. My father had to have known...and he never said a word. How could he do this to my mom? To me? To Willow? Not to mention, poor Mr. Outlaw. He loves his children more than any man I've ever met. His heart must be breaking...or did he already know the truth?

"I'm sorry to unload this on you both like this, but I didn't know what else to do. I couldn't show up to your game after hearing that; I knew that if you saw my face, you'd immediately know something was off. I'm sorry I lied, I may not have been physically sick but I felt like I was after I left her house. My head hasn't been right since," Willow confesses with another sniffle.

Nate pulls her into his chest again. "Shhh, don't apologize, I get it. I was so fucking worried about you when I didn't see you in the stands, and Dad sent some elusive texts today that had me on edge. Speaking of, have you talked to him? What's he saying about all this? Do we even know it's true?"

Her head bows slightly. "Yeah, I called him as soon as I left Mom's. I was so distraught, I didn't know who I should talk to. I didn't want to unleash on him, but deep down, I had a feeling he already knew. Still, when I told him, he got really quiet. I drove straight home to talk to him, and he was waiting on the porch for me when I got there. He was quiet for several minutes before he started crying as he hugged me. He let me know how much he loves me and that it doesn't matter who my biological father is; he will always be my dad, and he will always be there for me, no matter what. He wants us all to talk about it, but he didn't want to ruin your game weekend. I didn't tell him I was coming here. I just needed to see you both."

I have a half-sister, and she's Nate's half-sister as well.

Leaning across the gap between the two beds, I wrap my arms around Willow. Her body shakes as all the revelations from the day seep in. "We'll figure this all out. I promise, okay? I love you," I whisper into her hair as she hugs me back.

My mind reels with so many emotions; I'm unsure what to do with myself. But I know one thing that must be done, and it's something I've been putting off for way too long.

I stand abruptly, and Nate's attention flies to me. "I-I'm going to leave you two to talk for a bit. I need to go do something..."

He eyes me for a moment, and then his attention is back on Willow, where it should be. I'm thankful for the distraction, since I know he would want to be by my side for where I'm going. But I need to face this on my own.

The crunching of the gravel driveway announces my arrival. I've been trying my best to string cohesive thoughts together during the forty-five-minute drive over here. I'm halfway up the front steps when the screen door opens, and my father steps outside.

Now, I'm not a violent person by any means, but seeing his face right now makes me want to throw my best right hook at him. He eyes me for a moment, and I wonder if he can see the anger radiating from every pore in my body. "Baby, you've finally come to visit me," he says, stepping outside and letting the porch door swing close behind him.

"Don't you dare *baby* me. Not right now."

"What's wrong? What happened?" he asks, concern etching his face, but I can also see he's bracing for whatever wrath I'm about to unleash. How could he not? I haven't spoken a word to him in months, and I just show up out of the blue.

"When were you going to tell me? Huh? Or did you want to try to bury that secret, along with your long list of fuckery you've done to our family over the years?" I poke my finger into his chest, pressing harder with every word. Tears prick my eyes, but I refuse to let them fall.

"You watch your tone with me, young lady," he demands, taking a step back from me. "And keep your voice down." Making sure Angela isn't within range to hear me, he peeks inside the house.

I stare at him for a few moments, leaving the window open for him to air out any of his grievances, but he stays silent. *Fuck this.*

"How long? How long did you know Willow was my sister?" I explode, my arms crossing over my chest. The position gives me the shield I need to have this conversation.

He startles at my revelation; guess he didn't think that secret would get out. "Baby, I—"

I hold up my hand, stopping the excuses I know he was trying to come up with. "Was it weird watching Nate and I fall in love, knowing you were fucking his mom all along?"

"Berkley Jay Black, you do not speak to me like that. I will not stand for such disrespect."

I scoff at his attempt to scold me. "You lost my respect the moment I realized what kind of man you truly are."

He stiffens, turns, and looks inside the house once again. It's funny how he'd rather have this conversation outside than in the privacy of his own home. I guess he'd like Angela to remain in the dark about his past. But how could she? Their current relationship was built on their indiscretions.

"So, Angela doesn't know?"

He shakes his head.

"About what, exactly? That you cheated on your wife for God knows how long? That you have another child who no one was made aware of? Or that you're still probably fucking around with Nate's mom to this day?"

His hands go up to placate me. "Please, let me explain. But not here...not right now." He looks so defeated that if I weren't so pissed, I would possibly feel bad about the way I'm speaking to him.

But the rage inside of me doesn't give a fuck who hears me. Why should I protect him? All my pain over the last few years is a direct result of his behavior... I don't owe him anything.

"I hope Angela realizes soon enough what kind of man you are... Actually, scratch that, she's just like you. So, I'm sure you two are perfect for one another."

He doesn't talk, but he doesn't go back inside either. Allowing me to speak my peace, so I leave him with one last thing.

"I don't think I could ever forgive you for putting Mom through all of that. Not to mention, the pain you've put me through. And most importantly, I'll never forgive you for keeping my sister away from me. I'm done."

Without another word, I storm off his front porch, finally allowing my tears to fall freely as I mourn the loss of our relationship, because I know it'll never be the same again.

I speed away and drive the short distance to the marina. A place that has always brought me peace, somewhere I can sit and be in my feelings. I take out my phone to text Nate and let him know where I am, because I'm sure he's worried.

But of course, my phone is dead.

After plugging it in, I lean my head back onto the headrest and replay the events that have just transpired, and allow myself to break. It's cathartic in a way. Knowing what just happened was needed in order for me to move on in my life. But that doesn't mean my heart doesn't ache with every breath. It hurts for the little girl who looked up to her father with rose-colored glasses, blinded by her adoration for the man she loved. It hurts for the wife who knowingly stayed in a marriage to try and save her family, or what was left of it. But most of all, it aches for the woman who will have to go through life never being able to trust her father's words again.

My phone finally powers on and a slew of text notifications fill my screen. Before I read any of them, I snap a picture of the view with the gorgeous sunset sky and send it to Nate.

ME

[Picture message]

ME

Miss this place.

NATE

ONE HOUR EARLIER

ME

Where'd you run off to, BB?

My mind is all over the place, even after Willow's cries have calmed down. I've never seen her so distraught. Not even when Dad and Mom told us they were getting a divorce. It kills me she had to bear that news on her own. I wish I could've been there to help shield the blow of my mother's venom.

"I'm okay now, I promise," Willow says after I hand her a bottle of water and a snack.

ME

Just let me know you're okay?

I was so distracted by Willow that I didn't protest when Berkley left, but I didn't think she was going to leave, leave. Where could she have gone? I assumed she just needed air, but the fact that she's not responding has me worried. I know this news must've hit her hard, especially after just recently learning about more of her father's discretions.

Willow stands and walks to the bathroom while I pace around. My chest aches when I think of my dad and what must be going through his mind. My father is the best man I know. He's always the first to show up and the last to leave. I can't begin to imagine how he feels.

Willow exits the bathroom and goes back to sit on the bed. Eying her cautiously for a moment, I take out my phone and check to see if Berkley has responded to me.

"Has she texted back yet?" Willow asks, and I shake my head in response as I reread the unanswered messages.

ME

> Baby... Whatever it is, we can face it together.

My last notification is colored green, which means she has no service, her phone is dead, or maybe she's hurt. I refuse to acknowledge the small dip in my stomach at the idea of the latter, so my mind races with where she could have possibly run off to. It takes less than a minute before I realize where she's gone, and within seconds, I'm packing up my bags.

"Wha—what are you doing?" Willow questions.

"I need to go talk to Coach for a second. Let him know I had a family emergency, and I won't be taking the bus back... Can you go to the girls' room down the hall, room 455, and get Berkley's bag for me?"

"Uh, sure, but where are we going?" Willow asks again.

"Berkley went to her father's, I'm sure of it."

"Alright, I'll get her stuff."

"Perfect, I'll meet you back here in five minutes," I say, handing her the spare keycard so she can get back in.

Opening the hotel door, I startle at the sight of Nola sitting in the hallway. I wasn't expecting anyone to be there.

"Is she okay?" he asks as he stands.

"Yeah, she'll be okay. Thanks for bringing her up here for me.

I appreciate it, man," I say, slapping his hand and bringing him in for a quick hug.

Willow steps out of the room a moment later and stops short at the sight of the two of us. Her red swollen eyes go wide. "Oh uh, hi," she says to Nola. "I never said thank you earlier..."

"Listen, I'll be right back... I need to go tell Coach I have family shit going on and will need to drive back separate from the team."

Nola looks at me, assessing my mental state, then his gaze flicks to Willow. "Hey, man, let me drive you guys. I don't think either of you should be driving right now."

"You sure? I would hate to put you out like that." Even though I'd hate to admit it, he's right.

"Of course, brother. Would you mind telling Coach I'm going with you?"

"Sure thing. Thanks again, for everything," I nod in appreciation and then head to the elevators, my chest swelling with gratitude.

After receiving Berkley's text, we bypassed her father's house and headed straight to the water. Pulling up to the marina, we spot her car and pull up next to it. A nervous energy picks up when I notice her driver's seat is empty. *Where are you, BB?*

I get out of the car in record time, not even bothering to tell them where I'm going. Making my way down the beach, my heart stops when I spot her wild ponytail blowing in the wind. I jog the short distance and plop down on the sand beside her.

Not even bothering to look my way, she leans her head onto my shoulder, and I wrap my arms around her.

"You okay, baby?" I ask, breaking the silence while I rub her shoulder gently.

She nods slowly but continues to stare out at the waves lapping at the shore.

"Did you see him?"

Berkley lets out a long sigh.

"Yeah, didn't deny anything either," she scoffs. "Didn't even go inside to talk. I wound up unleashing everything on him on his front porch."

"Did you not want to go inside the house?" I ask, because I find it odd that he would want anyone to hear what Berkley was claiming.

She shakes her head. "Angela was inside… My guess was, he didn't want her to find out what a piece of garbage he truly is." Berkley sits up and turns slightly to face me. My thumb brushes along her cheek, trying to wipe away the streaks of mascara.

"He was surprised when I mentioned Willow. Almost shocked that I even knew that piece of information."

"I wish you would have told me where you were going. You didn't have to do that alone," I say, cupping her cheek. Her beautiful eyes drink me in, and I get lost in them. She's the most precious thing in the world to me, and I hate that she had to face him on her own. I would give anything to take on the hurt he's caused her, to relieve some of the pain in her heart.

"I needed to do it. I've had so much pent up inside of me, I had to face him alone. It felt good, letting it all out." A sad smile graces her gorgeous face as she leans into my hand.

A cold gust of wind hits us, and Berkley shivers. "Come on, let's go to my dad's. I called him on my way here, so he knows we're coming."

When we approach the parking lot, Berkley peeks at Willow's Jeep, spotting Willow and Nola inside. She turns to me with a raised eyebrow.

"He insisted on driving. Said I wasn't in the right mindset to drive."

"Well, he's not wrong," Berkley huffs, and I chuckle.

"I'm not sure what that is." I jut my chin toward the white Jeep. "Or why Willow had his number, but I'm thankful he was there for her. He was really worried."

"I'm glad he was there...he's a good guy with a big heart," she says, and her fingers lace with mine.

"Yeah, a heart that better stay far away from my baby sister unless he's serious..."

She nudges me in the shoulder. "*Our* baby sister."

"Fuck, that sounds so weird." I push out a breath, and she smiles softly, nodding in agreement.

TWENTY-FOUR

BRIAN

There are things in life that nothing can prepare you for, and things you know will forever change you.

From the moment I heard Willow's shaky voice over the phone, I knew whatever she was going to say was going to devastate me. Then she confirmed my biggest fear since learning about Jane's indiscretions over the years.

Willow is not my biological daughter.

As I stand, looking out my front window, I await a conversation no parent ever plans to have with their children. But unfortunately for me, my life's path was never fully in my hands. I was married to a selfish, unworthy woman, who didn't care about the impact of her actions, nor her words.

I spoke with Jane briefly after Willow left earlier today. Not only to confirm the news, but to chastise her for what she did to our daughter. For the further damage she's caused in their lives. In what world would a grown woman unleash that type of news on their child without a proper discussion?

When I hear the rumble of an engine approach, I brace myself. Because now I know the truth…and the kids deserve to know the whole story, from the beginning. Nate gave me a heads-up that it wasn't just him and Willow coming here, that Berkley and his teammate Nola will be joining them too.

I'm down the front stairs and wrapping my arms around my kids as soon as they're out of the car. Unable to stop the tears from welling in my eyes at the sight of them. They're strong, and resilient, but still, no one should have to bear that news alone.

Berkley stands off to the side, where I see her staring off in the distance in order to give me time with Nate and Will. With a wave of my hand, I motion for her to come into the hug. There's no doubt in my mind she's feeling just as much betrayal as my two. I look around for their friend Nola as well, who's still in the driver's seat of the car. "Come on, let's get inside," I suggest, waving for Nola to join us.

Once we're gathered in the living room, Nola excuses himself to the back deck. I make a mental note to thank him later for being there for my kids on a day like today.

"Did you speak with her?" Willow asks.

I nod, but I'm unable to speak the words. The confirmation that the poison her mom spewed to her earlier is a hundred percent true.

Nate looks at me, concern etched on his face, and it hurts my heart that my children are suffering.

My voice cracks as I speak, "It—it doesn't change a thing for me, Willow bug. You're still my baby girl. Always have been, always will be."

As my eyes flit between both my children, my hand reaches for theirs where they sit across from me. Gently squeezing once, reassuring them that we're in this together.

"Did you ever suspect…?" Nate asks. I notice Willow's eyes don't meet mine with the question. Almost as if she can't stand to look at me while I answer.

"She always looked like her mother, but then I met Berkley…" I remember that day so vividly. We were about to have lunch, and Nate had mentioned his new girlfriend was coming over before they went to the beach. He was so excited for us to meet her. Lovesick from day one. I could tell… I was the same once.

"It's their eyes…such a clear blue. One you don't see very often. At this point, I had known about Jane's affairs, so I did feel a bit of paranoia, but despite the similarity, I brushed it off as a pure coincidence. Again, because it didn't matter." I try to reiterate that fact as many times as possible. "Your mom and I at that time had been in counseling for over five years. We started right after I found out about the affairs." I situate myself in my seat, getting comfortable before I tell them the full truth of our relationship.

"When I first met your mother, she had recently had her heart broken. We took it slow, and eventually, our friendship grew into something more, and we got pregnant with you, Nate. Then soon after, we got married. Of course, just like every relationship, we had our ups and downs, but we were happy together. A few years later, we found out we were pregnant with you, Willow. I was so ecstatic to finally have a little baby girl. No offense, ol' buddy," I say with a lighthearted chuckle. I love my boy ferociously, but I always dreamt of being a girl dad.

I take a deep, steady breath and continue as all three sets of eyes remain focused on me. "It was around the time of your seventh birthday that I found out about your mom's relationship with Wade. It was later brought to my attention that Berkley's father was the man who had originally broken her heart. She swore it was over between the two of them, that he was moving away, and it was a slip-up never to be repeated."

Berkley's eyes go wide with realization. "I had overheard my aunt discussing this but had no clue who it was about until Nate told me the truth."

I nod my head slightly. "Your mom had found out about the relationship, and they moved to Raleigh to try to repair their marriage. I didn't even know you guys had moved back until Nate mentioned your last name one day, and I put it all together." Not wanting to further upset Berkley, I don't go into details about her mother being the one who came to me about their infidelity a few days after Willow's seventh birthday. She made me aware of the first affair that had apparently happened eight years prior and apologized for not letting me know sooner. She never mentioned anything about Willow being Wade's, but I think that was the first time I considered it because of the timeline. Even though I chose to ignore the thought, likely not wanting to know the truth, because no matter what, she's my daughter.

"You never questioned if you were my father after finding out about the affair," Willow interjects.

"After the secrets came out, the thought briefly crossed my mind, but I was so naïve and in love with your mom and the family we had built; it was almost like I didn't want to know. I'm sorry, maybe that wasn't the right way to handle things."

"Daddy, none of this is your fault," Willow says, and her tone reminds me of the sweet little girl who used to run through the halls.

"Dad, don't question yourself; you have always been the best to us. I couldn't imagine being in such a one-sided relationship for so many years," Nate says, and I see the genuine remorse he's feeling.

"It was after the third offense a couple years ago that I finally decided to end it. I was no longer going to be the doormat to someone who didn't care about me or my feelings."

Berkley's eyes overflow with tears. "I'm so sorry my father ruined your family. I can't believe you can even stand the sight of me after everything he put you through."

I shake my head vigorously, "I could never blame you. We're all just innocent bystanders to their toxic adultery," I say, knowing all the times I was ready to call it quits, but I stayed and truly tried to make it work...for my kids.

I reach for her hand. "Plus, I knew from the day you and Nate met that you were something special, and I would never stand in the way of my son's happiness."

"I love you, Dad, so much. I'm sorry you had to suffer in silence all those years. You will always be my daddy. The first man I ever loved and the man I know will always be there for me." Willow hops out of her seat, wrapping her arms around me.

"Listen, me telling you all this has nothing to do with making you feel bad for me. It was so you'd know why I never thought for a moment you weren't mine. Because you'll always be my baby girl." Kissing her head, I try to hold back my own tears.

"All of you are my family, and I'm always here for you," I say, looking at the other two, who are just as emotionally wrecked from the day.

"We've all had a long day. Let's call it a night, okay?"

They all agree. Willow tells Nate and Berkley to go get some rest and that she'll let Nola know he can come in. She gives me a long hug before heading out back. I make my way to my front porch and sit, digesting the reality of things. But instead of getting down from the turn of events, I count my blessings... I have amazing kids who I know can and will do anything they set their minds to. I'm finally free of Jane and all the heartache that came with her. And I feel like I'm finally ready to move on.

But my first focus is making sure my kids thrive and know their worth. My happiness with the right person will come... one day.

TWENTY-FIVE

Berkley

I try my best not to make a sound as I slip out of bed, knowing Nate has got to be exhausted from his game and the heaviness of yesterday. Quietly, I creep downstairs, not wanting to wake anyone else up either.

Pouring myself a cold glass of water from the pitcher in the fridge, I notice movement on the screened in patio.

Nola and Willow are sitting across from each other with coffee cups in hand. Part of me doesn't want to interrupt, but a bigger part of me wants to talk to Willow, one-on-one. So, I slide the glass door open and join them.

"Did you guys even sleep?" The bags under Nola's eyes tell me the answer.

"There weren't any tattoo shops open, so Brody went for a midnight walk on the beach with me to clear my mind. We were just saying we should really go take a nap, at least."

I don't miss the way she says Nola's real name. A name I've very rarely heard anyone even mention, much less use when speaking to him.

I smile at them both and look at Nola. "I can drive back to school later so you and Nate can rest." I'm so glad Nola was here last night. I think it was important for Willow to have someone not in the family to talk to about the shit that went down yesterday.

Willow's eyes fill with emotion as she looks at me and my chest aches with pain for her.

"Brody, if you want to go take a nap in my bed for a little bit before y'all head back, you can."

He stands, likely reading that we need a minute together.

"Upstairs, second door on the right," she says, passing her empty coffee mug into his waiting hand, and he gives her a reassuring wink before heading in.

The door closes behind him, and Willow is the first to speak.

"So how are you feeling about all this? I don't think it really hit me what it meant for you and your childhood until last night." Her sad eyes break my heart, and I'll never forgive our parents for putting her through this.

"Willow, don't worry about me. My fairy tale childhood was shattered the day I lost my mother. And then again, when I found out about his affairs. If anything, you're the best thing I've discovered during the whole mess."

She smiles, but it doesn't quite hit her eyes. "It's so crazy. I have always looked up to you and considered you as my sister. Thirteen-year-old me wanted to be just like you. And now to know all this time, we were more alike than I ever could have imagined."

I squeeze her knee. "I loved you from the moment I met you. I think our souls knew what we didn't."

"I just don't want you to resent me or cause more problems for you and Nate. He filled me in on the real reason he broke up with you during the drive here last night, and it only added fuel to the fire I'm feeling toward my mom and your dad."

"I promise you, Will, not one fiber of my being resents you. I love you too much for that," I say, standing and reaching for her. She joins me, and we immediately embrace, just holding each other.

I wish I could take the pain pouring off her body and wash it all away in the tide, never to return again.

"And as for me and Nate. We may not be perfect, but I think we've discovered we can't live without each other. Us sharing a sister isn't going to change that. I'm done letting *their* actions affect our happiness." I kiss her cheek.

Our arms hold on to each other's and her eyes harden. "I'm not sure I'll ever be ready to face my mom again, and from the way your dad handled things yesterday, I'm not sure that I want to even attempt a relationship with him either..." She pauses, and the thought of him hurting her the way he's hurt me makes my empty stomach sour. "I just don't think I can take the rejection right now, but maybe one day."

I nod and reassure her. "Whatever you decide, I'll always support you, but I will tell you, the man I thought he was when I was a kid, he no longer exists, and I'm honestly not sure he ever did. But with that said, do what feels right for you, but just be careful, and please don't shut me out."

Willow smiles, nodding. "I won't."

Holding each other for seconds or maybe minutes, Willow whispers, "I love you, Sister."

Tears well in my eyes. "I always prayed for a sister when I was a young girl. And little did I know, I had the very best one waiting for me right down the road, being loved and protected by the boy I would one day fall head over heels for."

She leans back and smiles a genuine smile this time, one that brightens her eyes. "Sounds like destiny to me."

Hours later, Nate and I have our legs tangled as we lie in each other arms under his sheets. The drive back was a quiet one, and the guys slept on and off. Nate insisted on me taking a nap while he drove part of the way. I think we were all decompressing.

When we got home, Graham, the twins, Bellamy, and Darby were waiting on us with a home-cooked meal from Gigi Leblanc. We had debriefed them slightly on Saturday night's events after Graham called us, frantically searching the hotel for our whereabouts, but we promised to explain further today.

They're all like family to us at this point, so we wanted them to fully understand what was going on. We explained the situation to all of them and they respected us not to pry deeper into things.

Nate squeezes me to him even tighter. "I know that our argument from the other night got lost in the chaos of things, but I owe you an apology."

This is one of the things I digested on the quiet drive home.

I shake my head. "I would have done the same thing. And honestly, I'd been wanting to bring the situation back up so I could explain to you that nothing happened for a very long time after we broke up, but I never wanted the mention of his name to ruin our time."

"After the bomb Willow dropped this weekend, Carter Graves seems a lot less important. As long as I'm who you want now, that's all I care about."

"You are what I always wanted, Nathan," I whisper, nuzzling my nose into his chest.

"Even after everything from this weekend?" he asks, but doesn't give me time to respond before he continues, "I've been anxious since Willow told us, and I think a lot of that is because of what happened the last time a revelation like this occurred involving our parents."

I tilt my head up, kissing his chin. "Baby, you have nothing to worry about. I'm not going anywhere. I barely made it through the last time I had to live without you; I don't ever want to do it again."

Nate's hazel eyes blur with unshed tears. "I'm not sure I can put into words how much hearing you say that means to me," he smiles through the emotion. "Maybe I'll write about it later when I can get all my thoughts out."

"I'd like that," I whisper, running my fingers through his hair.

I love this man so much.

"It shouldn't have taken me so long to say this, but…"

The anticipation shining in his eyes makes my heart skip a beat.

I kiss his chest. "I…"

Then I shimmy up the bed and kiss his cheek. "Love…"

Trailing a line of kisses across his jaw, I whisper, "You," across his lips before I fuse my mouth to his.

He kisses me back, and it's hard to describe, but I feel his love pouring into me. Since the moment he stepped foot in Mountain Ridge, his actions have shown me nothing but the purest love. I just wasn't ready to see it.

We break apart for air, but he keeps his forehead against mine. "I love you, BB."

I smile, my lips barely centimeters from his own. "Thank you for coming back to me." My thumb finds the spot on his skin where my initials are etched.

He glances down at the octopus inked on his arm. "Want to know another thing I remembered from the aquarium field trip that day?"

I quirk my eyebrow at him. "Yes, please tell me, Mr. Marine Biologist."

Nate grins, chuckling. "I learned that sea turtles can find their way home from anywhere in the ocean."

He brushes a piece of my hair out of my face. "You're my home, BB. No matter what, I was destined to always find my way back to you.

THE WOLVES ARE ON A ROLL

It's a beautiful fall day folks, who's ready for some MRU sports...

We hope Outlaw, Wynn, and Leblanc have been eating the same wheaties as their roomies whose hockey season just started with a bang.

The crash brothers aka the Leblanc Twins and their teammates are currently on a 5 game winning streak.

It's been a great week so far for MRU athletics and we have a feeling the boys of fall will end it strong out there today.

Will the Wolves get the W today for Outlaw's birthday?

TWENTY-SIX

Nate

"**H**ell of a game, guys!" Coach shouts from behind me and Nola as we enter the locker room. We are the last ones here since we did the post-game interviews.

Everyone cheers and shouts, all of us on a high from the last-minute touchdown Nola scored to win the game for us.

"QB, anything you want to say?" Coach Price asks.

I give him a smile, so fucking proud of my team tonight.

"Every single person busted their ass out there. From the O-line protecting me, to our defense, who shut them down in the second half, to our special teams." I see Pike beside me and pat him on the shoulder. "This dude right here...he doesn't miss. You kept us in that game, buddy."

The team goes crazy again, and then I spot Nola standing beside the coach, and I drag him out in the center. "We already know Leblanc is going in the draft from the way he's been killing it all year," I say, winking at Graham. "But we might have to hide this guy for a few more years so they don't take him too." I throw my arm around his neck, pulling him into me. "Nola made me look good tonight. Mark my words, he'll go down in history one day."

He playfully pushes me off him, and everyone joins in, jumping around him until Coach whistles.

With a jolly grin on his face, his loud voice carries throughout the room. "Leblanc just reminded me we have a birthday boy in the house today."

I roll my eyes in Graham's direction as a few guys from my O-line pick me up, placing me on top of their shoulders, and the whole team starts singing "Happy Birthday" to me.

Shockingly, my eyes land on Carter's, and he may not be singing, but he's actually smiling and enjoying himself.

"Okay, okay...I have one more announcement," Coach yells over our loudness.

We all quiet immediately.

"We got the call earlier, but wanted to wait to tell y'all... We are going to the Carolina Bowl. You'll get a second chance at taking down East Carolina."

Cheers erupt again, and I'm thrilled with this news. I have no doubt we can beat them and this second chance to do it feels like it's meant to be.

"Redemption! Redemption! Redemption!" is chanted over and over in the locker room, and I wholeheartedly believe we'll get it just by how badly I know we want it.

Today has been the best birthday I've had in a while, and the greatest part is coming when I walk out those doors and into *her* arms.

Berkley

I've been wearing Nate's old practice jersey to every game for the last month, but this past week, I made a purchase for his birthday party, and I can't wait to see his eyes when I walk into their house.

"He's going to go insane when he sees you," Willow coos from where she walks beside me, and Darby agrees from the other side.

"Damn right, he is," Bellamy calls out. She's walking behind us with Shay, who Darby invited tonight because her boyfriend and the men's team are at an away game.

I have on an oversized Outlaw jersey, and I'm wearing it as a dress with little black spandex shorts under it. I paired it with over the knee black boots.

My belly churns with excitement at the thought of his reaction as Darby opens their front door to an already crowded Wolves Den.

"Birthday boy!!" Bellamy sing-songs over the loud music. "Your dessert is here."

I smirk, shaking my head at my best friend, but her antics get his attention, and when it lands directly on me, it's like everything else fades away. I stop in my tracks, my blue eyes locked onto his hazel ones until his begin their admiration down my body. His appreciation stops on the number two covering my torso before he meets my gaze again and a smile transforms his handsome face. He bites his lip and peruses lower to the skin between the top of my boots and the bottom of his jersey.

His eyes roll back in his head, and he runs his palm over his jaw. I swear I hear him groan, but I know that's impossible from where he stands. Then his large strides are eliminating the distance between us faster than I can think.

Nate's hand goes to my lower back, and he pulls me into him. I instantly feel his hard cock, and I can't help the little whimper that leaves my lips. I'm so pent-up after watching him on that football field today.

He places a kiss just below my ear, barely nipping the skin. "Is this another torture plan?"

I laugh and shake my head.

Nate's hand slips down to my ass, and he growls, "You're fucking killing me, BB."

I turn my head to whisper seductively in his ear, "It's not torture if I plan on taking care of you later, birthday boy."

Without hesitation, he takes my hand in his and starts dragging me to the stairs.

"But it's your birthday party," I say, but by the way my center clenches, I know I'm not that worried about the party.

"We'll come back." He gives me a sexy grin and presses his lips into mine. His tongue promises what's to come, and there's no doubt my panties are beyond wet at this point.

He pulls back to look at me. "I want to bend you over my bed, with my name on your back, my handprint on your ass, and my cock deep inside you. But first..." He bites my lip and whispers into my mouth, "I want to eat my birthday dessert."

"Please," I moan, and it's my turn to take his hand, pulling him up the rest of the steps.

But yelling at the end of the hall halts our movement, and we both look at each other, confused.

"Fuck both of you." It's then that I register the hysterical female voice is Tori's.

"Maybe if you didn't want to fuck your stepsister so bad, you'd have actually paid me attention and this whole thing would have never happened."

I look at Nate, wide-eyed and unsure of what to do. Nate's room is directly across from Cash's, but that's when I notice Bellamy standing there against the wall. For a second, a twinge of worry runs through me until I hear her voice.

"Fuck off, Tori. Don't blame me for this."

"You are such a cunt, Bellamy," she sneers, and Bellamy steps in her face.

"Trust me, you haven't seen shit yet, but I suggest you leave before you find out what a real *cunt* I can be. I'd hate to really hurt your little feelings."

I'd be scared shitless if I was Tori.

Tori storms away, bumping into my shoulder as she moves past us, and that's when Cash and Bellamy notice the two of us standing there.

Cash's head thuds back against the wall. "Fuck, dude. Please don't let this shit mess up your birthday party." Cash points toward the stairs Tori just descended. "Hopefully, she just leaves."

I notice Bellamy's hands are shaking, and there's no way I'm not checking on my friend right now.

"Give us a few. Go have a drink with the boys, and I'll see you back downstairs." I wink at Nate. We have all night to fuck each other's brains out, but my best friend needs me.

Cash looks at Bellamy, and I can tell he doesn't want to leave her. She must feel it because she speaks up. "Go take a shot with the birthday boy, and we'll talk more later. I'll be down in a few."

He stares at her for what feels like minutes, but he relents and follows Nate downstairs.

Bellamy immediately goes into Cash's ensuite bathroom, and I follow her. She splashes water on her face, holding on to the side of the sink as she takes deep breath after deep breath. I know she has panic attacks at times, but I've never actually witnessed one.

"You okay?" I ask quietly, rubbing her back.

She nods. "I will be." Further smearing her mascara, she splashes water on her face.

"Do you need to sit?" I put the lid of the toilet down in case she decides to.

"I'm okay. I'm not having an attack. It was close, but I'm okay," she nods repeatedly, like she's reassuring herself as well.

Her eyes meet mine in the mirror, and she turns around to face me, leaning against the counter.

"It's easy to blame Tori in all of this, but…" She hesitates.

"But what, Bell? You can tell me anything, you know that. It's pretty obvious there's more to your relationship with Cash."

"I'm definitely not innocent in the Tori-Cash saga."

"They're toxic and have been since high school, from what it sounds like," I say, because I've witnessed them fight so many times, it's ridiculous. Bellamy and Maverick always pass it off as their normal.

"Yeah, but even in high school…" Again, she pauses, and it breaks my heart that she doesn't feel comfortable enough to tell me, but I remind myself this isn't about me.

"Put it this way, from the day I moved there when I was seventeen years old, Cash and I...we never saw each other as siblings."

Okay, so this has been going on for a long time, even longer than I had always assumed.

"I'm not going to push you, but you know I'm here. Hell, you know all my dark family secrets. I'd never judge you. Never."

She smiles and reaches for my hand. "I know you wouldn't."

"But tonight's not the night. Let's go celebrate your man."

Nodding, I take her hand. "Even the strong ones need a shoulder to lean on sometimes." I kiss her cheek before we head downstairs. "I'm always here."

TWENTY-SEVEN

Nate

SPRING BREAK- FIVE MONTHS LATER

"I wish I was going to get one year with *all* of you at Mountain Ridge," my sister says from her spot on the edge of the pool.

Graham tosses her the football. "Aw, little Outlaw, you know you'll still get to see me."

She throws it across the pool to Nola, who came home with us for spring break.

"I know, I know. Just try to get drafted somewhere on the East Coast."

"I'm hoping for New Orleans. That's a quick flight."

"You know damn well my parents will expect to see your ass on the regular," Nola chimes in.

Graham chuckles, "That's a given."

"Let's hope our bye weekend next season lines up with a Sunday game day so we can all come to at least one," I say, knowing Coach would give us leeway if it's possible for us to go to one of Graham's games.

"That would be awesome," Graham smiles proudly.

I lift myself out of the pool to sit beside Willow.

"Since you and Berkley won't be here the whole summer, I think I may talk to Dad about moving up there earlier in the summer too."

I nod, because I think it will be good for Willow to get away from the town that holds so much pain for her.

"Have you decided where you are living yet?" Nola asks Willow.

She shakes her head. "Still waiting to see what the girls are going to do since Darby is moving into the basketball house."

"I do know...I'm not living in a dorm." Her nose crinkles. "I don't like people I don't know."

I chuckle, nudging her arm. "Well, how are you supposed to decide if you like them if you don't talk to them?"

She side-eyes me. "I can determine a lot from afar."

We all laugh. I never knew there was such a thing as an anti-social extrovert until my sister grew up.

The back door to my dad's house closes, and the most beautiful girl in the world walks out with a tray of food.

"Who wants a sandwich?" Berkley calls out, setting them on the patio table.

Graham hops out of the pool and over to the food before she even finishes her sentence.

"Nate, I'm glad you got your shit together because you are the luckiest son of a bitch I know," Graham mumbles with a mouth full of food.

"Trust me, I know," I say with pride as I stare at my gorgeous girl, who gives me a knowing wink.

"I just got off the phone with Bellamy. She can't come tonight, but she'll be here tomorrow," Berkley tells us.

"In time for our appointment, right?" Willow asks.

Berkley nods, chewing a bit of her sandwich before she can speak again.

"Yep, she said she'll get up first thing, so she'll be here in plenty of time."

"Is Berkley getting a tattoo too?" Nola asks from where he sits, tossing the football in the air to himself. The girls have been planning a matching tattoo for a few months now, so Willow was super excited to get them on the books for her artist during our spring break.

Willow shakes her head, briefly glancing in my direction, like she's embarrassed of what she's about to say.

"We're getting our nipples pierced together."

My eyebrows raise in surprise, about the same time Graham chokes on his sandwich.

Welp, I didn't see that coming.

"You know no one can touch them for, like, months after, right?" Graham asks, and Berkley lets out a laugh, pointing at the incredulous look on my face.

"Graham, shut the fuck up," I growl, because nipple play discussion involving my baby sister was not on my bingo card today.

"What?" He holds his hands up in an innocent gesture. "Sorry! I just wanted to make sure her and Bell knew that."

Willow smirks. "Yes, we both know about the aftercare. That's why Berkley isn't getting hers done."

Berkley covers her face. "Willow…good lord."

That's right, my baby can't go that long.

When she looks up, our eyes meet, and I wink knowingly at her.

We all sit around the outdoor table, eating our lunch. It's been fun to have Nola here with us this week. The whole crew was invited to stay either with us or Graham for the break, but the hockey team made it to the playoffs so the twins couldn't make it.

"Now I could go for some ice cream." Willow pats her stomach after we finish eating.

"I think I'm ice creamed out," Berkley huffs. We've been down to the boardwalk almost every day this week, thanks to Willow's sweet tooth.

"Anyone else?" Willow asks.

"I'm down," Nola says, at the same time Graham stands, "I'll drive."

I smile at Berkley, because that means alone time with my girl.

"Wanna go for a swim, Outlaw?" Berkley smirks, and for the first time today, she pulls her coverup over her head.

Holy. Shit.

It's the fucking blue bathing suit.

"Baby…" I groan, standing from my seat.

She does an innocent spin, which makes her ass bounce.

"Fuck..."

She stretches her hand out for me, and I take it, but instead of letting her lead me to the pool, I'm tugging her in the opposite direction.

"What are—" She doesn't finish her sentence because her eyes likely land on exactly where I'm headed.

The outdoor shower.

I turn around, pulling her into me and grabbing her ass, searing my lips into hers. Berkley opens up immediately for me, like she always does. Her nails claw down my shirtless chest, marking me as I suck on her bottom lip. Then she throws her leg over my hip, her heat meeting my hard cock, grinding against me.

So ready. So needy.

"I've been waiting all week for the right time to fuck you on that shower bench."

Her breasts rise and fall against me, and I can't help but take an eyeful. I push one triangle to the side and gently rub my thumb over her nipple.

"I've thought about it so many times," she moans as I walk backwards, pushing the door open but not taking my hands off her.

"Do you remember what I told you I wanted to do to this bathing suit the next time you wore it?"

Her clear blues dilate, and she nods with a whispered, "Destroy it."

"Hmmm." I pull us farther into the shower, latching the door behind us.

I sit down on the bench. "You want me to stretch them to the side so you can sit on my cock?"

She nods, sitting down on my lap, twirling her hips over my dick.

"You want me to come so deep in you that it drenches these little bikini bottoms?" I ask, dipping my finger down the back and running it along the center of her ass.

"Please, Nate." She stands back up to untie my swim trunks, and I lift my ass for her to pull them down.

Dropping to a squatting position, her mouth lands on the top of my dick.

"That's it. Get him nice and wet, BB," I command, and she purses her lips, letting her saliva drip down on my cock before her mouth seals around me, spreading it out.

My ass clenches at the sensation of her hot mouth and the sight of her in the little bikini between my knees.

"I jacked off so many times to visions of you in this bikini before you let me back in this pussy."

She moans around my dick, swirling her tongue around me.

I pull Berkley up, ready to be inside of her, slipping my fingers through her slit. "Is this pussy ready because my cock is the needy one today?" I ask as I stroke my dick with my free hand.

"So wet." I bite my lip and push her bathing suit to the side as she sits. Her insides flutter as she slowly adjusts to my very hard dick entering her. When she's fully seated, she moves her hips in small circles, and I push both sides of her top aside so her tits pop out, the perfect angle for me to suck and lick.

She rolls her body over me, and her pace picks up. I lean back, loving to watch all the control leave her body. "That's it. Let that needy pussy take over."

"Oh fuck, that's the spot," Berkley says, bowing her back just slightly as, over and over, she bounces up and down. Perfecting the angle of my cock hitting her G-spot, I swipe my thumb across my tongue before pressing it into her clit in a quick, circular motion.

"Yes, Nate. Yes!" she cries out, and I push the bikini bottom farther to the side.

"That's it, baby, keep going," I groan at the sight of her pussy swallowing my dick.

"Fuck…" I howl, knowing my orgasm is going to rip through me any minute.

"I've had you so many times this week, but I'm already so close to busting," I tell her, knowing she loves hearing how much she affects me.

"I'm about to… Oh yes… I'm… Come with me, baby," she whimpers as her body spasms around me, and I lose myself, releasing so deep inside of her as I roar things I can't even decipher.

Berkley's head leans into mine, both of us panting, our chests rising in tandem.

"That was… Wow…" she whispers as her body slouches and her head falls to my shoulder.

I kiss the side of her blonde hair. "It's always like this with us."

"I can't get enough of you."

"I hope you never do," she whispers.

And I already know to the bottom of my soul, I won't. I

learned a lot in the two years I didn't have her. The main one being…I can't and won't live my life without her again.

EPILOGUE

Berkley

ONE MONTH LATER

April 10th

I hope you know how much I love you, not by the hundreds of times I tell you a day, but by my actions. Thank you from the bottom of my heart for giving me another chance. I will be forever grateful for that and for you.

Also, thank you for loving our sister (that's still a little weird to say sometimes) the way you do. I truly believe this past year, you didn't only save me, but you saved her too. She looks up to you and loves you so much.

You are my family, my best friend, my home, my treasure, and the love of my life.

You are also sexy as hell. Just wanted to make sure you knew that.

PS: Are we signing this lease today or what?

I'll pick you up in a few hours. Here's a Diet Coke to start your morning.

I'm convinced there's nothing sweeter in this world than being loved by Nathan Outlaw.

On the mornings Nate and I don't spend the night together, I live for his early deliveries.

I look around at the dogwood trees in full bloom. It's hard to believe we're finishing up the end of our junior year of college. There's an excitement in the air that's different from the past few springs I've lived here. I know a lot of it has to do with the joy Nate brings to my life.

We're currently about to head to the airport for our flight to St. Louis to see Mav and Cash play in the frozen four. Then later this month, we'll watch as one of our best friends gets drafted to the NFL. And by the summer, we'll be moving our sister here to Mountain Ridge, and Nate will be preparing for another season of football.

He and Nola are gearing up for the NCAA championship after they lost out in the second round this past year. They also have 'beating East Carolina for a second time to break the tie' at the top of their manifestation board that Willow made them.

Thanks to Brian, we have everyone manifesting all the things. Just last week, I learned that one of my big ones came true. I'm starting an internship that Tiffany helped me land at the kids' school as a part-time assistant to some of the early education teachers.

Movement out of the corner of my eye draws me away from the dogwood tree to the sexy quarterback heading my way. And in that moment, I can honestly say, the thing I'm most excited about is dangling in between Nate's fingers.

A huge smile takes over my face when I see his free hand is holding up a half heart, like he does when he's on the field. I lift my hand, mimicking his as I always do, but this time, there's no jumbotron to capture the gesture, and even though I love being able to watch our moments on replay, this one feels even more special.

"Got 'em," he says, hopping into the truck and tossing me the keys before he pecks my lips.

We were so excited when we signed the lease, talking the realtor's ears off, we walked right out and forgot to get the keys to our new place.

"I still can't believe I talked you into moving in with me." He wiggles in his seat before reaching across to hold my hand.

"My besties kinda helped you out with that plan," I tease.

Which is true. I would have never initiated us girls not living together senior year, but that doesn't mean I'm not beyond excited to have a place of my own with Nate.

"True, but I promise there are lots of benefits to living with me." He waggles his eyebrows.

"Oh, I know, that's why I agreed to it," I deadpan.

He chuckles, and I feel it in my very soul.

I squeeze his hand. "But I do have one nonsexual requirement?"

"What is it, BB?

"I still expect letters and snacks waiting on me every now and again."

"That was always on the table. I won't stop doing that until I can't walk anymore, and by then, hopefully, we'll have a couple kids I can make do it."

"Aw, you planning our future already, babe?"

He raises our clasped hands and kisses the back of mine. "BB, since the moment I had you back in my arms, I knew I was never letting you go. You're my future."

And just like every other time this gorgeous man speaks to me like this, my heart soars. I love him with everything that I am and can't wait to face the days to come with him by my side

Afterword

Thank you so much for reading Replay. It means the world to us to have your support.

Reviews are everything to us authors. So, if you enjoyed reading, please consider leaving a review!

We have so much in store for our readers…
Sign up for our Newsletter so you don't miss out on book news or new releases.

AFTERWORD

ACKNOWLEDGMENTS

First and foremost, we want to thank our readers. From the bottom of our hearts, we thank you for taking a chance on us.

Thank you to my ride or die, LOML, my husband, for always supporting me and loving me through everything. Also, for the writing inspo :)

Shout out to my best girl for entertaining herself when I needed to fit in some writing and for inspiring me to be the best version of myself. I love you both forever and ever.

Thank you to my book bestie, now co-author, for riding this wild roller coaster with me and being the other part of my brain. Can't wait to see the next cover you design, you are so talented. -A

I want to thank my husband for dealing with my many late nights filled with writing and half-watched shows. Thank you for encouraging and supporting this crazy dream of mine.

Thank you to my two little ladies for understanding that "I need just a few more minutes" really means "until I get this scene finished." You two are the reason I'm shooting for the stars. I want to make you proud.

Eeep! My other half, thank you for doing this with me. You're an amazing partner, and I'm so thankful to have you by my side. We make one kick-ass team, and I'm so proud of what we've accomplished so far. With every book, I grow more and more excited to see how far we can go! xox — L

We also want to thank those closest to us for their support and love throughout this dream of ours.

To our editor Mackenzie, thank you for always making sure our words flow the best they can. Your suggestions and keen eye are top tier, and we are forever grateful to you.

To our PA, Kenzie, thank you so much for all your help in the background. We are so thankful for your friendship, insight, and creativity. The constant text, reels, graphics, and voice memos keep us on track, and we love having you as a big part of our journey. Love you babe.

Lizzy- Your attention to detail is amazing, and we are so grateful for the time you took to proofread Replay. Thank you for all your help and friendship.

To our Beta team — Thank you to Mackenzie, Erica, and Courtney for Alpha reading and giving suggestions in the early stage. We are also grateful for each of you and the content you create for us monthly. Thank you to Kelsey, Lauren, and Anja for beta reading our book babies, and always being amazing hype girls. Each of you made an impact on Nate & Berkley's story, and we are so thankful for each of you and the time you took to do this.

Thank you to our ARC/Street team. We appreciate each and every one of you for taking the time to give us honest reviews and promote our book. Reviews help authors more than people realize and we are so appreciative.

We especially love our street team group chats… when it pops off in there, it's the best. You babes are so fun, and your encouragement has been the best part of our busy days in the writing cave.

Thank you to Tori and Maddy at The Bubbly Bookshelf for all your work behind the scenes. You are both so creative and fun. We are thankful for you both and can't wait for more fun collaborations.

Shoutout to Mikaela and the babes at Chasing Books PR. You have been a pleasure to work with so far. Thank you for your time and effort in creating an amazing arc signup for this book.

To our book cover illustrator Concepts by Canea, you did amazing making our vision for this couple come true. We cannot wait to see what you create for the rest of the couples in this series.

Our author besties, you know who you are… from the group chats to the long voice memos, venting sessions, collaborations, and more, we thank you from the bottom of our hearts for your support and friendship.

To everyone above, you inspire us to continue this journey.

Thank you all for being a part of something that we cherish. We're truly grateful.

About the Author

A New Yorker and a Southern Belle.

Two Book Obsessed Babes that became lifelong best friends over their love for a good romance novel.

When they're not writing, they're devouring a good book or spending time with their family and friends.

Total opposites in some ways and exactly the same in others, making them a dynamic author duo.

Let's keep in touch... Follow our Socials

ALSO BY L.A. SHAW

Make You Series

#0.5 Make You Miss Me (Trent & Ashley)

#1 Make You Love Me (Greyson & Lottie)

#2 Make You Want Me (Nox & Emerson- Book 1)

#3 Make You Keep Me (Nox & Emerson- Book 2)

#4 Make You Mine (Trent & Ashley)

Reckless Hearts Series

#1 Reckless Abandon (Sloan & Wesley)

#1.5 Reckless Obsession (Blossom & Dalton) .

#2 Reckless Impulse (Quinn & Eli)

#3 Reckless Encounters (Ava & Parker)

Mountain Ridge University

#1 Replay (Nate & Berkley)

#2 Trick Play (Cash & Bellamy)

Made in the USA
Monee, IL
13 May 2025

17306551R00203